Praise for *Deadly Intruder*:

"In *Deadly Intruder*, Anne Kelsey has given us a delicious serving of intrigue, mystery, romance, and edge-of-your seat excitement. This book sent chills up my spine as I began to see how easily lives can be destroyed or turned upside down by Internet stalking. *Deadly Intruder* was a book I simply didn't want to put down. Kudos to Anne Kelsey. I will be looking out for more from her."
—Maureen McMahon, author of *Shadows in the Mist*

"*Deadly Intruder* is a tense, taut thriller that's all too possible in our electronic age. As the tension rises in each scene and chapter, I found myself looking over my shoulder to make sure no one was watching ME. It's been a long time since a book has drawn me so deeply into its dark, sinister web. Check it out…but make sure you have your phone shut off and your doors locked! I'll be watching for the next book from author Anne Kelsey."
—Elizabeth Delisi, award-winning author of *Fatal Fortune*

Deadly Intruder

Anne Kelsey

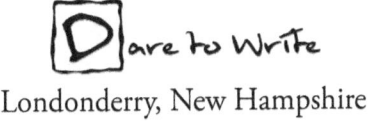

Londonderry, New Hampshire

Deadly Intruder
by
Anne Kelsey

Paperback ISBN-13: 978-0-9864046-0-3

Cover Design: Pamela Marin-Kingsley
Interior Design: Cathy Colbert

Dare to Write

P.O. Box 785
Londonderry, NH 03053
On the web: www.daretowrite.com/

To Elliot, Justin, and Brandon.
Sometimes the best dreams take
a little longer to come true.

Acknowledgements

Special thanks to my wonderful and patient editor Mandy Brown, to Cathy (Cat) Colbert who painstakingly typeset this book (despite my insistence on multiple fonts), and to Pam Marin-Kingsley for her superb cover design.

Also a heartfelt thanks to my readers Cynthia Hoest, Kim Smith Yergeau, and Mary Johnson for their insight and guidance as well as the Southern New Hampshire Women's Writing Group and the Rockingham Writers Association for their support throughout this journey.

Prologue

April 11 - Monday

Hands clasped in front of him, on his knees in his den, Brent looked up into his tormentor's eyes. "Kill me. I beg you." His voice cracked. Unable to stop the tremors that shook his body, he pleaded with his captor. "If you kill me, you'll still win the game."

Instead of replying, the man reached down and grabbed Brent by the back of the neck in a vice-like grip, lifting him up onto his feet. The pain was excruciating, and it shot straight through Brent's temples. The edges of his vision began to darken, but he fought through the pain. He had to stay conscious. He had to get to Amanda.

"Losers don't call the shots. Haven't you figured that out by now?"

Without warning, his assailant shoved him down onto the straight-back chair and slammed his head down onto the oak desktop. "Look. Look again." The man tapped the corner of the monitor with the barrel of his gun.

The computer screen was so close to Brent's eyes that everything on the screen was a mass of meaningless dots.

"How does the game end? The answer is right there." He tapped again. "Right in front of your face."

Brent blinked repeatedly, forcing his eyes to focus until he was able to distinguish the ghostly infrared image on the screen. "Amanda?" he whispered. Brent held his breath and looked for signs that his wife was still alive.

"Come on, college boy, figure it out," his captor said.

The man released the hold on his neck, and Brent cautiously straightened. "What is that?" Brent asked, his voice hoarse with dread. A thin line snaked from Amanda's hand up and out of camera range.

"It's an IV."

"What...why?" He turned toward his captor and stared into the man's cold, blue eyes. He knew without question that he was about to hear Amanda's death sentence.

"It's a brilliant idea, and how fitting to end the game with such an ironic twist."

"What do you mean?" Brent was having trouble following this madman's logic. He spoke sheer lunacy.

"I've figured out how to win the game without you or your wife." He let out a burst of maniacal laughter.

Comprehension suddenly dawned within Brent. He retched as hot bile rose, burning the back of his throat.

"No! You can't mean..." His limbs began to tremble. He was in the presence of pure unadulterated evil. God help them all.

Chapter 1

December 3 – Thursday

Brent looked around the plush surroundings of the Italian restaurant and made a mental note to bring his wife here sometime. The quiet ambiance, the chic décor, the linen tablecloths, she'd love it. This place was a far cry from his usual lunch of pork lo mein at the Wok and Roll with Todd. Nevertheless, Brent was savoring every bite of his lobster ravioli. *Was that a hint of nutmeg?*

"So, what do you think?" Clive asked.

Brent pulled his thoughts back to the conversation and laid down his fork. "Tell me the name of the game again?" He looked across the table at Clive, the newest hire at his firm, Revolution Advertising and Creative Company.

"It's called a deadpool," Clive said.

"And you get points for guessing when someone is going to die?"

"Right." Clive twirled the last of his linguini around the tines of his fork.

"That's just sick." Brent shook his head and picked up his knife and fork, cutting his next ravioli neatly in half. "How long have you been playing?"

"Come to think of it," Clive laughed, "a long time."

"Have you ever won?" Brent studied the man across the table. Mid-forties, he'd guess. Big guy, overweight, with the ruddy complexion of a dedicated drinker.

"No." Clive bent his head and shoveled in an enormous mouthful of pasta. "I finished in the top ten once, but out of the cash."

Clive talked throughout the entire lunch with his mouth full. *How the hell had a guy like this had a successful career in sales?* "Then why do you keep playing?" Brent noted a barely discernible bald spot Clive had attempted to conceal with a comb-over. He amended his guess about Clive's age to early fifties.

"Maybe this will be my lucky year." Clive tore off a chunk of bread and mopped up the remains of his marinara. "This particular deadpool has a huge payout."

"You mentioned that. Up to a half million dollars." Brent chuckled and pushed his plate aside, leaving several ravioli untouched. "I think you're full of it."

"Hey look, pal. We're both salesmen. I'm quite certain you can shovel the shit with the best of them, and so can I, but I'm not bullshitting you on this one." Clive pushed his ample frame away from the table and looked around, snapping his fingers for the waiter.

"You got some marinara on your tie," Brent said.

Clive looked down. "So I do."

"Sir, how may I assist you?" The waiter materialized out of thin air, a crisp white towel folded over his left forearm.

"Here." A platinum credit card bounced across the white tablecloth landing near the edge, upside down. "I'll make sure to apply the same lack of attention to your tip that you showed my very important client."

Brent looked away embarrassed. *Was this guy for real?* He folded his napkin and tucked it under the edge of the plate.

Clive waved his hand, shooing away the tuxedo-clad waiter. "Entry into the game is by invitation only, but I'll finagle you a spot." He dipped his napkin in his water glass and started dabbing at the spot on his tie. "The game's a hoot. A bit twisted. But no harm's done."

"Thanks for lunch," Brent said as they walked through the parking lot to their cars. The sun held no warmth, and a bitter wind sent Brent's unbuttoned trench coat flapping around his legs. "I should have taken you out. You're the new hire."

"Forget about it." Clive waved the comment away. "Besides, I refuse to be taken out to lunch by a colleague half my age. What are you, twenty-one, twenty-two?"

"Twenty-four. I take it you're anticipating a record second month on the job since you treated me to lunch at a four-star restaurant."

"Please!" Clive rolled his eyes. "I'm writing that meal off on my Revolution expense report first thing tomorrow morning. In case anyone asks, you were the president of First Fidelity Bank."

"You're kidding, right?"

"Come on. You're going to stand here and tell me you're not playing games with your expense account?"

Instead of answering, Brent asked another question. "So how was your first commission check?"

"I did all right, although according to the other salesmen at Revolution, not as well as you. In order to beat your sales number, I guess I've got my work cut out for me."

"You planning on giving me a little competition?"

"You bet your ass."

Brent smiled. "Get used to seeing the name Brent Darby at the top of the leader board. It's been there for a while, and I don't intend for that to change."

"We'll see." Clive put his hands in his pants pockets and rocked back on his heels, peering up into the sky. "Looks like we're in for a storm."

Brent followed his gaze to a bank of black clouds darkening the western sky. "It never snows this early in Boston."

"The Farmer's Almanac claims we're going to have a snowy winter."

"I hope not." Brent patted the top of his red Dodge Viper. "I'm not ready to put this baby up on blocks."

13

"It's a beauty." Clive placed a hand on the roof of the sports car, tracing the edge of the black racing stripe that ran bumper to bumper.

"Thanks. My wife has asked me to take the car off the road when the first snowflake flies."

"That's a damn shame. I wouldn't if it were mine."

Man, this guy was arrogant. "See you back at the office." Brent pulled a pair of black leather driving gloves from his pocket and slid behind the wheel.

"Why? The better part of the day is over."

"It's two o'clock."

"Yeah, well, I'm headed home anyway."

"Then I guess I'll see you tomorrow."

In the rearview mirror, Brent watched Clive give the Viper a last lingering look before he turned into the wind and opened the door of an ugly mud-brown Ford four-door sedan.

"You might want to rethink not locking your car," he called over.

Clive turned and gave him a quizzical look. "Why is that?"

"Let's just say pranks are a way of life if you work at Revolution. You don't want someone to put a duck in the backseat of your car. From what I heard, neither the duck nor the car survived."

Brent couldn't help smirking at Clive's expression. He turned the key in the ignition and listened with satisfaction to the purr of the high-powered engine. *This guy wouldn't last six months.* He flipped down the visor and finger-combed his hair. It could use a trim. When he got back to the office, he'd make an appointment. Slapping the stick shift into first, he couldn't resist blowing by Clive and peeling out of the parking lot.

An occasional snowflake drifted down as Brent crept through downtown Boston traffic. The stereo was cranked, and he hammered out an accompanying drumbeat on the steering wheel.

By the time he reached the office, the snow had really started coming down. Unable to pretend to ignore it any longer, he was forced to flip on the windshield wipers. The thought of taking the car off the road was heartbreaking, but he'd promised Amanda. He sighed; it looked like winter had arrived early, and with a vengeance.

• • •

Brent stoked the fire before returning the poker to the stand and plopping back down on the couch beside Amanda.

"Isn't the snow beautiful?" She motioned out the window where the flakes were coming down in a torrent, illuminated by the back porch light.

"It's a bit early for me."

"I know, but it's the first snowfall since we moved into our new house." She picked up the half-empty bottle of wine and poured them each another glass before leaning back. "This is what country living is all about. Snow that stays white instead of turning black."

"It's only December third. That's too early for snow, even in New England."

"I think it's romantic."

"You're right." Brent dropped his arm from the back of the couch down onto Amanda's shoulders, drawing her close. "We don't have anywhere to go, and this is nice, sitting here in front of the fire." He idly ran his fingers through her hair, noticing how the firelight glinted off the honey strands. "Thanks for making dinner, hon."

"My pleasure. I know how much you love frozen chicken fingers and French fries." She chuckled.

"Good thing I had a big lunch."

Amanda elbowed him in the ribs. "You knew when you married me that I didn't cook."

"Right. I keep forgetting." He propped his feet up on the coffee table. "Actually, I had a fantastic lunch. I went to Ristorante Lucia in the North End."

"Really? Didn't the *Globe* just do a write-up on that restaurant? I'm jealous. Did you take out a client?"

"No. That place is too expensive, even on an expense account, but it was bravisimo." He made a show of kissing his fingers.

"That's one of the few things I miss about living in Boston, the ability to walk to so many great restaurants. People born and bred in Garnet, New Hampshire think Mac's Place on Route 28 is fine dining. Ugh. So how did you end up going there for lunch?" She leaned forward and took a sip of wine.

"Revolution hired a new salesman, and he took me there for lunch. He's going to be sharing my territory."

"Are you okay with that?" Amanda looked up at him.

"He was hired strictly to drum up new business, which is great for me. I hate cold calling. Now I can concentrate on doing what I do best: growing my established accounts."

"So what did you think of him?"

"He seems like an okay guy, although a bit on the arrogant side. I'm sure he took me out to lunch to pick my brain. Toward the end of the meal, the conversation took the oddest turn."

"How so?"

"Have you ever heard of a deadpool?"

"A what?"

"A deadpool. It's sort of like a football pool. Except, instead of betting which team will win, you bet on a list of people you think will die within the next twelve months."

Amanda sat up and twisted toward him, her face aghast. "I hope you're kidding."

"That was my reaction too," Brent said. He stood up and walked over to the fireplace. "Clive's been betting on deadpools for a long time," he said over his shoulder, poking at the fire. "Since college anyway, and I'm guessing he's in his mid to late fifties."

"I'm sorry, but that's appalling. How can a game like that even be legal? Are these games played out of Vegas?"

16

"The one he plays is on the Internet. If it's true, it's pretty creepy." He pulled the mesh fire screen closed. "It's possible he was just pulling my leg."

"Did you say this guy's name was Clive?"

"Uh-huh. Clive Ellis. Why?" Brent walked back to the couch.

"It's just such an unusual name. I overheard a woman in my kickboxing class mention that her boyfriend's name was Clive. I wonder if it's the same guy."

Brent shrugged.

Amanda picked up her plate and wineglass and stood up. "I hope I don't get nightmares about deadpools tonight. In fact, to take my mind off it, I think I'll work a little more on my drawing before I turn in. My customer wants the portrait of her schnauzer done before the little darling's birthday next week." She rolled her eyes.

Brent picked up his own dishes and joined her in the kitchen. "I've got a better idea. Why don't I throw another log on the fire, and we get naked?" He pinned her against the counter and wrapped his arms around her, trailing kisses down the side of her neck.

"Hmmm." Amanda leaned back against him. "Maybe we don't need another log…"

Brent swung her up into his arms and strode back into the family room. "Better luck next time, pooch," he said stepping around the leg of the easel. He and Amanda collapsed in a heap on the couch and began pulling off each other's clothes.

• • •

December 24 – Thursday

It was just after eleven p.m. when Brent waved goodbye to his in-laws and closed the front door. With an audible sigh of relief, he leaned against it. He could think of several ways to start his Christmas vacation, and none of them had anything to do with his in-laws.

His mood on the upswing, he headed down the hall. In the kitchen, Amanda stood with her back to him at the sink. "Ah… alone at last with my ravishing wife!" Brent crossed the room, grabbed her from behind in a bear hug, and nibbled on her earlobe. "Care to leave this mess and join me for some fun and games in the bedroom?"

Amanda picked a dishtowel up from the counter and slapped it playfully onto his shoulder. "Not until after the dishes are done. I'll wash. You dry."

"Spoil sport." Brent laughed and reached around her for a crystal wineglass on the drain board.

She turned off the faucet and looked at him with a serious expression. "Why were you late getting home tonight?"

"I'm sorry, hon. I'm just buried in stuff."

"What stuff? You knew what time my parents were coming for dinner tonight. Plus, I was worried to death about you driving that stupid racecar in the snow."

"You worry too much. Besides, it was only a dusting."

"So why were you late?"

"I got caught on my way out the door."

"On Christmas Eve?" Amanda gave him a look of pure skepticism.

"Honest. In fact, I was in such a rush that I forgot my laptop." Brent felt a twinge of conscience at the white lie. He had forgotten his laptop, but Revolution had been all but deserted since early afternoon.

"Or maybe you weren't all that excited about having dinner tonight with my folks." Amanda lifted the corner of the towel off Brent's shoulder and dried her hands.

"Well, maybe there is a tiny grain of truth to that, but Todd did stop by. I'll admit that we started talking, and I sort of lost track of time."

"I knew it." Tears welled up in her eyes. "I don't see why it is such a struggle for you to get along with my folks."

"I don't but—"

"Especially since…"

"Since what?"

She hesitated a moment. "Since both your parents are gone. I wish you'd let my parents help fill that void."

He tried to change the subject. "And I didn't appreciate you making me look bad in front of your dad tonight. Did you really have to drag out a bunch of travel brochures?"

Amanda put the last plate in the dishwasher and started loading glasses into the top rack. "Can't you try to be a little more tolerant? After all, we see them so infrequently."

"We see them every few weeks. I'd hardly call that infrequent."

"It's Christmas Eve. It's part and parcel of being an only child. I just wish you'd be more considerate."

"Considerate?" Brent's temper flared again. "Your dad was grilling me about our finances in the middle of dinner. While we were eating the filet mignon that I paid for."

"And I politely asked him to drop the subject. I know how to handle my dad. He's just worried—"

"Not that you came to my defense or anything." He set the last crystal wineglass on the countertop with a bang.

Amanda flinched. "But Brent—"

"But what? Your father all but asked me how much money was in our checking account. Jesus!"

"He did not."

Brent spread his arms out to encompass the spacious kitchen. "Doesn't this prove how well I'm taking care of his precious daughter?"

"Of course, but—"

"A custom-designed, custom-built house?"

"Dad's afraid we may have gotten in over our heads, that's all." She crossed her arms. "We're so young to have such a big

19

mortgage, along with all the other monthly bills. The money I bring in from selling my artwork barely covers my paint and supplies."

"I can make the payments," Brent said with an edge to his voice. He reached for the serving platter Amanda was rinsing.

"Now we have the Viper payment too."

"I knew you were going to throw that car in my face again." Brent put down the wet platter and threw the wet dishtowel into the sink. "Was I so wrong to buy something for myself after winning Rookie of the Year? You didn't complain about the diamond necklace I bought you at the same time."

"Oh, Brent." Amanda reached for his hands. "The necklace was beautiful, and I know you love the car. It's just that—"

"Oh, so you think winning was a fluke?" He spun on his heel and slammed the dishwasher closed, rattling the glasses inside. "It wasn't."

"You don't need to prove anything to me, Brent. I love you."

"My career isn't impressive enough for either of you two to discuss over cocktails at the club."

"Now you're just being ridiculous. This whole fight started because—"

"I was late. And I apologized for that. But no matter what I do, it never seems to be enough." Brent saw genuine hurt cloud Amanda's eyes, but he turned away from her.

"You're the one who keeps trying to one-up my father."

"Well, I've got a hell of a long way to go to catch up to the bank president with the private plane and the fleet of cars."

Amanda sighed. "He's just a little concerned about our financial situation, that's all."

"Not to mention the lake house."

"Brent, stop it."

"We are fine. Trust me."

"I'm trying, but we still have your school loans to pay off and—"

"Thanks for reminding me that I'm the one who came into this marriage with all the debt." Brent leaned back against the counter and crossed his arms.

"There's no need to get sarcastic."

"You always forget the upside to working on commission. I have the opportunity to make a whole lot more money than I did when I was on straight salary."

"But there is risk involved too." She began wiping down the counters. "If you fall short of your quota, you have to sell more the next pay period to make up for that."

"And if I sell over my quota, my commission is added to my base. Since Revolution doesn't have a cap on commissions, I could double my gross income."

She turned to face him, sponge in hand. "But you fell short in November."

"Oh, come on, Amanda. Are you going to micromanage every penny I bring in each month?"

"Maybe I should get a real job."

"There is no need for you to do that. You love painting. I promised you on our wedding day I would take care of you."

"I don't want to be taken care of, Brent. I'm not a pet," she fumed, slapping a hand on the countertop. "And please don't talk about my artwork like it's a hobby. It's not a hobby. It's my career."

"That's not what I meant." He saw the tense set of her shoulders. "Come on…" He began to massage her neck, and moments later she began to relax beneath his fingers. "I don't want to fight. Especially on Christmas Eve."

Amanda turned in his arms and leaned her head on his chest. "I brought out the brochures because I want to plan a weekend away for the two of us. With the hours you put in at Revolution, we hardly see each other."

He held her, his fingers stroking her back. "Go away for a weekend? I thought we agreed that we'd put any extra money toward paying off my loans."

Amanda let out a cry of exasperation and pushed out of his arms. "Well, did you consider how much extra money you put into the racecar before you bought that?"

Brent threw up his hands. "I love that car. How many times are you going to throw the Viper in my face?"

"Until you *get it!*" Amanda cried.

Brent felt his anger rise. "What do I need to *get?*"

"You never should have bought that car." She shook her head. "Not that car. I can understand that you needed to buy a new car once you became a salesman, but why not a Honda or a Buick—"

"You know I wouldn't be caught dead driving a Buick—"

"You would have gotten a new car, and I would have been able to plan a trip."

Brent snorted. "A Buick? Come on."

"Forget about the Buick. I just meant that maybe a family car—"

"Are you kidding? A family car? My career just kicked into high gear. The word 'family' is not on my radar screen."

"I'm not talking about starting a family tomorrow, but—"

"I've apologized over and over again for not discussing the Viper purchase with you before I bought it. I'm sorry you didn't like the necklace. I'm sorry I didn't buy tickets to Cancun instead. No matter what I do, I'm always wrong. I am always in the penalty box." He spun on his heel and walked to the doorway.

"And I've told you over and over that the necklace wasn't necessary. It hardly makes up for the car. We need to talk about these things!"

Tears glinted in Amanda's eyes, but Brent was too angry to stop the flow of words. "I can't be your dad. I can't seem to be whoever it is you want me to be." He turned away from her, his gut churning. "I need to go cool off."

• • •

22

Brent slid behind the wheel of the Viper and took off down the quiet street. He might as well head back to Revolution and pick up his laptop. He wound through the dark neighborhoods, occasionally catching a glimpse of a decorated tree in a front window. His thoughts floated back to that last Christmas with his parents. He'd been halfway through his junior year at Brown, and he had never been happier.

He'd loved being back home for the holiday break, able to compare notes with his two best friends from high school. The three of them had it all. They tried to one-up each other, each bragging—that their school had the prettiest girls, the toughest professors, that they lived in the crappiest off-campus apartments—and joking about who was going to have the highest starting salary after graduation.

As Brent drove up the entrance ramp for 93 South, he couldn't keep his thoughts from moving on to the following April, just four months later when both his parents were killed in a car accident. But this time during his return home, he was listening to his older brother, Jimmy. *"You mean to tell me that you were totally unaware of Mom and Dad's financial situation? I find that hard to believe. Every penny they had went to pay for that ivory tower school you got into."* Those words still reverberated in Brent's head. Even after all this time, he couldn't shut them out.

The honest truth was, after he'd been accepted to Brown, his dad had never said a word to him about how his education was going to be paid for. *And he'd never asked.* Instead he remembered the pride in his father's voice when he'd call him at school, sometimes in the middle of the day, to ask about classes or if he was leaning toward a specific major. *Do you need anything, son? Anything at all?* His dad never hung up the phone without telling Brent how proud he was of him.

Entering the parking garage, Brent drove up and around the multiple levels before pulling into his assigned parking spot. The entire level was empty, save one car parked a few spaces away

23

from his in the CEO's spot. He recognized the car, and it definitely was not the CEO's.

Stepping out of the car, Brent walked toward the entrance of the building, his mind still in the past, in that late-night phone call midway through finals week at the end of his junior year when his life had come to a sudden halt.

Jimmy had stuck a "closed for family emergency" sign on his mechanic shop for a week. Brent had made phone calls to his professors arranging to return after the funeral to make up his two remaining finals.

Then the obligatory meetings had begun. They'd spent hours listening to the lawyers and the bankers and the loan officers. Suit after suit stared at their computer screens and explained about second mortgages and equity loans and how a year ago his parents had cashed in their retirement account. His brother glared at him. *See?* Jimmy's gaze seemed to say. *For you. So you could go to Brown.*

ID badge in hand, Brent shook off thoughts of the past. The door latch clicked, and he yanked it open, entering the office building and stepping into an open elevator. Moments later the elevator opened onto the twenty-sixth floor, the main sales floor of Revolution. He passed the empty reception desk, somewhat surprised the overhead lights illuminating cube city were on at midnight on Christmas Eve.

He wound his way through the myriad of cubicles where his desk had been last year and toward his office. He unlocked his door, taking in the panoramic view of the Boston lights out the window before he flicked on the light. It still gave him a rush of pride that he had earned the top spot among all his first-year colleagues, and this office was one of the benefits. So was his equally coveted assigned parking space.

He reached over and grabbed the handle of his soft sided laptop case. It was sitting on the file cabinet just inside the door where he'd rushed out without it earlier. He turned off the light and pulled the door shut.

"Hey, Brent."

The voice startled him, and he whipped around. "Clive, you scared the shit out of me!"

"I heard a noise, and I thought I'd come and investigate. What are you doing here this late?"

"Forgot my laptop. I—" At that moment Brent's cell phone rang. He pulled the phone from his pocket. "Hey, Todd. Aren't you in the middle of a wedding?"

"Yeah, and I only have a second." Todd spoke quickly. "We're at the Sheraton off exit two. I want you to get your ass down here."

"You want me to come down now?" Brent glanced up at the clock on the sales floor. "Why?" Clive hadn't moved, he stood listening to the conversation.

"I'm not telling you over the phone, just get down here."

Brent started walking toward the elevator. "No way. I've got to get home to Amanda. We had a f—" He bit off the word, then cursed himself when Clive's eyebrows shot up.

"Did you have a fight with Amanda?" Todd asked.

"Look, it's just not a good night, okay?" Brent responded. "It's Christmas Eve. It's late."

Clive reached out and pushed the call button for the elevator.

"Where are you?" Todd asked.

"I stopped to pick up my laptop at Revolution. Clive is here too."

"Who?"

"It doesn't matter."

"You did have a fight, didn't you? And you went to work to hide, you big coward. Look, call Amanda and have her meet us down there."

"She is not going to—"

"I'll call her. I can get her to come down."

Brent heard muffled voices through the phone and someone strumming an electric guitar in the background.

"Chris, I heard you, already," Todd shouted. "Give me one sec. Brent, we've got to get back on stage. I'll convince Amanda to meet you down here. I promise. I've got big news. Bring whoever else is there too. The more the merrier."

"Amanda is not—"

"Sure she will. She'll come down if I ask her."

The call disconnected. If anyone could convince Amanda to do anything, it was Todd. Maybe his buddy could help him salvage the mess he'd made of Christmas Eve.

"Wherever you're going, would you mind if I tagged along?" Clive asked.

Brent shrugged as he opened the door to the parking garage. "Suit yourself. I'm just going to meet Todd for one drink."

"I'll buy the first round."

"What is it with you offering to pick up the tab all the time?" Clive waved the comment away, and Brent watched him open the door to his car, parked in the CEO's space.

• • •

By the time Brent reached the hotel, it was starting to snow again.

He thought about leaving his laptop in the car, but he decided against it. There was virtually no storage in the Viper, and he wasn't going to risk someone busting out a window and stealing it. Clive pulled into the parking lot a moment later.

Laptop in hand, Brent stood in the lobby of the hotel for a moment before he caught sight of a small neon Coors sign. He pulled open the large medieval-looking oak door, and Clive followed him into the dimly lit space.

A half dozen men and one woman sat around a U-shaped bar. Brent walked to the only unoccupied side and set his laptop on the bar. Before he'd even taken off his coat, Clive signaled with one hand for the bartender.

"Get me a Bud on tap" Clive called out, sliding onto a barstool. "And a couple of shots of Jack."

The bartender put a cocktail napkin down in front of each of them and looked at Brent.

"I'll have a Corona."

"And start a tab for us, please."

"Why?" Brent asked, reaching for his wallet. "I told you I'm only staying for one beer."

Clive put a hand out to stop him from paying. "Right, and I offered to buy the first round."

"Sorry to disappoint you, but this is the only round I'm having tonight."

"Whatever you say." He shot Brent a grin.

"I wonder if Amanda's here yet?" Brent shoved his wallet back into his pocket and glanced over his shoulder toward the door. *What kind of a man got into an argument with his wife on Christmas Eve?* He felt like a jerk.

The bartender set both beers down and reached overhead for a glass, but Brent waved him off and picked up the bottle, taking a long swallow. The bartender took a few steps over to a woman and began refilling her empty beer glass.

"Hey, buddy!" Clive said, snapping his finger at the bartender's back, "where are those shots of Jack?" Clive stood up on the rungs of his barstool and called over to the bartender. "And my friend here needs another beer before his wife arrives."

The bartender looked at Brent, raising both eyebrows.

Brent shook his head firmly. "No, I'm good."

Clive held up his palms to Brent in apology. "Look, I'm sorry. You asked why I was at work tonight? Where else would I go? I'm a three-time loser at the happily-ever-after thing, and with three ex-wives, you can understand why I'm a little bitter. Especially around the holidays."

The bartender approached with the two shots.

Clive tapped the bar in front of him. "Looks like I'm going

to have to drink alone tonight. Put 'em both down here. Can I borrow a pen?"

Brent considered getting up and walking into the ballroom. At least he could enjoy his beer and listen to the band. The last thing he wanted to do was sit here and listen to this blowhard.

"Would you mind helping me out with something?"

"What's that?" Brent replied, not really interested. He took another sip of beer. Except for seeing Clive at a couple of department meetings and lunch that day, he hadn't had much contact with him. Still, the guy must be a hell of a salesman in order to have gotten in the door at Revolution. Time would tell if he'd have to worry about Clive causing him any serious competition.

"I'm looking for a couple of names to add to my deadpool list."

Brent looked toward the door again, hoping to see Amanda. "Any names come to mind?"

Clive's voice cut into Brent's thoughts. "What's that, again?" Brent asked, deciding he might as well finish his beer. As soon as Amanda got here, he'd get a room and make it up to her.

Clive leaned toward him and slid a cocktail napkin he'd been scribbling on between them. "I'm looking for some suggestions for my deadpool list."

"You've got to be a sick bastard to play that game."

Clive picked up his beer, drained a third of the glass before letting out a belch. "Lighten up. Plus I have a feeling this will be my lucky year." Clive shoved one of the shot glasses over to Brent. "Come on. Let's drink to one of us bringing in a half million this year."

Brent made no move to pick up the shot glass.

"You might earn what, fifteen percent of that figure at Revolution this year?"

Instead of answering, Brent did a quick mental calculation and came up with seventy-five thousand. He'd better bring in a hell of a lot more money than that.

Clive continued, "After all, you're the big Rookie of the Year winner."

Brent wasn't going to deny it. "True. I had a good year."

"So I heard, but no matter how good you are, or were, you're not going to see a check for five-hundred-thousand dollars anytime soon." Clive paused and drained his glass. "And neither am I, even if I am a better salesman than you."

"Which you're not."

"So I hedge my bets and try to bring in money a few other ways as well. If I win, I'll take the money and run. If someone questions my taste level or calls me a sick bastard, I don't give a damn."

Brent quickly ran through the numbers again in his mind, remembering that Clive told him it cost five grand to join and that the winner could net a half a million dollars? No way. No online game was going to offer odds like that. He shook his head.

Clive picked up a shot glass and knocked it against the one closest to Brent. "This one's for real."

Bullshit, Brent thought.

"Come on. One drink. To getting rich." Clive raised his glass. "By whatever means possible."

Oh, what the hell. "I'll drink to getting rich." Brent downed the shot. *After all, he was going to spend the night at the hotel with Amanda, so he didn't have to worry about driving.* He glanced at the door.

"Atta boy." Clive slapped him on the back.

"Who's on your list so far?" Brent asked, as he signaled the bartender for another beer. *This whole deadpool game could be a great conversation starter at the monthly business-to-business meetings he attended.* Then he remembered cold calling was Clive's job now.

"Open your laptop. I'll pull up my roster."

"There you are!" Todd called out, sliding onto the empty bar stool to Brent's left. "You are not going to believe what happened tonight!" With his drumsticks, he beat out a riff on the top of the bar.

"What?" Brent asked, taking a swig of his fresh beer.

"This frigging wedding, right. I hate weddings. We all hate weddings, but Chris up-charged the hell out of the gig because it was on Christmas Eve. Father of the bride went for it, so we were stuck playing at the Sheraton, right?"

"And," Brent prompted.

"After our first set, this guy walks up to Jordan and asks him if we'd be interested in recording a demo for him. We'd just finished 'Glamour Girl,' and he must have liked the sound of it. Check it out." Todd laid his sticks on the bar and pulled a business card out of his back pocket. "Capitol freaking Recording Studio. Los Angeles, California." He let out a whoop.

Brent took the card and read the front. Larry Conrad. Executive Producer.

"Can you believe that?" Todd grinned. "A demo! The guy wants Chris to call him in January to set it up. This may be our big break."

"Congratulations," Brent said, picking up his beer and saluting Todd. "It couldn't have happened to a better, more talented guy."

The bartender walked over. "Sounds like you guys have something to celebrate."

"Line 'em up," Clive said. "First round is on me."

"Jack?" the bartender asked, holding the bottle of Jack Daniels aloft.

"Yes, sir," Clive responded, holding his hand out toward Brent to take a look at the business card.

"No argument here, but who the hell are you?" Todd asked, leaning over Brent to see who was sitting next to him.

"Sorry," Brent said. "This is Clive Ellis. He's the guy that was burning the midnight oil at Revolution tonight when I stopped in to pick up my laptop. Clive just started a couple months ago. I thought maybe you guys had crossed paths at work. He's the newest member of the sales team."

Todd leaned over, his blonde ponytail falling over one shoulder, and shook Clive's hand. "Todd Tanklefsky. I work in information systems."

"Tanklefsky? What kind of a name is that?"

"It's Russian," Todd replied. "Thanks for the drink."

"My pleasure," Clive responded. He raised his glass. "To fame and fortune."

"What are we celebrating?" the bartender asked when the empty shot glasses were back on the bar.

"The start of my music career," Todd said. "I'm with On The Rise, and we were just asked to cut a demo for Capitol Recording Studios."

"I'd say that's worth a round on the house." The bartender gave a furtive glance around and then added a clean glass to the three on the bar and filled them up. He raised his shot glass, and they followed suit, clinking them together before downing the amber liquid.

"What makes you think this guy is legit?" Clive asked, handing the card back to Todd.

Brent saw Todd's face darken.

"What makes you think he's not?" Todd shot back.

"I'm just saying…"

"What is your problem?" Brent asked, turning to face Clive.

"Trust but verify," Clive said. "Open your laptop. You'll feel ten times better than you do now once you know he's the real deal. It'll take two seconds."

"Do it," Todd said.

Brent leaned forward and opened his laptop. A few keystrokes later he was logged into the hotel's wi-fi. Todd held out the business card, angling it so he could read the letters in the dim light. After typing the first and last name into a search engine, Brent held his breath.

A second later they were looking at a bio on the Capitol Recording Studio website. "Executive Producer Larry Conrad,"

Brent read aloud, "responsible for signing such bands as White Tornado and First Street Heat." He paused and turned to Todd, eyes wide. "Holy shit!"

"You're up, Brent," Clive said, grinning. "Now we really have something to celebrate."

Todd let out a raucous yell, and they all traded high fives.

The bartender walked back over with the bottle of Jack.

Brent pumped a fist in the air and nodded at the bartender to pour another round of shots. Then Todd asked the bartender to set them up again. And Clive offered yet another round.

Brent was feeling more than a little drunk, but Clive was right. Todd was his best friend, and Todd had certainly bought him more than a few rounds of drinks the night they'd celebrated him winning the award from Revolution.

"One last round," Brent said, speaking slowly and carefully. His tongue felt as if it had grown two sizes too big for his mouth. "Here's to my best friend, Todd," he wrapped his left arm around him. "T-to making it big in the music industry. I always knew it was just a matter of t-time." He downed the drink and watched Todd do the same. *I am so wasted.* They slammed their empty shot glasses upside down on the bar.

"It's about time someone finally discovered the band." Todd had a look of pure delight on his face. "I know we can make it. I just know it. You…" he gave Brent a playful punch in the arm, "get awarded a permanent backstage pass for years of listening to us play in crappy venues all over New England." He paused. "Speaking of backstage passes…"

Brent followed Todd's gaze.

The door to the bar was partially open, and Todd's eyes were locked on a petite woman peering in. When her eyes found Todd, she smiled and motioned for him to join her.

Brent slapped Todd on the back. "Go."

"You don't mind after I dragged you all the way here?"

"No. Go enjoy yourself."

"Okay. The band and a few friends are going to have a little celebration," Todd said. "Thanks again for the drinks. I'll see you guys after Christmas."

A moment later Todd had one arm wrapped around the girl's tiny waist, his sticks protruded from his back pocket. He raised his free hand as he departed.

"Shit! I forgot to ask him about Amanda." Brent slid off the barstool and took a step, nearly stumbling before he caught himself by grabbing the back of Clive's stool. He steadied himself a moment and then pulled a credit card out of his wallet and tossed it on the bar, signaling the bartender. "I'm going to hit the head, cash out, and go home."

The walk to the bathroom made him realize just how intoxicated he was. He washed his face and blinked in the mirror trying to focus. *Where was Amanda?* He leaned against the bathroom wall and called Todd to find out. All three calls went to voicemail. Next he spent a laborious few minutes typing out a text message, but he got no response. Finally he walked back to his stool in the bar.

Cell phone still in hand, Brent sat back down. "Shit."

"What?" Clive asked, looking up from the laptop.

"Hey. What the hell are you doing on my computer?"

"I just pulled up my roster on the deadpool site."

Brent's cell phone vibrated, and he read the message from Todd: "Sorry. She decided not to come."

Brent sighed. "Shit. Shit. Shit." He closed his eyes but when the room tilted, he opened them again. He was definitely too drunk to drive at this point. He checked the time on his phone, not really surprised to see that it was two a.m. *Way too late to call Amanda.*

He remembered her mentioning that her stomach was slightly upset after dinner. And he felt yet another twinge of guilt. Amanda wasn't big on red meat, but he'd bought the steaks trying to impress her father.

Well, at least Todd had called Amanda so she knew where he was. Tomorrow he'd share Todd's good news and apologize for being such a jerk on Christmas Eve. He'd make it up to her and treat her like a queen all day on Christmas.

"Is everything okay?" Clive asked.

"Yeah." Brent had no intention of sharing any of his personal life with this loser.

"All right, help me put together this deadpool list. I've got to get this roster in before the deadline, which is on December 31st."

Brent rubbed his eyes. *Maybe he ought to get a room and crash?* But on second thought, spending money on himself was pretty selfish. He could doze in his car. He made a mental note to buy a bouquet of flowers on the way home.

"Earth to Brent?"

"What?"

"Are you going to help with my deadpool roster or not?"

"I guess." He'd drink a couple glasses of water and then catch some sleep in his car until he sobered up.

"Okay, throw a name at me," Clive said.

"How about the Pope? He's got to be dead soon, right?"

"Yeah, but the guy's ancient, so he's hardly worth anything," Clive said. "You've got to get more creative than that. Who else?"

"Let's see…how about that guy on death row? The one that murdered those sorority girls last summer?" Brent picked at the label on his beer bottle, trying to remember. His brain was running in slow motion. "You know the one."

"Phillip Travia?"

"Yeah. They're about to fry that bad boy."

"Good one." Clive used two fingers to hunt and peck for the letters to enter the name.

"How about Paul Newman?" Brent suggested.

"He's already dead."

"He is? When did that happen?"

Clive shrugged.

Brent kept tossing out names.

"You're pretty good at this. So if you did play, who would be on your list?"

Brent thought for a minute. "How about the leader of some third-world country, like Fadhl Sharma? Isn't he the President of Yemen? A guy like that is always a heartbeat away from getting blown away by a random assassin."

Clive nodded. "Not bad. Who else?"

"I don't know, the Vice President?"

"I have to disagree on that one. Have you seen the Vice President lately?" Clive asked. "He's taken up jogging, and his wife has him on that rabbit-food diet she invented. He doesn't look that bad anymore."

"He's already had one heart attack," Brent countered. "It's only a matter of time before—"

"Okay, I put him down."

Brent realized he had another fresh beer in his hand. *How had that happened?* The rest of the night continued in a blur.

• • •

December 30ᵗʰ – Wednesday

Removing all but the slightest bit of gray oil paint from the liner brush, Amanda studied the tilt of the kitten's face. With a delicate hand and holding her breath, she drew the brush across, barely touching the canvas as she added one last whisker. Exhaling, she sat back, studying the overall effect with a critical eye.

Satisfied, she swished her brush around in a glass jar half filled with turpentine and then wiped it on a wadded-up Brown University t-shirt. When Brent found out she'd turned them into paint rags, he'd responded by staggering around their bedroom, clutching an invisible dagger stuck in his chest. "Wiping paint on my t-shirts from Brown? Have you no respect?"

"You graduated two years ago," she'd teased, "this is a much better use for them." He'd grabbed her, and they'd gotten into a wrestling match that ended with great sex on the family room floor at the foot of her easel.

"What do you think, you cute little fluff ball," she asked the calico kitten with the green eyes who stared back at her from the canvas. "We've been married for two years. Is that still considered the honeymoon phase?"

She selected another brush and dipped it into the dark gray paint, painting a squiggle on a piece of drawing paper to check the color. Too dark. With a toothpick Amanda added white until she was satisfied with the color.

The morning after the big fight, Brent had come home with his tail between his legs, along with a beautiful bouquet of roses and what looked like a hell of a hangover. Served him right for abandoning her on Christmas Eve.

Looking up at the clock, she was surprised to see it was already past four o'clock. It got dark so early now that it was past Daylight Saving Time. She stretched her neck, working out the kinks as she continued to clean her brush, swishing it again and again in turpentine. It was time to quit before she made a mistake. When the brush left no trace of paint on the rag, Amanda laid it aside and screwed the top on the turpentine.

She pondered the bottom of the canvas, around the kitten's feet, wondering if it needed something. "A clump of yellow dandelions, maybe? Or how about a hint of beach sand?" No, neither one was right. Both ideas were too pedestrian for a socialite of her client's status. Mrs. Wagner lived in a four story mansion on Brattle Street in Cambridge. She decided to call and ask her.

She pulled out Mrs. Wagner's business card, which was thick enough to be used as a doorstop and dialed her client's number.

"Hello, Mrs. Wagner, this is Amanda calling from Artful Paws."

"Who, dear?"

"The pet artist."

"Oh, of course. You were painting my Ginger."

"Yes, and I wanted to give you an update."

"Oh." Pause. "Well, actually, it's rather a good thing you called. I'm terribly sorry to tell you that I have to cancel the painting."

"Cancel?" Amanda's heart sank. "But why?"

"It's just this terrible economy, darling. My husband had an absolute fit when I told him about it the other day."

"But you commissioned me to do the painting and—"

"Yes, dear, but my husband has forbidden any further conversation on the matter."

"But…" What could she say? She hadn't gotten a deposit up front. "Perhaps we could set up a payment plan."

"Milton has put his foot down. Something he rarely does, but you can understand that I am left without options."

Which is better than what I'm left with: a half finished painting of your cat.

"I do appreciate you understanding my position."

"It's just that my position is equally—" *Click.* Amanda stared at the phone. The woman had hung up.

Amanda stood with the phone in her hand and felt a knot of anxiety harden in her stomach. She'd been so sure that this job was going to lead to others within the wealthy art-loving community outside of Boston.

Over the half wall, her eye fell on the canvas, assessing, critiquing. And the painting was good. Really good.

Or was it? Biting her lip, she forced her eyes to move elsewhere. Her gaze stopped on the one-hundred-and-ten- dollar bottle of cognac she'd bought Brent for Christmas.

Now that she'd lost the sale, she wished she hadn't let her dad talk her into such an expensive brand, even if she had loved the ornate bottle the cognac came in.

Brent was the top salesman at Revolution. And now Todd had gotten his break—poised to cut a demo track with the band. So what had she accomplished in the last two years? Maybe she simply wasn't talented enough? Amanda returned the phone to the charger and slumped down onto a kitchen stool before folding her arms on top of the countertop and rested her forehead against them.

The front door slammed, and Amanda felt a tear roll out of the corner of her eye.

"Hey, honey," Brent called out. "I'm starving. How about we order a pizza?"

She lifted her head and swiped at a tear as his footsteps neared the kitchen.

"Honey?" he repeated.

Amanda tried to blink back the tears.

Brent rounded the half wall separating the kitchen from the family room. "What's wrong?" he asked.

Amanda heard the worry in his voice. "I'm okay."

Brent dumped everything he was carrying onto the kitchen counter: his laptop, gray wool jacket, two binders, and an enormous stack of files. "Talk to me." The second he let go of the pile, the manila folders cascaded down onto the floor, but his gaze never wavered.

"I've had a lousy afternoon." She sniffled.

"Can I help?" He reached out and took one of her hands, rubbing his thumb over her fingers.

"You can listen."

"Okay. What happened?"

"The painting I'm working on…the kitten in the other room…" Amanda sniffled.

"Yes." Brent sat down on the other stool, her hand still captured in his. "It's okay. Breathe."

"It's my first art commission in months." Amanda felt a fresh tear slip down her cheek. "Remember the lady I told you about who lived in that mansion on Brat—"

"That rich wacko with the two-story totem pole in her entryway?" Brent leaned over and wiped the tear off her cheek with his thumb.

Amanda nodded. "I called her this afternoon to tell her how well the painting was coming along and she...she..." A tiny sob escaped. "She doesn't want the painting anymore. And I think the painting is really good, don't you?"

"Why did she cancel?"

"She said her husband put his foot down, and it couldn't be helped." Amanda pulled a tissue from the box on the counter and blotted her eyes.

"She can't just cancel a commissioned piece of artwork. You wrote something up when she agreed on the price, right?"

"No."

"Oh, honey..." Brent sighed. "You have to—"

"But she was so nice. She made me tea and—"

"Well, at least you have her deposit. What do you ask for up front, fifty percent?"

"No. I didn't get a deposit because—"

"Why not?"

Amanda closed her eyes. "Brent, please don't interrogate me. This woman is clearly a millionaire. I told you about the inside of that house. I wasn't going to ask for a deposit."

"Well, clearly you should have."

"Well, I didn't. My business is different than yours."

"Getting a deposit and a signed contract is the only way to close a sale."

"My business relies on word of mouth and referrals, not paperwork."

"Word of mouth isn't the way to run a business. It's not sustainable." Brent gestured with both hands.

"I'm an artist. I'm not a salesman."

"It's not a good business model."

"Brent, please. I don't need a lecture."

"But you asked for my advice."

"No, I didn't. I asked you to listen to me. Why do men always want to solve everything? I don't want advice. I want...I want…" She broke off and another sob escaped. "I want a hug."

Brent got off the stool and held out his arms. "You're right, you did just ask me to listen. But I want to help. It tears me up when I see you cry."

"I know." She nodded and slipped into his arms. "But it's what women do," she murmured into the nubby fabric of his suit coat. Amanda burrowed into Brent as close as she could, willing his warmth to seep into her. She stayed in his embrace for several minutes, inhaling his comforting scent.

She was going to have to make a decision about Artful Paws. Her business was going into another month without a single commission. Maybe it was time to put her dream of being an artist away for good.

• • •

January 8th – Friday

The sun was already setting when Brent swiveled around in his high-back leather chair, staring out the window of his office. Only the top of the Hancock Tower remained ablaze from the last rays of the sun. The rest of the city was already awash in the deep blue shadows of early winter. The cars heading north on I-93 already had their headlights on.

When they decided to buy the house in New Hampshire, neither had realized the traffic that backed up into Massachusetts every Friday afternoon. In winter it was the skiers, in summer it was the vacationers heading to the Lakes Region. Brent knew that if he headed out now, his sixty-minute commute would take at least an hour and a half. Better to wait it out a bit. If he kept an eye out the window, he could leave as soon as the traffic let up.

Turning back around to face his computer, Brent decided he might as well go through his email. He reached for the mouse and groaned as thirty new messages lined up in his mailbox.

Brent deleted a half dozen automated emails unopened. Everything from his wine-of-the-month newsletter to his daily Merrill Lynch stock tip. It was four-thirty by the time Brent double-clicked on the last unopened note. It was a memo from finance with more stringent rules about submitting expense reports. He chuckled to himself. *Looks like Clive would be paying for all those drinks at the Sheraton out of his own pocket after all.* He looked forward to busting Clive's chops about that.

Opening a folder titled Policies and Procedures, he dropped the finance email inside. He was about to close his laptop down when a chime signaled the arrival of a new message. "Speak of the devil," Brent said aloud, noting Clive was the sender.

Brent,

Thanks for the help with my roster for this year's deadpool. I'm happy with our picks. I may be a contender this year. What do you think? Attached is the link to DieorDieTrying.com. Check it out.

Clive

After a moment of contemplation, Brent double-clicked on the embedded link, and macabre laughter began pouring out of the tiny speakers on his desk.

There was a rap on Brent's open office door, and he looked up.

"Hey, man," Todd said, walking into Brent's office. He stood twirling a drumstick wrapped in green metallic tape through his fingers. "I just wanted to stop by and remind you that IT will be doing some system updates during the next few days—"

"Check this out!" Brent interrupted, motioning Todd over. Transfixed, Brent watched a rotating skull drop slowly from the top of the screen.

Todd ambled around behind Brent's desk. The skull had grown in size until it filled the screen and it was no longer rotating. Both eye sockets filled with blood then slowly overflowed down the skeleton's face, materializing into wavy letters below that spelled out "DieorDieTrying.com."

"Awesome," Todd replied. "Sweet graphics."

Brent grinned up at Todd, but as usual, his friend's face was hidden behind the curtain of dirty-blonde hair that fell to his shoulders.

"Is this that deadpool game you were telling me about? The one that Clive plays?" Todd asked. He grabbed a metal folding chair that was leaning up against the wall.

Brent nodded. "He just forwarded me the link."

Todd flipped open the chair and sat backwards on it, his long arms dangling over the back. "How do you get points?"

"Someone on your list has to die."

"Right."

Brent began to move the cursor around the screen, exploring.

Todd reached up and pointed with one drumstick to a smiling skeleton, its skull cleaved by a bloody ax. "What's that button?"

Brent rolled the mouse over the graphic and clicked. "Looks like last year's winner. Some guy by the name of Frank Miller. Let's look at his roster." Brent clicked on another button, and a list of names popped up. The first three names on the top of the list had a blood-red line through them, and each one had a red number beside the line. "Looks like Frank had three people on his roster actually die last year. What are the odds?"

"Shit, man. He had Ryan Donoghue on his list."

"Who is that?"

"Are you serious?" Todd gave Brent a look of disbelief. "Heat Sensation?"

Brent shrugged. "Given your limited areas of expertise, I'm

guessing Heat Sensation is a band and that Ryan is a member of that band?"

"Was a member of, you mean," Todd said. "And yeah, Donoghue was the lead singer. He was like, twenty-one. He was run over by the driver of his own tour bus. It was tragic, man." Todd shook his head.

"Sounds like it," Brent replied.

"Do you recognize the second name on the list, 'Jim Carlton'?" Todd pointed again. "Who the hell is that?"

"No clue." Brent rolled the mouse over the second name on the list, which was also crossed out with a thick red line. As he hovered over the name, applause began to emanate out of his speakers.

"Man, they must have a pretty twisted programmer on board," Todd said.

"Not to mention pretty twisted players."

"Like Clive?"

"Like Clive," Brent agreed. He reached over and turned his speaker volume to the off position.

"Click down below the second guy's name. Over there in the lower right-hand corner," Todd instructed.

Brent moved the cursor over and a pop-up box appeared. "I get it." Brent said, nodding. "For the guys that died, these are the details about their deaths. Jim Carlton was a reality TV contestant."

"Yeah, for Top Cadet," Todd read over his shoulder. "Is that show even on TV anymore? No wonder we've never heard of him. Scroll down further."

"He died in a skydiving accident. That's a nasty way to go. He was worth sixty-one points."

"Why sixty-one points?" Todd asked.

"You take the age of the dead guy and subtract it from one hundred," Brent answered. "Get it?"

"Yeah. I got it." Todd shoved his drumstick back into the side pocket of his cargo pants.

"Cool in a creepy sort of way, huh?" Brent asked.

"You got that right," Todd answered. "So skydiving guy was thirty-nine when he died?"

"Exactly." Brent rolled the mouse over a gravestone with a smiley face on it and clicked to open it. "This looks like a comprehensive list of every person nominated last year. You can see how popular some folks were, like the Pope, who is still alive and kicking." He laughed. "A ton of people had him on their rosters. But look…" Brent used the arrow keys to page down. "The guy who won last year was the only player that put Jim Carlton – i.e., skydiver - on his roster. That's why he won. Those sixty-one points were huge."

"Well, huge when added on top of the seventy-nine points for the kid from Heat Sensation. Plus whatever points he got from the third guy on his roster who died."

Brent continued to scroll up and down the list. "Actually, two people picked the lead singer of Heat Sensation. But no one else on the other guy's roster died, so he didn't even finish in the top ten."

"Remind me again why this game is fun?" Todd said standing up and collapsing onto the metal chair with a bang.

"According to Clive, it's all about the money." Brent spotted a graphic that looked like a pirate's treasure chest. Blood was seeping steadily from beneath the partially open lid and forming the words "DOLLARS FOR DEATH." He clicked on the treasure chest and a photo came up of a scanned check. "Four hundred and eighty-two thousand dollars," Brent read aloud. The check was made out to Frank Miller.

"No freaking way!" Todd exclaimed, leaning down to stare at the image on the screen. "The winner got a check for that much money last year?"

"Looks like it."

"Frigging unbelievable."

"When Clive explained the game to me, frankly, I didn't

believe him. That guy talks so much bullshit. I honestly didn't think this deadpool game really existed."

"That is some serious cash." Todd whistled softly between his teeth as he walked around to the other side of Brent's desk.

"I guess now I understand why DieorDieTrying.com is by invitation only. Clive offered to get me in."

"Really? You didn't take him up on it, did you?"

"No."

Todd nodded. "The guy was an asshole the other night. I don't even know him, and he starts giving me crap about my contact at Capitol. What the fuck was that?"

"Yeah. I plan to steer clear of him outside of the office. Although that night at the Sheraton, after you ditched me, he asked me for a few names for his roster which I graciously provided."

"Like who? You were pretty hammered that night."

"Speak for yourself."

"So who did you end up recommending for Clive's list?" Todd asked.

"I don't remember. I can pull it up though." Brent was using the arrow keys to page back when his phone rang. He grabbed the receiver, securing it between his ear and shoulder, and checked caller ID. "Hey, what's up?"

Eyes still focused on the computer, Brent did a search on the name Clive. A roster popped up entitled Clive's Crypt. He hit the print key. "Yeah, he's here. Do you need him?"

"Who is that?" Todd asked. He reached over and grabbed a red paperclip from a box on Brent's desk. He lined it up on the edge of the desk and flicked it at Brent's head.

"Yeah, I know. Those guys in information systems are frigging useless."

"Oh. You think?" Todd said. He grabbed the box of paperclips.

Brent ducked as a barrage of multicolored paperclips rained down on him. He laughed and gave Todd the finger.

"Can you still enter a roster?" Todd asked.

Brent shook his head no and covered the mouthpiece. "The deadline was December thirty-first. Why? Were you thinking of entering?" Then into the phone he said, "Sure. I'll send him right over." Brent hung up.

"Who desires my invaluable expertise now?" Todd asked, heading toward the door.

"Max." Brent swept an arm across his desk scattering the paperclips to the floor. "The sixty-four-inch color printer is down. He yelled something about being an hour past his deadline. Max is clearly in meltdown mode."

"So what else is new?" Todd paused, pulled a drumstick out of his pocket, and began walking it through his fingers. "Don't forget we're updating the system. In case I don't see you tomorrow, you won't be able to log on either Saturday or Sunday. Major system upgrade."

Brent waved a hand in his direction. "Yeah, I heard you. That will give me a rare weekend to play instead of busting my butt for Revolution."

"How does Amanda put up with you, anyway, you workaholic?"

"You should talk."

"Yeah, but my boss forces me to come in and work the occasional weekend. You do it by choice. So I assume you and Amanda made up after the fight on Christmas Eve? What was that about?"

"Yes, we made up and none of your business." Brent looked up at the clock; it was almost five-thirty. "No thanks to you, since a night at the Sheraton would have gone a long way toward getting back in her good graces."

"Well, you shouldn't have started a fight with her on Christmas Eve, dumbass."

"I know. I know. I was being stupid."

"I don't know why she puts up with your sorry ass." Todd shook his head.

Brent laughed. "Sometimes I don't either, but thank God she does."

"You've got it all, man. Can you please make an effort not to screw things up from here on out?"

Brent laughed. "I'm trying. I really am."

"If you were just a little more chill, like me, you and Amanda wouldn't fight all the time."

"We don't fight all the time."

"Compared to what, the World Wrestling Federation?"

"Anyway, things are really good between us right now. And it isn't like you haven't had your share of screw-ups."

"Hey, rock stars play by different rules. And once I start putting out platinum CDs and going on world tours, I'm not going to be around to give you my sage advice. Best enjoy it while you can."

"I'll make a note."

"Yup, my life is pretty sweet right now. Lots of girls, lots of free drinks. I can't even say I hate my day job. And it's only a matter of time until I have a rider requiring my dressing room be filled with caviar and premium champagne."

"Well, at the moment, pal, about all you can afford is M&Ms and Mountain Dew."

"All things in good time." Todd walked back to the window and pointed with his drumstick. "Traffic's a nightmare. It's going to take you a while to get home, my friend."

"Damn skiers," Brent said as he rapidly closed files and shut down his computer. He'd call Amanda as soon as he got on the road. "Hey, I meant to ask you. Did your band play anywhere on New Year's Eve?"

"Just a small local deal. But we've got an upcoming gig at The Jail in February. Have you heard of it?"

"Doesn't ring a bell, but Amanda and I haven't been out clubbing in a while."

"It's on Tremont."

Brent nodded, reached for his laptop case, and shoved his computer inside before zipping it up.

"The place is known for hosting up-and-coming bands." Todd walked over and slouched against the doorjamb. "Our new California connection helped get the booking."

Brent looked up, "That producer is making things happen already. Congrats." He grabbed his coat from the back of the door, and as he reached for the light switch, his eye fell on the single sheet of paper sitting in the outbox of the printer. The deadpool roster for Clive's Crypt.

"We're playing on a Sunday night in February. On the fourteenth. The Jail is not exactly a great place to bring a Valentine, it will probably be dead. Still, I'm hoping for the best-case scenario, not to mention fighting off lovesick groupies half my age!" He backed out the door, grinning.

"In your dreams, rock-and-roll boy! Besides, that would make the girls what…twelve? For your information, the cops call that statutory rape."

"What are you, my freaking lawyer? I promise I'll check IDs first."

"You better," Brent said. "I have no intention of hauling your useless butt out of jail." Brent grabbed the paper and pulled the door shut.

"And make sure you invite Amanda," Todd said, walking backwards down the hall.

"Will do." Brent grinned as Todd gave him his customary one drumstick salute before he turned and headed off down the hall, his flip-flops slapping against his heels.

Brent turned in the opposite direction, scanning Clive's roster as he walked down the aisle between the rows of cubicles. He noticed that two of his suggestions (at least the two he remembered making) were listed on Clive's final roster. Maybe he should ask for a cut if, by some miracle, Clive won some money?

Passing a blue recycling bin, he dropped the sheet of paper inside and made a run for the elevator.

• • •

January 9th – Saturday

Midmorning on Saturday, Brent stood barefoot in the kitchen making a sandwich. He slathered mayonnaise on one piece of the bread and mustard on the other. As he waited for the pot of coffee to finish brewing, he licked a bit of mustard off his thumb before wiping the back of his hand across his worn gray sweatpants. He poured himself a steaming cup of coffee and then piled ham and cheese high on the sandwich.

Not bothering with a plate, he ate the sandwich standing up at the sink in six huge bites while looking out the window. A blue-and-white bird hopped upside-down along the trunk of one of the large oak trees in the backyard.

Brent washed his sandwich down with a slurp of coffee and glanced over at the thermometer attached to the corner of the house. The temperature hovered around the twenty-degree mark. So much for his plan to change the oil in the Viper. That could wait for another day. He'd freeze his butt off in the garage on a day like today.

Being alone in the house was a treat. Amanda and one of her new girlfriends were off getting their hair done for a neighborhood party tonight. Since he was unable to log onto the Revolution site, he decided to treat himself and just kick back.

With a fresh cup of coffee in hand, Brent wandered into the den. Maybe he could get in a game or two of RISK before Amanda got home. With a sense of guilty pleasure, he sat down at the computer. Amanda thought Internet games were a colossal waste of time.

The ancient machine labored through its startup mode,

and Brent held his breath as he fiddled with a paperclip. It was hard to let this computer go since it was the last gift his folks had given him.

When the desktop popped into view, Brent went directly to his email folder. The oldest note was from several days ago. It was from Amanda's mom, and as expected, it was a thank-you note for the Christmas gifts they'd received. He hit the print key and a single page rolled into the tray of his desktop printer. The other dozen or so messages all looked like spam. Everything from ads for lonely singles, to discount Viagra. About to delete the lot of them in one keystroke, Brent saw something.

The last email had no sender name and no date. In fact, all the columns from left to right were blank. *How was that even possible?* Brent sat back and contemplated the email for a moment. Lots of emails arrived with a blank subject line, but how was it possible to send an email without a date stamp?

He stared at the unopened envelope wishing he were just a bit more computer savvy. Technology was so screaming fast these days that it was hard to keep up. He was a big Facebook fan, and he had a Twitter account, which Amanda thought was absolutely silly. He was even thinking of starting some sort of sales blog. The purpose was the same for all of them: to generate sales leads.

Still, he didn't always have a handle on the behind-the-scenes technical stuff. He knew enough to carry on a conversation, but more than a cursory knowledge seemed a waste of time, especially since Todd was brilliant in that arena. Todd would make sure he was aware of the must-have free app or whatever.

Still, he sat fascinated by the anonymous email. Perched on the edge of the desk chair, tapping a pen, he pondered whether or not to open the note. *Could there be any harm in opening it?* Since there was no attachment, he had to assume it was safe. Still, he paused since he was on his personal laptop. At work he never worried about this stuff since the IT department was just down the hall. Eventually curiosity got the better of him.

The note was short, only two lines:

BRENT,

WELCOME TO DIEORDIETRYING.COM.

I TRUST YOU WILL BE A WORTHY ADVERSARY.

INTRUDER

Intruder? Who the heck was Intruder?

Brent stared at the note. Besides not knowing who Intruder was, he thought the wording was strange. And the font was strange, too. It was certainly not your everyday Helvetic or Courier. He couldn't quite place it.

He studied the lack of serifs and the broad style. Very dramatic. Completely over the top. Most people couldn't care less about what font they used to type an email. It was rare to see anyone go with anything other than the default font. The fact that this person had chosen a specific font, and an odd one at that, was unusual. Plus, it was really only appropriate for Halloween, and January was a long way away from Halloween. Brent knew this font. *What was the name of it?*

All of a sudden he slapped an open palm down on the desk. "Showcard Gothic," he said out loud. A few clicks later, after confirming his guess, he gave himself a mental pat on the back. *Damn, I'm good!*

Font recognition was part of a well-rehearsed sales presentation Brent had perfected over the last year for prospective clients.

Near the end of his presentation, Brent would ask one of the decision makers to pick a random headline out of a magazine. If Brent was unable to correctly identify the font, he would take ten percent off the initial consultation fee. The ploy often worked, and he would land the account on the spot.

On occasion he failed to correctly identify the font, but that wasn't the point. The point was to be remembered. That was half the battle in a sales job. And his success lately seemed to bear that out.

Brent leaned forward again and continued to study the note. *Why such a huge font size? Why all caps?* He hated that on principle, likening it to yelling in a conversation.

He drummed his fingers, guessing Clive was behind the anonymous email. It seemed like a parlor trick he might have up his sleeve, and even the all capital letters seemed to make sense with Clive's in-your-face personality. After all, Clive seemed to love throwing down the gauntlet.

Curious to see if a reply would go anywhere, Brent hit the reply-to-sender key, even though there was no information visible. It would probably come back as bounced.

From the drop down menu, Brent chose Arial Narrow for his reply. It was his current favorite: clean and simple. Also, since the list was alphabetical, it didn't require scrolling through pages of font choices. He banged out a quick response:

Intruder—or should I say Clive—

Maybe you were drunker than I thought on Christmas Eve. I declined your invitation to play the DieorDieTrying.com game. Good luck with your roster. If you win, do I get a cut?

Brent

Without reading the note over, he hit the send key and closed out of the email program. That bit of business completed, Brent jumped onto the Internet and opened his favorite multiplayer game site. Lots of people were online. The RISK site was humming.

A dozen or so people were milling around who were not involved in a game yet. Brent was about to start up another game when his computer chimed, and he was invited to join five other players. Several keystrokes later, he ran his index finger down the list of the screen names of the other players in the room. Two were familiar to him, regular online gamers. Because he was the last person in the room, he was stuck with gray, an unlucky color for him.

The fighting was fast and furious, with countries changing hands and armies being obliterated right and left. Players ganged up heartlessly against the orange player, and he was ousted early from the game. Purple was eliminated soon after. The remaining colors fought to the death, showing each other no mercy. Between turns, as the number of remaining players dwindled, the online chat increased. Everyone began to heap insults on their opponents, curse their own bad luck, and share adolescent sexual exploits. That was part of the fun.

Brent kept an ear out for the garage door, wanting to log off before Amanda walked in the house. He knew she'd be shocked by these conversations. She just didn't get the whole concept of guys trying to one-up each other. Ninety-nine percent of the stories these guys were telling online were total bullshit. His own certainly were. But what did you expect on the Net?

Halfway through the game, the dice started to roll in Brent's favor, despite his unlucky color. The trick was you had to win Australia early. Didn't these people know that? He was now confident he would claim victory. Sometimes it was just too easy.

An hour later, Brent had overthrown the last of his enemies and conquered the world. He was feeling good. Red suggested a rematch, and they agreed to another game the next day.

Brent's stomach growled, and he looked at his watch, surprised to see it was after three o'clock. Amanda must be on her way home by now. He hoped her girlfriend hadn't talked her into getting her hair colored, or worse, cut.

As he started closing folders and files, his thoughts returned to the note from Intruder. He checked his email. Nothing new, nor had the reply he'd sent to Intruder bounced back as undeliverable. *Interesting.*

Brent jumped back on the Internet, deciding to check out Intruder's roster on the deadpool site. The now familiar maniacal laughter burst from the desk speakers, and the skull began its slow rotation.

From the home page, Brent clicked on the master list of rosters. He scanned the titles players had given their lists of nominees. A few of the more clever names jumped out at him. "Grateful When They're Dead" was a good one. So was "Cash for Cadavers." *People must really get into this game.* But after an outlay of five grand, that made sense.

The online rosters didn't appear to be in any particular order. He pulled up a search box and began to type in the word Intruder. He cocked an ear for the garage door, but all was quiet.

The search feature found an entry called Intruder's Chalk Outlines. *So, whoever Intruder was, he had a deadpool list. Was it Clive? Did Clive have two rosters?* Then Brent dismissed the idea. The guy wore polyester suits. There was no way he'd drop ten grand playing an Internet game. *Who was this guy?*

Maybe the names on the roster would give him a clue. Brent was about to double click on the roster when something at the bottom of the screen caught his eyes. *No! It couldn't be!*

He stared at a roster entitled "Darby's Death List." *The name Darby wasn't that uncommon. It didn't necessarily mean…* With an unsteady hand, he double clicked. Fadhl Sharma was the first name on the list. *Oh my God!*

Brent struggled to remember what happened that night at the bar. Images raced through his mind: fresh bottles of beer appearing in front of him, tossing his credit card on the bar before heading to the restroom, making suggestions for Clive's deadpool list. But most damning of all, Brent recalled returning to find Clive typing away on *his* laptop.

Brent knew he had suggested the name Fadhl Sharma. He wasn't into international politics, but a customer the previous week had mentioned the name of the President of Yemen, and it had stuck with him. Somehow, that night at the bar, Brent became the newest player with a roster on DieorDieTrying.com. *Shit!*

The garage door rumbled, and Brent let go of the mouse and dropped back in his chair. *Clive, you conniving bastard!*

In a daze, Brent exited off the site. His heart was racing as he jogged to the garage to meet Amanda. He had no doubt his credit card had been charged the five thousand dollar entry fee.

• • •

January 10th – Sunday

Careful not to awaken Amanda, Brent eased back the covers. The bedside clock read seven-thirty, and he had a hell of a headache.

They'd gone to the neighborhood party last night, and he'd put deadpool rosters and Clive's ugly face out of his mind for a couple of hours and enjoyed himself. Toward the end of the evening, the men had snuck down to the basement to play pool and smoke cigars. His jacket had reeked so badly that Amanda made him hang it outside when they got home, which was well after one in the morning.

After a hot shower, Brent dipped his head under the faucet and swallowed four aspirin. He threw on jeans and a sweatshirt and padded downstairs barefoot. The day was overcast and dreary. The thermometer read exactly thirty-two degrees. It looked like either rain or snow was on the way.

He tried not to think about how hard his head was pounding as he waited for the coffee to brew. He contemplated pouring in a little hair of the dog, but his stomach flip-flopped at the mere thought. Instead, he took the whole pot and his favorite mug into his office. He snapped on the desk light and jiggled the mouse to bring the computer out of sleep mode.

He'd gotten up before Amanda so that he could resolve this deadpool situation.

After breakfast, he was going to explain everything to Amanda. How Clive, without his knowledge, had signed him up to play the game that night at the Sheraton. The fact that he now had a roster, Darby's Death List, on the site was a little unnerving. *Was there even a possibility he could win?* No, he couldn't think that way. He needed to undo what Clive had done, first and foremost because they sure as hell didn't have an extra five grand in their checking account to pay the credit card bill when it arrived.

The conversation with Amanda wasn't going to be easy, but after all, none of this was his fault. Well, except for getting hammered at the bar, and he'd already apologized to her for that. He felt good that he was taking the high road. But first things first, he had to get the roster taken down.

This time, before he logged on, he remembered to twist his computer speakers to off. When the skull began its slow rotation, it did so silently. Brent began searching through the various pages of the site looking for contact information.

Fifteen minutes later, he had come up empty. The DieorDieTrying.com site listed virtually no contact information. Not a name, not an email address to send questions or complaints, not a phone number. Not even the standard link most websites had to opt off the mailing list. Nothing. With no other options, Brent bounced over to his email and pulled up the welcome note he'd received from Intruder and hit the reply key.

Brent pulled down his law textbook from the shelf above his computer, studying, selecting, and finally paraphrasing an appropriate sounding legal passage. Satisfied, he typed his reply:

Intruder,

Please remove my roster from the

DieorDieTrying.com site and issue a credit to my MasterCard immediately in the amount of $5000. I have chosen to terminate said agreement and the user's account at this time, as is my legal right, with or without cause. Due to unauthorized access to the service, a breach of this agreement has occurred, which is a violation of law. I have copied my lawyer on this email, and he will be in contact with you if you do not comply with the above request within thirty days. Any further communication, if imperative, can be sent to me at Revolution Advertising and Creative Company.

Sincerely,
Brent Darby
cc: Charles. L. Courtright, Esquire

He thought the last bit, adding in the name of a fictitious lawyer, might be advantageous in speeding the process along.

Okay, hopefully that email would serve to end the matter. He made a mental note to call his bank to let them know that a credit should be coming through on his MasterCard. He assumed he would get an email at work when Darby's Death List was removed from the game site. In fact, that was why he'd listed his company. *No sense in Amanda stumbling over DieorDieTrying.com emails now that this whole thing was going to go away.*

Feeling some of the weight lift off his shoulders, he clicked back to the game site to log off. His hand hovered over the log-off button. This was the last time he would go to this site. *Who played this game anyway? Movie stars? Rock stars? Could he even tell?*

Brent went to the master list of all rosters before he remembered he'd reviewed this list before. Although some had last names, like his roster, most were a play on words about death. There were few clues here about the real identity of the player behind the roster.

Brent gave himself five more minutes to fool around. Then he'd log off. He clicked over to the master list of nominees entered into this year's game and used the mouse to do a quick scroll from the top to the bottom of the list. No red lines, apparently none of the nominees had died during the first ten days of the game.

The list had a built-in sort feature, and Brent did an ascending sort, showing the most popular pick, down to the least popular. It irritated him that Clive had been right about the Pope being a popular selection; the Pope was the fifth most popular nominee.

Brent noticed there were other sort features as well. A sort by oldest nominee showed a surprising number of players had chosen picks in their late nineties. Points in this game, even two or three, must be harder to come by than he originally thought. Brent reversed the order of the list, putting the youngest nominee on top. The name Drew Vanderhorn, with a point value of ninety-two, popped to the top of the list. Which meant...

Brent did the math and grimaced before shoving the mouse away, disgusted. *Who the hell would put an eight-year-old kid on a deadpool list?* The trackball rolled across the mouse pad sending name after name scrolling past. *In fact, how could DieorDieTrying. com even allow players to nominate children? That was just sick. Didn't this game have any rules?*

Brent decided to take a quick look at his own roster before it was taken off-line. Fadhl Sharma was the only name he'd seen on his roster last Thursday because he'd logged off when he'd heard Amanda come home. Back at the list of rosters, he quickly found Darby's Death List and double-clicked. He scanned the list of the ten names, recalling some of the discussion at the bar. The sorority killer was listed, as was the vice president.

Brent caught himself wondering again if there was any possibility that he could win, and then he shook his head violently.

No! The concept behind this game was sick and wrong. And he certainly did not have five thousand dollars to spend on anything —especially not a demented game like this.

It was imperative that he get himself free and clear of this game as soon as possible. He needed to do whatever was necessary. Brent reached for the mouse to log off when something further down on the monitor caught his eye. His hand froze in mid-air, and he leaned closer, staring at the screen. He had sorted the list of rosters alphabetically, and now he zeroed in on the word Intruder. The roster for Intruder's Chalk Outlines was listed two rosters below Darby's Death List. Without thinking twice, Brent clicked the mouse, and Intruder's list popped up on the screen. Like a knife cut to his mid-section, Brent stared at the screen. Nestled into the sixth position on Intruder's roster was Brent's own name.

Chapter 2

January 11th – Monday

The doctor entered the examination room and shook Amanda's hand, his eyes crinkled at the corners.

"Amanda, it's good to see you. Happy New Year," he said.

"Happy New Year to you too, Dr. Shelby."

"So how are you?" The doctor asked, looking down at an electronic tablet.

"Good."

"Apparently so. Your last visit to the office was a year ago, for your last physical. Married life must agree with you."

She smiled. "Brent is doing great at Revolution. We bought a house too."

"Great. And how are you doing?"

"Good."

"Your vital signs look good. Height, weight, blood pressure. We'll send the blood and urine samples to the lab for the usual tests: diabetes, cholesterol, triglycerides, HDL, LDL. A nurse will call you in a few days with the results. Are there any medical issues you'd like to discuss before the pap test?"

Amanda shook her head and felt a trickle of sweat roll down between her breasts. *Why did women always get so worked up over a simple pap test?*

"Okay, we'll have you out of here in no time. I'm breaking in a new med student. Would you mind terribly if I had him do your pap?" Dr. Shelby asked.

Amanda groaned audibly. "I guess it's okay," she shifted on the table, causing the paper beneath her to rustle. "They have to learn somehow, right?" A moment later the door opened, and a dark head appeared. The white medical coat was so new it still had creases in it. The young man approached her, his hand outstretched.

"Good morning, Mrs. Darby."

"Good morning." He introduced himself, but Amanda didn't catch his name. She gave him a limp handshake, wishing she hadn't agreed to this. She kept her other arm tightly wrapped around her middle in a vain attempt to keep the paper gown from opening and exposing every inch of her naked body.

"Lie back, please, feet in the stirrups," Dr. Shelby said.

Amanda settled into the position and let her mind float away from the indignity of the procedure.

"Relax. You'll feel a little pressure here…"

She pictured herself lying on a deserted beach in St. Lucia. She wore a pink bikini, and a light breeze was blowing.

"A little scrape. You may feel a small pinch."

The water was turquoise, and she could feel the warm sun on her skin. Tiny waves lapped at her toes. Off in the distance she heard a question asked and answered.

"It's called a Chadwick sign. The cervix is softer and on the bluish side," Dr. Shelby said.

"Is everything okay?" Amanda asked. She opened her eyes, and the fantasy evaporated. The med student was studying her crotch, and she quickly closed her eyes again.

"Everything is fine," Dr. Shelby said. "Amanda, you can sit up now."

By the time she'd struggled into a sitting position, only Dr. Shelby remained in the room. He sat on a rolling stool, inputting information into her electronic chart.

"You told the nurse you were unsure of the date of your last period?"

"It's been a couple of months, but my periods have never been regular."

"And you're not taking any medication?"

"No."

"Are you currently using any kind of birth control?"

"A diaphragm. In college I was on birth control pills, but I used to get headaches, migraines sometimes, so I switched. Why all these questions about my period? What's going on?" A knock sounded on the door, and the medical student re-entered the room. He nodded at Dr. Shelby, handing him a yellow slip of paper.

"Would you like to give her the news?" Dr. Shelby asked him.

Amanda felt a nervous flutter in her stomach. "What news?" She looked back and forth between the two men. "I thought you said everything was fine?"

Dr. Shelby nodded for his medical student to continue.

"Mrs. Darby, you're pregnant."

Amanda gasped. "What?" She looked at Dr. Shelby for confirmation, feeling a host of conflicting emotions sweep over her.

"You're the first woman I've had the privilege of saying that to," the student continued.

"Yes," Dr. Shelby nodded. "It's one of the best parts of the job." He beamed at Amanda. "Congratulations."

"But how could I...I mean..." A smile spread across her face. "I can't believe I'm pregnant."

"About six percent of women become pregnant using a diaphragm, even with consistent use," Dr. Shelby stated.

"How could I not know?" Amanda looked from the doctors down to her abdomen, placing both hands on her flat stomach.

"Your baby would be impossible for you to feel at this stage," the medical student answered.

"A baby," Amanda repeated softly. "I'm going to have a baby."

"I'm sending you down for an ultrasound to pinpoint your due date. I'll want to see you monthly for pre-natal checkups through your second trimester," Dr. Shelby continued, handing her a stack of pamphlets. "I'm sure you know the basics. Eat healthy. No alcohol. And stay clear of smokers." He opened a cabinet and gave her several clear sample packets. "These are prenatal vitamins—"

"These things are huge."

"If you have trouble swallowing the pills, you can try crushing them up in applesauce. But it's important to take a prenatal vitamin every day. Do you exercise?"

Amanda looked up at him, still dazed. "Exercise? Kickboxing at the gym twice a week."

"Hmm." Dr. Shelby rubbed his chin. "I'd feel more comfortable if you switched to something a little less physical. How about swimming? Or yoga?"

Amanda nodded, barely taking in the doctor's words when she heard a light knock on the door. An African-American woman wearing plum-colored scrubs stepped partway into the room.

"We just had a cancellation in ultrasound," the woman said. "If you're finished here, Doctor, I can walk her downstairs, and we can get her right in." She smiled at Amanda.

"Thanks, Estelle," Dr. Shelby replied.

The rest of the appointment passed in a blur. Now she was glad she hadn't had time to find a new OB-GYN in New Hampshire. Dr. Shelby told her she'd have the baby at Brigham and Women's Hospital in Boston. The commute into the city for appointments would be a minor inconvenience, but she was happy to make the drive in order to ensure great medical care for her baby—and peace of mind for herself.

With the engine idling, she sat in the medical center parking lot, staring at the black and white ultrasound image. Ten weeks' pregnant, she couldn't get over it. Propping the grainy image up in front of the radio, she put the Jeep in drive. She checked her mirrors as she pulled out of the lot, catching her own goofy grin in the side-view mirror.

With one hand on the wheel, heading north up I-93, Amanda slid her other hand inside the warm recesses of her black cape, protectively pressed up tight against her belly. Against her baby. Their baby.

How would Brent react to the news that she was pregnant? The smallest trace of doubt brushed the nape of her neck.

• • •

January 14ᵗʰ - Thursday

Brent stood in the break room at the office, watching Todd pour the last of the milk into his coffee. Another sleepless night had him in a foul mood. "Well, how would you feel if you saw your name on a deadpool list?"

"Come on, Brent." Todd laughed, pulled open the refrigerator, and stuck the empty carton back on the top shelf. "It's a joke. And a pretty good one at that."

"A joke? I don't think it's a joke. I think it's pretty damn sick."

"The whole game is sick," Todd shot back. "That's the point, remember? Players betting on when people are going to die."

Brent glared at him.

"Clive is playing, and his name isn't on the damn list."

"Did you ask him about it?" Todd asked.

"Yeah. He thought it was hilarious."

"Well…" Todd poured spoonful after spoonful of sugar into his coffee. "You have to expect guys that play a game like that are going to have a warped sense of humor. Did he at least admit to signing you up when you were at the bar?"

"No," Brent said. "Clive claims I did everything myself, including typing in my credit card number. He said all he did was type up the roster at the bar as we were throwing suggestions around."

"Do you believe him?" Todd asked.

"No."

"I wouldn't either."

"Clive thought that maybe the owners of DieorDieTrying.

com may have inserted the names of all the first-time players to get a rise out of us."

"Looks like it worked." Todd stirred his coffee before he dropped the spoon in the sink and snagged a chocolate doughnut from a box on the counter.

"Which would explain why Clive's name is not on anyone's roster. He's not a newbie."

"So why are you in such a panic over this?"

"Several reasons, but most importantly I'm worried about Amanda. Do you know that someone has an eight-year-old kid on their list?"

"Ouch."

"Yeah. And that's not all."

"Fill me in on the way to the server room," Todd said.

Brent fell in step next to him. "There is no contact information on the website. I replied back to the email Intruder sent using some legalese from an old law text book. I demanded that my roster be taken off the site and my money refunded."

"Did you get a response?" Todd asked through a mouthful of doughnut.

"Not yet. What if Intruder sends me another email and Amanda reads it?"

Todd shrugged. "Nothing much you can do."

"This could really get ugly. Do you think she'd divorce me?"

"Stop being melodramatic." Todd stopped abruptly at the door of the server room and swung around. "You told her you're in the game, right?"

Brent shook his head.

Todd stared at him. "What have you told her?"

Brent shook his head again.

"Not even about the five grand?"

"How am I supposed to explain any of that?"

"You're in deep shit." Todd licked his fingers and wiped them off on his pants. "She's going to find out."

"She can't," Brent said. "She absolutely can't."

"Hang on one second." Todd darted through the door of the server room and stopped in front of one of the computers.

Brent caught the door before it closed. "One individual seems to be behind all of this. Who is this guy, and how did I end up on his roster?"

"The same way everyone ends up on a roster, I imagine." Todd spoke loudly over the noise of the equipment. "Someone nominated you. Someone wants you dead." He shot a grin over the top of the equipment stack.

"Funny," Brent said. He stepped into the server room and let the door close behind him. "But who?"

"Someone who wants to have a little fun at your expense. Who have you ticked off lately?"

"I'm serious. Someone is targeting me."

"I'm telling you, just ignore it," Todd said. He yanked open the door and walked out into the hall.

Brent followed him, allowing the door to slam shut behind him. "I doubt you could forget about it. Just let it go."

"It's a stupid game."

Brent lowered his voice in the quiet of the hallway. "I was kind of hoping you might...you know..."

"Don't." Todd sent an angry look his way.

"You don't even know what I was going to ask," Brent said.

"Yes I do. And the answer is no."

Brent sighed.

Todd took a step toward Brent. "I haven't done any hacking since high school," he hissed at him. "And even mentioning that word in this building could get me fired."

"I know. It's just that I didn't join the damn game to begin with. This is all Clive's fault."

"So go figure it out with him. Stay off the stupid site and just forget about it."

"But—"

"Look, Brent. It's his word against yours. I'm not saying I don't believe you, but you're not exactly blameless here. You egged Clive on with suggestions for candidates, and somehow or other you ended up with a roster in the game. It's a bit late for regrets now, don't you think?"

• • •

Spotting a parking space directly across the street from Brent's office building, Amanda parallel parked and shut off the engine. After several minutes, she laid aside the paperback she'd brought and instead watched for Brent to emerge from the glass doors at the base of the high-rise.

In an uncanny coincidence, earlier in the day Brent had dropped the Viper off for an oil change and maintenance check. Since the garage was keeping the car overnight, Amanda suggested the two of them have dinner in Boston.

She'd called ahead to Bricco's on Hanover Street, one of their favorite restaurants, and made a reservation.

Where was he? She was going to burst if she had to wait much longer.

Her stomach grumbled. *Maybe after dinner they could walk over to Modern Pastry and have a celebratory dessert?*

Amanda craned her neck to study the pedestrians scurrying across the street, their collars turned up against the raw, wind-swept January evening. She switched on the dome light and reached for her book when she heard the click of the back hatch. In the rearview mirror she saw Todd standing next to her husband, both illuminated by the street light.

"Hey, honey. Thanks for picking me up," Brent said. He threw his briefcase inside. "I invited Todd to grab a bite with us. Is that okay?"

Amanda blinked. *Todd?* She hadn't thought to tell Brent she wanted it to just be the two of them.

Brent slammed the hatch shut and climbed into the front seat and leaned over to give her a quick kiss. Todd had the back door open, waiting for Amanda's response as taxis and cars whizzed by him.

"Right." Amanda said. *What else was she going to say?*

"You sure, Amanda?" Todd said.

Brent twisted around in his seat. "Get in, you idiot. It's dinner. Not a date."

Amanda let out an inaudible sigh as she buckled her seatbelt. The guys began to talk shop as if she wasn't in the car. Feeling sorry for herself, she checked her mirrors and pulled out into traffic. *So much for a romantic dinner alone.*

• • •

After dinner, Brent drove, dropping Todd off at his apartment and nixing her idea to go out for dessert by saying he needed to get home to review an ad campaign for a meeting he'd set up the following day.

Feeling defeated, Amanda sat in the passenger seat, listening halfheartedly to Brent talk as they headed home. She hadn't been able to get a word in edgewise. He was rambling on, something about going to a bar called The Jail to hear On The Rise next month.

"This is so great for Todd and the band," Brent said. "He specifically asked that you be there. You're going to join us, right? This is the gig that music producer set up. The band wants a packed house which will be tough to get on a Sunday night."

Brent glanced over at her, and Amanda realized he was waiting for a response. "Sure. I mean, no. I don't want to go. But you should." The doctors' words about staying away from smokers ran through her head. Was she being obsessive wanting to avoid even the minimal smoke she'd encounter from those diehard smokers puffing away just outside the entrance to the club? Amanda paused, flustered. *Should she tell him now? Once they got home Brent was going to disappear into the den.*

68

Under the cape, she slid both hands over her belly, drawing strength from the baby inside. "Brent, I have some news I've been dying to tell you all night, but I wanted to wait until it was just the two of us." A shiver of anticipation ran up her spine.

"What," Brent said, as he reached over and interlaced his fingers with hers.

Amanda twisted in her seat so she was facing him. "I'm pregnant."

Brent chuckled and squeezed her hand. "No, really. What is it?"

"I'm serious." Amanda took a breath. "We're going to have a baby." Brent turned his head toward her. In the glare of the oncoming headlights, she saw his shocked expression.

"Pregnant? Are you sure?"

She nodded.

"Wow. I don't know what to say. How pregnant?"

"Ten weeks. Eleven now, actually. They did an ultrasound. I've got it in my purse."

For what seemed an eternity, Brent simply stared at her. Then abruptly, he broke eye contact and returned his attention to the road.

"Brent, say something. I'm so excited." Still trying to gauge his reaction, she chattered on nervously. "I found out during my annual physical. I had no idea I was pregnant. We're going to have a baby!" At that moment, Brent released his hand from hers.

"How did this happen?"

Brent's words hit her like a slap. "What do you mean, how?"

"Amanda, I mean…we agreed to have children when we were ready financially, but not now."

Amanda let her head fall back against the headrest. "Yes, but sometimes things happen. I—"

"Was this your decision?"

"My decision?" Tears filled her eyes. "Are you asking if I planned to get pregnant?"

"I'm just asking—"

"Asking what, exactly?"

"I didn't mean it that way."

"What did you mean, then?"

"It's just…I thought we were being so careful. I always asked—"

"Asked what?" Amanda demanded in an icy tone. "Asked me if my diaphragm was in?"

"Well, was it?"

"How dare you, Brent. Yes, I had my diaphragm in place every time we made love." A tear rolled down her cheek, and she wiped it away with the back of her hand as silence filled the car.

After several moments she spoke again. "We're pregnant." In the glow of the dashboard lights, Brent ran a gloved hand over his upper lip, eyes firmly glued to the road. "It may not be what you planned, what either of us planned. But why can't you just be happy about the baby?" she pleaded.

"Right now, I'm simply stunned. I honestly don't know what to think."

"What is there to think about?"

"I'm sorry, Amanda, but I need a little time to come to terms with it. That's all."

"I'm pregnant with our child. A couple of days aren't going to change that fact." Unabated, her tears overflowed and dripped down into the folds of her cape.

"Is it so unreasonable that I may need a little adjustment period? Christ, Amanda. You sprung this on me out of the blue."

"Are you saying…?" Amanda's voice broke. She swallowed a sob and forced herself to start again. "Are you saying you don't want this baby?" She held her breath as Brent hit the garage door opener and drove into the garage.

"I'm saying that I've been working really hard to try and be a husband and a provider and an employee. I don't know if I'm ready to be a father right now, too."

Amanda's heart wrenched. "Is anyone ever really ready?" The garage door rumbled shut behind them. The keys jangled as

Brent pulled them from the ignition. They both got out of the Jeep, and Brent held the door to the house open for her to enter ahead of him. He seemed careful to avoid brushing up against her.

Still gripping the paperback, Amanda forced herself to hang up her cape and walk into the family room. She switched on a lamp and reached for the box of tissues on the coffee table. After blowing her nose, she opened the paperback, but the words turned to fuzzy black-and-white caterpillars as her tears continued to flow.

With a wadded-up tissue she dabbed her eyes and watched Brent over the top of the book. Still wearing his overcoat, his back to her, he stood at the kitchen window. She willed him to turn around, to see the hurt in her eyes. Instead he remained ramrod straight, staring out into the black night.

• • •

January 21st – Thursday

A week had passed, and Brent sat in his office, staring at the clock on his computer, trying to get Clive off the phone. They were forced to work together because they shared a sales territory, but that was the extent of their relationship. The client meeting was in one of the lower conference rooms, and he was never late for a client meeting.

"Just one more thing…" Clive said.

"Sorry, I have to run…" Brent said, knowing it was useless. The only way to get rid of Clive was to hang up on him.

"I'll make it quick. I'm almost at my next appointment."

"Go. You have one minute." Brent opened his mail tool and listened with half an ear.

"I was wondering if you'd care to make a little wager?"

Brent snorted. "What now? You already conned me into putting a roster on the deadpool game. Great idea that turned out to be."

Clive let out a protracted sigh. "Will you stop stressing about that, you big baby? A man has to have some fun."

"The deadpool is not my idea of fun."

"Okay. Fine. But this bet I've cooked up is right up your alley."

"Have you ever thought about Gamblers Anonymous?"

Clive laughed. "You sound like my first ex-wife."

"What is it?" Brent asked, pretending to yawn. "The Patriots? The Bruins? Both teams are crap this year." He turned his attention back to his mail. He had several more notes from DieorDieTrying. com. He didn't even bother to open them anymore. With a few clicks he selected all three notes and hit the delete key.

"Hello? Did you hear me?" Clive asked.

"What?" Brent's attention snapped back to the conversation. "No, I didn't hear you. I try not to listen when you talk."

"The bet I'm proposing is simple. Whichever of us has the highest commission check first quarter, wins."

"Are you kidding me?"

"Nope. No secrets between friends, right?" Clive said.

"I don't know about that, but keep going…" Brent could almost taste revenge.

"We compare commission checks for January, February, and March. The winner is the person with the highest combined commission checks for all three months."

"And what does the winner get?" Brent leaned back in his chair, amused. He could easily kick Clive's ass.

"Well, if you win, I'm offering my timeshare in the Bahamas for a week. Oceanfront property, frosty drinks served on the beach by scantily clad women…" Clive trailed off.

"Not bad," Brent replied. *Amanda would be all over a week on the beach.* "And I assume if you win, you've got something in mind?"

"Yeah." There was a pause of several seconds. "Your Viper for a week."

"No fucking way!" Brent shot up out of his chair.

"Oh, come on," Clive whined. "It won't cost you a dime, and you can check my driving record. It's spotless, not even a speeding ticket."

"No way. Not a chance." Brent checked the clock. He had two minutes.

"Work with me here. I've got three ex-wives and a girlfriend taking every last dime I manage to haul in. I'll never be able to afford a car like that. I just want to drive it for a week. Just a week. What do you say?"

"No."

"What are you afraid of? I only get the car if you lose the bet. What are the chances of that?"

"No."

"The other day, didn't I hear you say you were in the doghouse with Amanda?"

He didn't remember saying anything like that. *Not in front of Clive.*

"Seven days in paradise would go a long way toward making things up to her," Clive continued.

Brent picked up a pen and wrote the word Bahamas on a Post-It note. He pictured Amanda in a skimpy bikini on the beach. Then he remembered she was pregnant and adjusted the image, envisioning Amanda in a one piece suit, high cut on the sides to show off her long legs and sporting just a bit of a baby bump. Either way, she was gorgeous as hell. There was something about the way she carried herself, those green eyes and that blonde hair.

"So, what do you think?"

"Total combined commission for January, February, and March. The entire first quarter combined, right?" *He had this. He had this!*

"That's the idea."

Brent flipped through his online appointment schedule. His accounts were solid. Sales were coming in steadily, and he would gain momentum into February and March. Clive was cold calling. No way could he come close to his numbers. The guy might be good, but he wasn't that good. No way.

"Well?" Clive prompted.

"I'm thinking. Give me a minute." Brent didn't want to make a mistake. *But this bet was like taking candy from a baby!* He wanted revenge so bad he could taste it. Plus he loved the idea of whisking Amanda off on a romantic getaway. It was exactly what she'd been asking for. He so wanted to do this for her.

"Brent? Can you hear me? Kshhhh. My cell connection is breaking up. KKshhh. Kshhh."

Brent shook his head at Clive's pathetic attempt to imitate static on the line.

"You asshole," Brent shouted into the phone. "All right, I'm in. You got yourself a deal. Do you hear that?"

Clive laughed, and the phone went dead.

Brent eyed the clock and grabbed his suit coat. He shoved an arm in one sleeve as he raced for the elevator. It was five past the hour.

• • •

February 1ˢᵗ – Monday

"Man, I can't believe it's Monday," Brent said as he leaned up against the wall of Todd's cubicle, arms folded over his chest. "I worked practically all weekend."

"I can relate," Todd replied. His head was down as he sat on the floor, unscrewing the cover from a CPU.

"Thank God it's the start of a new month. That last week of January just about did me in."

"These late hours during the week are starting to get in the way of practice time with the band."

"Are the guys still giving you crap about missing a couple of practices?"

"Oh, yeah."

"How serious is it?"

"Right now I'm ignoring them. Everyone will chill out once we get the demo cut."

"Amanda has been having a fit about all my evening appointments. I'm looking forward to some breathing room after the end of the first quarter. I can't wait to see my sales numbers for January. I had a killer month."

Todd looked up and did a double-take. "Is that another new suit?"

"It is." Brent ran a hand down his lapels. "I bought it at Brooks Brothers. Don't give me that look. I had to. I have two high-end clients, and both are ready to close deals with me. I can only show up in the same suit so many times. Have you ever shopped at Brooks Brothers?"

"I shop at Old Navy." Todd plucked at his t-shirt. "Ever heard of them?"

"Pathetic. You and your clothing. Come on, let's go."

"Where?" Todd asked.

"The all-hands meeting, remember? To meet the new CEO?"

"What a waste of time."

"Hardly. It's critical to learn the power players in the new regime."

"Trust me, it'll be a waste of time. You go. Fill me in later. I need to get this memory upgrade installed."

"How long can that take? Two minutes? Do it, and then I'm dragging your ass up off the floor and down to the main conference room." Brent picked up a silver Slinky from a collection of toys on Todd's bookshelf. He walked the spring back and forth from one hand to the other. "I wanted to run something by you."

"What?"

"It's about the deadpool game."

"Did somebody finally die?"

"I don't know. I actually took your advice, and I haven't even been online."

"So what's the question?"

"The original note I got from Intruder…"

"Yeah. The one you got on your personal computer, right?" Todd asked looking up.

"Yeah, at home."

"What about the note?" He snapped a memory card into place.

"It said, 'Welcome to DieorDieTrying.com. I hope you'll be a worthy adversary.' That's pretty weird, huh?"

"Why is that weird?"

"Well first of all, I thought the word choice was just plain odd. I mean, none of the DieorDieTrying.com players are adversaries. The game is total luck."

Todd shrugged as he snapped the cover back on the CPU. He picked up the screwdriver and began replacing the screws.

"Plus, the note was anonymous."

"What do you mean, anonymous?" Todd asked.

"That stuff at the top of the email, where it lists who it's from, the subject line, the date…"

"The header information."

"Yeah. They were all blank."

"Really?" Todd paused. The screw fell to the carpet and landed near a flip-flop. "Blank?"

"Blank." Brent set the Slinky back on the shelf.

"And you opened the note?"

Brent shrugged. "Yeah. Why?"

"Did it have an attachment?" He took another screw from the soda cap and twisted it into place.

"I don't think so."

Todd shook his head. "Did you delete it?"

"No. I was pretty sure the note was from Clive. At least I thought so at the time. I did a reply-to-sender and suggested the sender contact me at Revolution if there was a need for any future communication."

"Here?" Todd winced.

"I didn't want Amanda to see anything from the game."

"Thanks for that."

"Thanks for what?"

"Now you've made this deadpool shit my problem."

"Why is it suddenly your problem?"

"Because I'm a systems guy. I'm the last line of defense against the asshole that sent you that note. And now you've given him a way to track you down through Revolution."

"I don't see what the problem is?"

"The sender was probably some joker trolling for a warm body."

"Well, what should I have done?"

"You should have deleted the note without opening it. Come on. Even you should know better than to open emails with or without attachments from people you don't know."

Brent sighed. "Okay, that was stupid. I know. I really thought it was Clive."

"And now you're not sure?"

"I don't know. Clive just doesn't seem smart enough to be behind this."

"Well, since you replied to the email, the sender, whoever he is, now has a live address. By responding, you verified the portal, and now the system can be compromised. The original email was just a phishing attempt."

"Shit."

"Are you getting more spam now?"

"Yeah." Brent groaned. "I'm getting buried." He paused, embarrassed. "Both at home and at work."

Todd tossed the screwdriver on top of his desk, where it landed with a clank among a sea of tools and computer parts. "You got nailed by a cracker."

"A what? What's a cracker?"

"A cracker likes to go around causing trouble, sending spam, hoping to overload your system. This person, whoever he is, may try to hack into Revolution. So, like I said, thanks."

"Hey, I'm sorry," Brent replied. "I screwed up."

"Yeah, you did. Big time." Todd stood up and shot Brent a look of annoyance. "It's something you're pretty good at lately." He slid his feet into a pair of blue flip-flops.

"Can you stop the emails?" Brent asked.

"Probably, but I don't have time for this shit." Todd walked out of his cubicle and looked up at the clock. "And I am royally pissed off at you. I need some time to think this over. I can do that at the meeting as well as anyplace else. Let's go."

Brent nodded. "I appreciate you looking into it for me."

"Do you have a firewall installed at home?"

"I think so, maybe."

"You better hope so. A firewall should prevent this guy from accessing your computer systems," Todd explained. "You, of all people, since you don't know shit about computers, should have one."

"A firewall, right. I'll put it on next year's Christmas list. Right up at the top, along with trouser socks."

"You can joke around about it, but you're going to get screwed one of these days. Without a firewall your computer is vulnerable over the network to anyone twenty-four hours a day."

"Fascinating."

"You don't believe me?"

"I do, but…can you just frigging help me and skip the lecture?"

"I'm just saying, even if your computer is turned off, someone could waltz right into your system and steal your life. Bank account numbers, credit cards information, you name it."

"How is that possible?"

"That's why this company, and every other big company, spends major bucks to protect the computer system." He patted the top of the CPU. "I've watched the software work. Hackers bombard us constantly trying to break into Revolution. To them, the more sophisticated the protection, the bigger the challenge."

"Got it," Brent replied. "Can we go already?"

"Although with enough skill and time, hackers can break into just about anything."

"You'd know…"

"Hey!" Todd took a step toward Brent and stuck a finger in his face. "You know, you can be a real asshole sometimes." Todd shoved him aside and took off down the hall.

Brent caught up with Todd at the stairwell and put a hand on his arm. "You're right. I was out of line."

"You just love rubbing my nose in it, don't you? What is your problem? Here let me spell it out for you. This job is important to me. The last thing I need is you screwing things up for me."

"I'm sorry."

"Yeah? Well, apologizing seems to be your way of solving everything, and that is getting old." They walked the rest of the way to the conference room accompanied only by the rhythmic slap of Todd's flip-flops.

The room was packed. Brent followed Todd as he threaded his way down the aisle to two open seats. Clive was seated in the row behind them. Just as they sat down, Suzette Grant, the personnel director, walked up to the podium. Suzette, also secretly known as Mary Sunshine for her icy demeanor, tapped the microphone.

Brent caught an unpleasant whiff of sauerkraut as Clive leaned forward and spoke near his ear.

"The new CEO is the third guy from the left," Clive whispered.

Brent studied the distinguished gray-haired man sitting in the middle of the row of male executives.

"The guy's a real ball-buster," Clive said, loud enough for those in the near vicinity to hear him.

Todd slouched down in his chair. "Wake me when it's over, will ya?"

• • •

Two hours later, all three men were in Brent's office. Todd was sitting in Brent's desk chair typing away on his computer. Clive and Brent sat in the two chairs opposite the desk, rehashing the meeting.

"Unbelievable," Clive said, his voice rising. "The new CEO gave quite the little heart-warming speech, didn't he? I can read right through Phil Anderson's bullshit. I told you he was trouble."

"Keep it down," Brent said in a harsh whisper, walking over to close his door. The last thing he needed was Ed, the sales manager, thinking Brent was talking smack about the new CEO.

"Cost cutting. Productivity analysis. I'm telling you, jobs are on the line," Clive continued at the same decibel. "You mark my words, Phil came here to clean house."

"I didn't think he was so bad," Brent said.

"Then you don't know shit," Clive said. "You mark my words. Heads are going to roll before midyear."

"Well, frankly, that's the way it ought to be," Brent cut in, tired of Clive's whining. "I pull my weight and so should everyone else. What's the sense in dragging along a bunch of underperforming salespeople?"

"You never had a bad month before?" Clive snapped.

"I'm not saying that, but there should be a certain consistency."

"Easy to say when you've already proven yourself. I just got on board, plus I'm past fifty—"

"Pressure getting to you already, old man?" Brent replied, trying to lighten things up. "I thought we had a bet going? I thought you were going to blow my doors off this quarter?"

"You heard Phil. Mandatory time cards. Monthly call reports. Account analysis. When am I going to have time to make sales calls?"

"Yeah, they're putting the squeeze on all right." Brent looked over at Todd. "Better watch out, buddy. They may require all employees to start wearing ties next."

"No way, man." Todd laughed and swiveled back and forth in Brent's leather chair. "I don't do ties."

"How are things with the band?" Clive asked.

"Awesome," Brent replied for Todd. He stood up and gave Todd a high five over the top of his laptop.

"I forgot the name," Clive said

"On The Rise," Todd said. "Hey. I've got a gig coming up at The Jail on Tremont. You should go."

"He's too old for a night of hardcore rock-and-roll." Brent replied.

"I can make it," Clive said.

"Bring everybody you know. The Jail, on Tremont. February fourteenth. Got it?" Todd returned his attention to Brent's computer. "Okay, back to business. Come take a look."

Brent and Clive both came around the desk and looked over Todd's shoulder.

"See that?" Todd tapped an area of the screen with the eraser end of a pencil.

"Are you talking about those fuzzy lines?" Brent asked, leaning closer and pointing to one of several gray bars distorting the image on the screen. "Those random lines seem to pop up from time to time and then disappear. I think I need a new monitor."

"The screen resolution noise is probably not related to your monitor," Todd said. "It could be your graphics card overheating, which would cause the artifacts you're seeing."

"Artifacts?" Brent repeated.

"Yeah. Or maybe an intermittent connection to your external display. Or even be a problem with your onboard RAM."

"You mean that bunch of numbers and dots?" Clive touched the screen with his index finger, leaving a smudge.

"Yup," Todd answered. "That is the Internet Protocol

address. IP for short. Each IP is unique, but it's always a series of four numbers with dots between them. I've activated the full headers, but in this case, the sender bounced it through a re-mailer."

"A re-mailer?" Clive asked, looking blankly at Brent.

Brent shrugged. "I'm clueless."

"Someone is trying to cover their tracks," Todd said. He peeled off a Post-It note and jotted down the list of numbers. "Re-mailers are free online services that hackers take advantage of to try and hide their identity. I'll search around tonight to see if I can trace the note back to its original destination." He stood up and walked to the door.

Brent turned to Clive. "What's your take on all this?"

"I told you before. I think you're making a mountain out of a molehill."

"From what Todd is saying, this guy went to an awful lot of trouble to keep his address hidden," Brent said.

Clive walked back around the desk and sat back down. "It's not a virus or a worm, so what's the big deal?"

Brent returned to his own chair and propped one foot up on the radiator. "True. Pop-up ads are way more annoying."

"I'll let you know if I find anything," Todd said.

"Thanks," Brent said, as the door clicked shut.

Clive stood, rubbing his hands together. "Time for the big reveal?" he asked.

"Yup." Brent grabbed a binder off the corner of his desk and opened it. He'd never admit it, but he was a tiny bit nervous. "Well, old chap," he blustered. "Ready to divulge your January sales numbers?"

Clive smiled. "You first."

Chapter 3

February 3rd – Wednesday

Brent took a sip of cold coffee and swallowed with distaste. It was mid-morning on Wednesday, and he was at his desk in his office looking over his calendar for the last two weeks of February. By cajoling, arm twisting, and exchanging favors, he'd gotten appointments with the majority of his key accounts. His schedule was going to be brutal. He had a nice cushion already, but he had every intention of trouncing Clive and walking away with the bet. There was no way he was letting some corner-cutting, cold-calling, old-fart sales rep top his numbers or drive his Viper.

The appointments were all legitimate, but still his conscience tugged at him. He and Amanda had made up, but things hadn't been exactly warm and fuzzy between them since the fight in the Jeep.

He'd gotten into the habit of logging onto the office server from his home computer after dinner. For a couple of hours, he'd immerse himself in sales figures and projections. The upside, although Amanda didn't know it, was that in a few months, he'd be whisking her off to the Bahamas, courtesy of Clive.

A glance at the clock reminded him that the weekly department sales meeting would be starting in half an hour. *Maybe he could get a jump on the new call report before the meeting.*

Minutes later, happy with the layout of the sales data, Brent moved on to formatting. He wanted a one-page document that was both crisp and clean. He was beginning to think the new report was a good idea. After all, it gave him yet another way to shine above the other salesmen at Revolution.

Brent added borders and headings and then scrolled down through the various fonts once, before going back to the top, and deciding on Bookman. From the dropdown menu, he was about to select it when the name of the next font on the list caught his eye.

BRENT WILL DIE.

"Son of a bitch," Brent said aloud, as his heart skipped a beat. He shifted in his chair, staring at the three words on the screen.

He took a deep breath, trying to roll with it and find the humor in the situation. Who had he punked last, anyway? He couldn't remember. And as far as practical jokes, this one was pretty mild. *Marketing, maybe?* Something this lame was right up their alley. Except that right about now, after finding his name on a deadpool roster, he didn't find the word death and his name funny.

Brent dropped back into his chair and found himself staring at the ***BRENT WILL DIE*** font.

Was it possible all this deadpool stuff was tied into one big internal practical joke? Was it something Clive set in motion? Brent immediately discarded that idea. *The sales team would never target one of their own. Accounting?* No, they seldom participated, too many straight shooters. The production team was another possibility. Or more likely still, the folks in graphic design.

Brent looked over at his bookcase where his Rookie of the Year trophy sat. It was an actual size 32AA girl's training bra, which had been dipped in bronze and attached to a wooden plaque which said "Check out my RACC!" RACC was the acronym for Revolution Advertising and Creative Company. As unimaginable as it seemed, this trophy, along with the Salesman of the Year trophy (which was 36DD bronzed bra) came with a significant bonus check and were the most coveted prizes Revolution gave out each year.

When Brent brought the Rookie of the Year Award home, Amanda had immediately nixed his suggestion of putting it on the mantle in the family room. Instead, she banished it to the den. Still, every time they invited people over, Brent would haul it out. *Was he wrong to be so proud of it?*

When the award had gone missing, Brent was sure his wife had thrown it out. Eventually he found it on the passenger seat of his car. Amanda had placed an ivy plant on the base of the wooden plaque and trained the tendrils to wind themselves up and around the rigid bra straps. *It didn't look half bad.* Amanda had attached a Post-It note asking that he take it back to the office – for good.

Would the culture at Revolution change with the new CEO? And what else would change? Suddenly conscious of the time he had let slip away, Brent pulled his thoughts back to the present. First things first, he wanted the **BRENT WILL DIE** font off of his computer. *Right now.*

He wound his way laboriously through the start menu, settings, control panel, and finally down to the individual font folder. Still, it was unsettling to see the words **BRENT WILL DIE** sitting so casually, tucked among his favorite fonts. He shook his head at the idiocy of the prank and hit the delete key.

The phone rang, and he jumped.

He leaned over to look at the caller ID. The number was familiar, but he couldn't quite place it. The phone rang a third time, and he picked it up. "Brent Darby," he said.

"Hey, buddy, how's it hanging?"

"Clive." Brent cursed inwardly, wishing he'd let the call go to voicemail. "I'm swamped. I'll have to call you back."

"Actually, it's about Regency Auto."

"Did you say Regency Auto?" Brent caught a hint of unmistakable gloating in Clive's voice, and he was instantly on guard. *Why was Clive calling about the mega chain of Boston auto dealerships?*

"I'm in my car. Just on my way back from a meeting at their corporate offices."

"Excuse me?" Brent asked.

"Turns out the guy who owns Regency is the godfather of one of my girlfriend's kids. Her youngest, Zachary. Can you believe that? Anyway—"

"Why the hell are you making a sales call on my account?" Brent gripped the phone so tight his knuckles hurt.

"Your account? Now hold on just a minute. New accounts are my territory. As far as I can see, you've been chasing your tail on this one. There are no dollar signs after Regency Auto on your account list."

"I had a relationship—"

"But no sales. I'm right, aren't I? Fair is fair, buddy."

Blood thumped in Brent's ears. "You backstabbing, little…" He seethed as he pushed away from his desk and whirled around in his chair to stare out the window, imagining only Clive's smirking face.

"I stabbed you in the back? Are you kidding me?"

"It's my account," Brent spit back.

"It's not your account."

"I gave them a quote last year."

"So? I test drove a Maserati last year, and the salesman wrote up a contact. I never bought the car, and he didn't make a commission."

"You stole my account."

"I'm just trying to make a living here, same as you. I finally land a big fish with a cold call, and you're too jealous to congratulate me?"

"Fine," Brent snarled. "Congratulations. If you ever go near another one of my accounts, I'll rip your balls off." He slammed down the phone.

Brent rose out of his chair and paced back and forth, furious. Regency Auto was supposed to be the crown jewel of his accounts this year. He was sure a contract with them would have given him a lock on winning Salesman of the Year. *Damn!* If he hadn't been so distracted by the stuff going on at home and this deadpool nonsense, he would have seen this coming. He should have kept a closer eye on Clive, seen him for the snake he clearly was.

In a sour frame of mind, he closed the call report document, unwilling to send it to his boss without a final review. Now he'd have to run to make the meeting. Being the last one to arrive was becoming a habit.

Sifting through the sales printouts, quotas, and ad layouts on his desk, Brent finally unearthed his sales folder and headed for the door. He was getting further and further behind.

• • •

At two-thirty Brent came out of the meeting and strode down the hall looking for Todd. He wasn't happy, due in large part to the fact that there was a new name atop the leader board. As he walked by the department administrative assistant's desk, Claire called out to him.

"Hey, Brent. Can you grab your mail while you're here?"

"I'm on my way out the door. Can you just put it in my box?"

"Actually, it would be better if you took it with you now."

Brent paused before turning around. "Sure, I guess so. Why?"

"I only opened the first three." With an inch-long, hot pink fingernail, Claire pointed in the direction of the mail bins. On a table, beneath them, was a stack of magazines wrapped in brown paper.

Brent walked over to the table. The brown envelope had been slit open at the top. He pulled the magazine from the protective cover. *Penthouse? What the hell?* He felt Claire's eyes on his back. He verified the address label and then pitched the magazine into the recycling bin where it landed with a thud.

He slid the next magazine out only far enough to see the title: *Hustler*. It, too, he tossed in the recycle bin. Heat radiated up onto his face. He removed the lid from the recycling bin and picked up the entire stack and dumped everything into the blue bin.

"Brent," Claire called after him. "You better call and get those cancelled. From what I hear, the new CEO does not have a very good sense of humor."

Brent didn't bother to respond. He turned the corner and headed for Todd's office.

• • •

Once again Amanda swished her brush around in a jar half filled with turpentine, washing away all traces of the honey brown hue she'd spent far too long blending on her palette. The color wasn't right, and the terrier staring at her from the easel wasn't any better. She unclipped the half-completed picture, heavy with wet paint, and tossed it onto the table that held her two previous attempts. She was barely able to stop herself from snatching up all three and crushing them into a giant wad of crumpled paper.

In fifteen minutes she needed to be on the road to the OB-GYN in Boston, yet she couldn't motivate herself to move. She wanted to get over this hurdle of being dissatisfied with her artwork. *What was wrong with her? Why couldn't she paint?* It was becoming a pattern, another morning squandered at her easel with nothing to show for it.

She reached into the back pocket of her jeans and pulled out her cell phone.

"Hi, Dad, do you have time to talk?"

"I always have time to talk to you."

Amanda poured out her frustration to her dad. "Painting seems to hold more frustration than joy. I don't know what to do."

"How are things between you and Brent?"

Leave it to her dad to guess what the real problem was. "We're fine. He's under a lot of stress right now." She hadn't even told her parents she was pregnant. She was determined to wait until she was into her fourth month, but she couldn't hide it much longer. Besides, thinking about the baby—and Brent's reaction to it—just depressed her.

"Is there anything I can do to help?"

"I don't think so."

"You know your mother and I are behind you one hundred percent."

"I know, Dad. I'm just feeling blue."

She glanced over at the three half-completed drawings of the terrier she'd tossed onto the table. There wasn't a single thing she liked about any of them. She'd always thought her gift was her ability to bring any animal to life on the page. The last terrier she'd painted stared back at her with no hint of personality whatsoever. She wasn't digging deep enough to bring the dog to life with her brush.

"Do you want to come over for dinner tonight? I see on the calendar that your mom has something going on. It would give us a good chance to talk."

"No. Tonight Brent will actually be home. I think the two of us need to talk. Thanks anyway, though." *Maybe she would tell Brent that she had decided to get a real job. Despite his objections.*

"He's treating you all right, isn't he?"

"Yes, of course. We love each other, Dad. We are just going through a bit of a rocky road at the moment."

"There is rough water in every marriage."

"I know." Still, Amanda couldn't imagine her dad reacting as Brent had. Brent's reaction to the pregnancy had really scared her. Could it be that she didn't know him as well as she thought she did? *What if he never came around to the idea of this child?* She brushed a hand across the top of her belly, already completely in love with the baby within her. It was unfathomable to her that he didn't feel the same way.

"It's all going to work out, Amanda. Trust me. I'm always here if you need anything."

"Thanks, Dad. I'll let you get back to work."

"I'm never too busy to talk to my precious girl. I love you."

She pushed herself up off the couch just as the doorbell rang. "I know. I love you, too. Thanks for listening. You seem to be able to listen without offering advice. That makes you a very special man."

Her father chuckled. "It's a learned skill. Brent will be able to do that eventually. Keep after him."

Now it was her turn to chuckle. "Okay, Dad. I'll call you next week."

"I look forward to it."

Still lost in disquieting thoughts about her marriage, Amanda looked out the sidelight window to the right of the front door and saw the UPS man. She opened the door.

"Good morning," said the UPS man. "I have a package for Brent. If you could just sign on line number five for me."

"Sure." Amanda took the electronic devise he held out. "How are the roads?"

"Clear now. Although they were a little slippery this morning. It's nice to see the sun out today, even if it is still cold."

Amanda nodded and accepted the tiny package he handed her. "Thank you."

"Have a nice day."

Amanda closed the door, and looked at the return address. "Leather and Lace Lingerie?" She said the words out loud and then remembered that Valentine's Day was only two weeks away.

Clearly her fears about Brent and her marriage were the result of an overactive imagination. But still, she was surprised her husband was thinking about Valentine's Day so far in advance. *Why would Brent be buying me lingerie? Especially the kind of lingerie that fit in this small of a box when I'm pregnant.* The box fit in the palm of her hand. She was more in need of maternity underwear than a thong. More than a little curious, Amanda walked into Brent's office and placed the box on his desk, next to his computer.

Now she was really running late. Amanda grabbed her coat and keys and headed out to the garage, deciding to push the package and her troubles out of her mind. Worrying wouldn't change a single thing, and besides, if he bought her something for Valentine's Day, even if it was inappropriate, it was the thought that counted. She should be giving him the benefit of the doubt. Good things came in small packages, and she'd find out soon enough. Valentine's Day was only eleven days away.

• • •

"The recycling bin? What a waste. You should have walked that stack of porn magazines right down to my office," Todd said, picking up a pair of chopsticks.

"Very funny."

"You can't say I didn't warn you."

Sitting at a booth at Wok & Roll, Brent pushed his uneaten lo mein around his plate. He looked up at Todd. "But how could I have been a victim of identity theft?"

"It's a lot easier than you think," Todd mumbled, through a mouthful of egg roll. "A store clerk can swipe your number. Someone can capture the keystrokes when you type your credit card online to make a purchase. Your personnel file at Revolution can be compromised. Do you have any enemies at the office? Other than Clive, I mean."

Brent flipped him the finger.

Todd laughed. "Aren't you taking this bet with Clive a bit too seriously?"

"I have to win. This isn't just a stupid bet. He's messing around with my accounts."

"Right, I heard about Regency. That was brutal. Is there any way you can get that win back in your column?"

"No. I went to Ed, and he sided with Clive. Do you know what that's going to do to Clive's February numbers?"

"I can imagine."

"And my February is shit up to this point, and now I've got this identity thing over my head. I'm drowning, man."

"Look, about the identity thing, I understand why you're freaked out about this. You should be. It's pretty serious. You've got to make reestablishing your identity your first priority."

"My first priority is to find out who did this."

"Brent, listen to me. The fact is, there are a hundred ways your identity could have been stolen. We give out our personal information online all the time. We follow the instructions and fill in the little boxes on the screen without thinking twice about it."

Brent nodded in agreement, watching Todd wipe the grease off his fingers with a paper napkin. "Isn't there anyone stopping these criminals?"

Todd shrugged. "The problem is, by the time they stop one scam, ten new ones have already been invented."

"And that's supposed to make me feel better?" Brent pushed his plate away, no longer hungry. "All right, I've got the picture. Now, seriously, tell me how I backtrack and find out who did this to me."

"This is the problem with all of you damn salesmen. You never listen when anyone else talks. You just blast ahead and do everything your way."

"What do you mean? I will fix it, but I'm not letting whoever did this get away with it."

"There is no point in trying to track down the person who stole your identity. They are way too smart. They've covered their tracks. They've stolen what they wanted and moved on. You need to do that too."

"No way. With or without your help, I'm going to figure this out and bring this guy down."

"Has anyone ever told you you've got anger management issues?"

"No."

"You still think it's Clive, don't you? That's why you're like a dog with a bone. You won't let this go because now you're even more pissed at him."

"You're damn right."

"I'm only going to say this one last time."

"What?"

"Figuring out who did this is the least of your problems. What you need to concentrate on is reestablishing your identity." Todd held out the plate of fortune cookies.

Brent shook his head. "I'll do that too. How do I get started?"

"Net crimes have been rampant for more than a decade and nothing seems to be stopping them. Your bank may help. Or your credit card company. If money isn't an issue, there are a number of companies that will reestablish your identity and your credit for a fee."

Brent shot him a look of annoyance. "It's not like I have piles of cash sitting around."

"No, just enough for a Viper and a couple of custom-made suits."

"You sound like Amanda."

"Did you ever get the five grand back from the deadpool game?"

"No."

"I didn't think you would. Still, that blows. I just read online that it costs consumers thirty-one billion dollars each year to recover from identity theft. On top of that, it takes the average person one hundred and seventy-five hours to do a total cleanup."

"You're kidding, right?"

"Sorry, man. It's something of a nightmare."

Brent slumped back against the booth, feeling defeated. He didn't have time for one more crumb on his plate, much less two solid weeks' worth of work to put his life back into some semblance of order.

"Can Amanda help you?"

"You know I can't drag her into this," Brent dropped his eyes.

"Does that mean she doesn't know about the identity theft yet?" Todd asked. "And I take it she still doesn't know about the deadpool either?"

"No, I haven't told her anything."

Todd reached for the check. "My treat, for once. Are things okay between you two?"

"We're going through a bit of a rough patch."

Todd raised his eyebrows.

Brent was relieved Todd didn't push the issue. "Come on. I've got to get back to the office. I'm up to my ass in shit there too."

• • •

February 14th – Sunday

It was Sunday night, and Amanda sat at her easel, sketching. Her glance kept returning to Brent, who was stretched out on the couch, remote in hand, flipping channels. She couldn't help but notice how good he looked, wearing well-worn jeans and a navy polo shirt. With a pang, Amanda realized it had been weeks since they'd made love.

She set aside the piece of black charcoal and wiped her fingers on a damp rag. Barefoot, she walked over to the couch and laid a hand on Brent's arm. "Can we talk?"

His eyes met hers. "I'm sorry. I know I've been quiet lately."

Determined to break through, Amanda sat down beside him. "I'm worried about you." He leaned forward to pick up his wine glass, only to pull his hand back when he realized the glass was empty. Amanda took note of the scant inch left in the bottle. She certainly hadn't had any. Not a drop since she'd found out she was pregnant. *Had he opened a new bottle at dinner?* She couldn't remember. She hoped it was a partial bottle from the night before.

94

"I've never seen you this stressed out before."

Brent's gaze returned to the TV, and he resumed flipping channels.

Amanda reached over and pressed the power button. "Shutting me out isn't the answer," she said in a quiet voice.

Brent studied the floor.

"When we got married, we agreed that if we had problems, we'd work them out together. Can you share what's going on? What's upsetting you? I feel like we're becoming strangers."

He sighed. "Things are out of kilter. I need to get some things straight in my head first."

Amanda chose her words with care. "I have doubts and fears about the baby too. I'd hoped we'd turn toward one another. Not away."

"I need time."

"How much time? You're slipping further and further away from me, physically and emotionally. I want this pregnancy to be a joyous time in our lives."

"A better man would be ecstatic over this incredible news. I know that." Brent stood up and ran a hand through his hair. "I'm trying to get there. But if I'm being honest with you, this has been really hard on me. I'm working to come to terms with the idea of having a baby at this point in my life."

Amanda's heart sank. She searched his face for even a glimmer of hope.

"I know you want me to say I'm thrilled, but I can't. Not yet. Not until I know I can secure a future for the three of us." He picked his coat up off the chair. "Are you ready? We need to go."

"Go where?"

"Into Boston. Tonight is that gig the music executive set up for On The Rise."

"On Valentine's Day?"

"I can't help the date. That's what the music producer set up for the band."

"You can't be serious," Amanda said, out of patience. "The night I told you I was pregnant I also told you I wasn't going to go clubbing in Boston to see Todd play."

"It's hardly clubbing. It's going to one bar."

"Being in that environment is probably not good for the baby." She crossed her arms over her chest.

"Oh come on, Amanda! Besides, Todd needs our support," Brent said.

"So does your pregnant wife," Amanda shot back.

Brent reddened and turned on his heel. "We agreed to celebrate later in the week."

"God forbid you spend an evening at home with me," Amanda called after him.

The door to the garage slammed, and minutes later Amanda heard the Viper peel out of the driveway. She hoped he wouldn't drive like a maniac all the way into Boston. She eyed the almost empty wine bottle again.

What was going on with him? It wasn't unusual for him to have a glass of wine with dinner on occasion, but she'd never seen him take the bottle and continue drinking in front of the TV. *How much had he drunk? Damn him!* Now she'd worry until he arrived home safe.

She'd queued up an on-demand action movie, purposely avoiding a chick flick, but she had no desire to see it alone. Frankly, she'd forgotten about Todd's band playing tonight. And heaven knew that Brent went to every one of Todd's shows.

It wasn't that she intended to make a big deal about Valentine's Day anyway, but she had gotten Brent a card. All she'd hoped for was an evening spent together, cuddled up on the couch. Instead, another long, lonely night stretched in front of her.

Amanda walked back over to her easel, regretting her harsh words. She loved Brent and hated it when they fought like this. *Would he ever come around to the idea of being a father?* He'd told her he needed time. She hoped that was true. Then she pictured the Viper wrapped around a tree.

Unable to bring herself to pick up a piece of charcoal, she stared at the sketches of the Dalmatian puppy she had drawn and clipped to the easel with a clothespin. Angry hornets were flying around his head. "Caught in the act," she had penciled underneath. From the puppy's expression, he knew he'd gotten himself into big-time trouble. His friends would have to come in for a rescue.

Amanda felt the same way. Brent had a short fuse, and their fighting used to bother her. But this new silent treatment was worse. Brent was working later and later, and when he was home, he seemed to escape to his office right after dinner. The two of them never even went to bed at the same time anymore. Brent often stayed up until two or three in the morning. *Could he really be working all that time?*

A chilling thought popped into her head, and Amanda sank down onto her stool in front of the easel, shaken. *Had she missed all the obvious signs?* She stared at the puppy's soulful eyes. *Was it possible Brent was having an affair?*

A tremor ran through her. Was he anxious to get online so that he could talk with other women? Or with one woman in particular? She placed her hands on her stomach, forcing herself to consider the possibility. *Was that why he was angry about the pregnancy?* Her thoughts jumped from one dreadful possibility to the next.

If something was going on, she was determined to find out. She refused to be anyone's fool. If her husband had a lover, she would find out right now. She stood up and, with fierce determination, headed for the den.

When she walked in the room, she heard the familiar hum of the computer. She sat down and pulled the chair closer to the desk, wondering exactly what she should be looking for. With one hand on the mouse, she jiggled it back and forth and activated the monitor.

• • •

Brent got to the club around ten, paid the cover fee, and stepped inside. Assaulted by earsplitting music, it took him a moment to recognize the popular tune the deejay was spinning.

Brent shrugged out of his heavy bomber jacket and tossed it up onto a ledge along with several others. The place was far more crowded than he had expected. He turned to survey the crowd, already beginning to sweat in the sauna-like heat. They were mostly college students, although quite a few older men were scattered throughout, no doubt hoping to score with a female coed. Periodic flashes from the strobe light lit up the room, but Brent saw no sign of Todd's blonde ponytail. *He must be backstage, getting ready to go on.*

Brent bumped arms and sidestepped elbows, working his way to the main bar. The whole place reeked of stale beer and testosterone. He stood waiting impatiently for one of the bartenders to notice him. After several minutes, he pulled a fifty dollar bill out of his wallet and held it up. The bartender, wearing a black muscle shirt and jeans, motioned him over.

"What'll it be?" the bartender shouted at him, over the heads of three women pressed up against the bar.

"Corona," Brent yelled back. One heavily made-up woman turned around to glare at him, and he caught a glimpse of a snake tattoo emerging from her prominently displayed cleavage. He shuddered at the thought of raising a daughter.

The bartender disappeared a moment, then returned and set two open bottles on the bar in front of him.

Brent held up two fingers and raised his eyebrows at the bartender.

"Big guy paid for one." The bartender jerked his head toward the far end of the bar and snagged the bill from Brent's hand.

Brent let his gaze drift down the bar. He paused on a beefy man with chin studs and a nose ring before spotting Clive on a stool a few places down.

Seeing Clive didn't do anything to improve Brent's night, especially since he was still ripping mad at him for stealing his Regency Auto account. Clive looked out of place. He was wearing a long sleeve dress shirt with the cuffs rolled up on his forearms. *Had he been out calling on accounts? On a Sunday? On Valentine's Day?* The thought unnerved him.

Clive was chatting with an attractive woman on the next barstool, and he seemed to have captured her full attention. She wasn't a college student, but she wasn't fifty either. *What did women see in him?* Brent forced a smile when Clive looked in his direction and raised a hand in acknowledgement.

The bartender slapped his change on the bar and waited. Brent snuck his hand between the two women and shoved the five dollar bill on top back at the bartender. He grabbed the remaining bills, pocketed them, and raised the two bottles over his head and began working his way upstream through the sea of people.

The deejay announced the band, and the crowd surged toward the stage in anticipation. Brent fought a losing battle against the human tide. When he finally managed to pull himself free, his shirt clung to his back, and someone had upended a drink on one of his pant legs.

Brent rose up on the balls of his feet, craning to see over the crowd. He caught a glimpse of Todd, twirling a pair of red drumsticks high above his head as he climbed up onto the raised drum platform.

The band launched into one of its original songs, and Brent watched his buddy hammer the skins while he tapped his foot to the beat on the sticky floor. He had finished one beer and just started to relax and enjoy the music when he felt a tap on his shoulder. He turned to see Clive standing next to him.

Clive leaned toward him. "He's good," he shouted in Brent's ear, pointing toward the stage and mimicking Todd's actions on the drum set.

Brent nodded.

"The drummer is a friend of yours?" yelled the man standing next to Clive.

Brent nodded again. He shot the man a glance but didn't recognize him.

Clive leaned over again, yelling over the music. "Joe Kalaris. He's a buddy of mine."

Brent accepted the man's outstretched hand, guessing he was a college student with his spiky gelled hair and multiple bracelets on both wrists. He wore three shirts, layered one on top of the next. Brent was sweating bullets in a polo shirt. *Any minute, this guy would probably pass out from heatstroke.*

"Did you hear?" Clive said.

"Hear what?" Brent kept his eyes on the band and took a long swallow of the second beer.

Clive leaned forward and cupped one hand to his mouth. "Revolution is going to announce a layoff second quarter."

Brent flicked his eyes at Clive and mouthed, "Bullshit."

"The board of directors voted Friday. It won't be made public until April."

Brent turned to face him. "How'd you find out?"

Clive just smiled, his teeth glowing an eerie florescent under the surrounding black lights.

Brent shook his head. "I would've heard," he yelled over the music.

Clive shrugged. "Suit yourself."

The strobe lights in the club flashed, and spotlights began to spin in a dizzying display of colors as the band launched into their next song without missing a beat. Brent felt the wooden floor vibrate beneath his feet.

He listened to the end of the song but only joined in the applause halfheartedly, still mulling over Clive's words. *Layoffs?* Well, luckily he didn't need to worry. Certainly not after winning the Rookie of the Year award. Still, yesterday's sales didn't matter, it was all about tomorrow.

With an overextended credit card and a baby on the way, he didn't even want to think about the possibility. When the applause died down, the lead singer introduced the members of the band.

Clive spoke again in the relative calm. "Just get ready to hand over that Viper next month. I don't want to hear any excuses."

Brent let out a harsh laugh. "The only thing I'm going to hand you is your ass."

"We'll see."

The band played the familiar intro to a popular heavy metal tune, and the crowd went nuts, making further conversation impossible. Brent felt a slap on the back, and he saw Clive making a beeline toward the woman he'd been talking to at the bar. Clive's friend, Joe, gave Brent a nod and disappeared into the crowd.

Brent turned his attention back to the stage. Two linebacker-sized college kids stepped in front of him, and he found himself losing interest in the show. He glanced upwards, watching the pulsating lights illuminate a cloud of smoke that hung in the air from the smoke machine that had been pumping the stuff out nonstop. Maybe Amanda had been right after all, and he had made her feel guilty.

For the remainder of the show, Brent hugged the wall. As the deafening music pounded inside his skull, he wondered what Amanda was doing at home. *Alone. Again.* All he had wanted was to go out and have a good time, but it wasn't turning out that way.

Brent set his almost-full bottle of warm beer on a nearby table and with brute force plowed once again into the gyrating crowd. The bass player slid into the final riff of the last song in their set as Brent made his way across the room to the stage.

Todd, a huge grin on his face, ran offstage with his bandmates. The crowd stomped their feet and cheered, and moments later the band came back and played an encore. Brent stood at the perimeter of the crowd, waiting impatiently. Before the stage lights dimmed, the deejay cranked up another tune. The crowd headed for the various bars, anxious for more drinks, and Brent was relieved to have a bit of breathing room.

Waiting for Todd, he lounged against the stage. He was still irked about Clive's remarks, and he searched the bar until he caught sight of him. Clive hung over the shoulder of the woman, who stared adoringly up at Clive. Brent turned away in disgust.

"How'd we sound?" Todd asked as he jumped off the stage and landed next to Brent.

"Great," Brent answered automatically. "Did the record exec make it?"

Todd nodded. "He stayed for most of the first set. Thanks for coming, man," he shouted.

A girl who looked well shy of twenty-one sauntered up and held a drink out to Todd. She was wearing a thick layer of makeup and a short, black leather skirt.

Brent watched as Todd leaned over and whispered something into the girl's ear. She giggled and latched onto Todd's arm, batting her eyelashes.

Brent took his cue. "I've got to go."

"No sweat. I'll see you tomorrow." Todd drained the glass and wiped the sweat off his brow. "Or I'll call you tonight if we get a contract."

Brent grinned and nodded. "Do that."

Todd saluted him with his drumsticks and turned his attention back to the girl at his side.

The crowd had cleared out a bit, although the bartenders behind the main two bars had people three deep waiting for drinks. Brent made his way easily to the front of the club and unearthed his coat which now rested near the bottom of the pile. His ears were still ringing from the amplifiers as he pushed through the glass door, opaque with condensation, and emerged onto the dark street. The icy air enveloped him, and Brent took a minute to yank the zipper up and flip his collar against the subzero temperature. Then he started walking.

He headed in the opposite direction of the parking garage, wanting time to sort things out. It was one a.m., and he had the sidewalk all to himself.

He had gone to the bar tonight to support Todd, but he also realized he had gone to try and hold on to an image he had of himself, to prove that he was still cool, still hip, or at least hip enough to do the club scene. He wasn't a man tied down with kids, schedules, or getting up for two a.m. feedings.

Going out clubbing with Amanda used to be fun. But tonight, the whole scene didn't have much appeal. Todd and Clive might be trolling for a hookup with someone, but that was the last thing he was looking for.

What the hell was he doing here? There had been more than enough support at the club for Todd. His presence didn't matter in the least. He was kidding himself if he thought otherwise.

Brent should have been home with Amanda. She was his best friend, his wife, and she was pregnant with his child. She'd asked him to stay home. And the truth was, he'd rather be with her than anyone else. Why was he so convinced a baby would change that?

He turned right onto Boylston Street, continuing to follow the edge of the Boston Common. The park was bleak this time of year, with patches of dead grass showing in between the piles of dirty snow. He hunched his shoulders up to his ears against the cold as he passed the buildings of Emerson College on his left. There wasn't a student or even a homeless person in sight. Everyone, it seemed, was smart enough to have found a place inside on such a bitterly cold February night. Brent walked on.

He'd been angry with Amanda since she'd announced she was pregnant. As unfair as it was, he'd blamed her for the pregnancy. He'd held her responsible. It was easier on him that way, to make her the scapegoat so he could be the unwitting victim.

So why couldn't he open up and talk to her about his fears? *Why was he punishing her?* Brent came to the end of the block and jogged in place at the red light to keep warm, guilt heavy on his shoulders.

Pregnancy wasn't as easy to undo as a keystroke on his

computer. *What if he didn't have what it took to be a good father? What if he failed? Would he lose Amanda then too?* The light changed, and Brent made his way across the street.

What had Amanda asked him? Was anyone ever really ready to be a parent? He didn't know. All he knew was that Amanda was so close to her parents that sometimes he was actually jealous of their relationship. Was that what he was afraid of? That a baby would divide her love even further? Did he really believe Amanda's love for him was that shallow?

Maybe he was the shallow one, buying sports cars, getting drunk, and making stupid bets with coworkers who were even more immature than he was. He didn't want to end up like Clive when he was in his fifties, thrice-divorced and seeking out women in bars for one-night stands. A shudder went through him.

The baby would be here in August. He could change. He would change. He needed to accept that not everything was in his control.

Brent did an about-face and began striding back toward the garage. His ears tingled in the cold, but he felt some of the weight lift from his shoulders. Amanda needed and deserved his support. He jogged a half a block, his thoughts coming so fast they bumped up against one another. He had been punishing her for his own feelings of insecurity. He had been acting like a jerk, and it was time to set things right.

As Brent jammed his hands deep into the sheepskin-lined pockets of his coat, he felt a crinkle of paper. He paused under a streetlight and pulled a torn scrap of paper from his pocket. In ballpoint pen, in all capital letters were the words "PLAY THE GAME."

• • •

Amanda sat down at the computer in Brent's office. She double-clicked on the word processing program, forcing down the guilt she felt at snooping. Word was one of the few programs she used regularly. On the dropdown menu she opened a list of previously viewed documents. A quick glance confirmed that all documents were related to Revolution. She opened a few just to double check.

Next she moved on to their email, feeling her nerves ratchet up. She knew, if something was going on, she would most likely find it here. Her heart sped up to jackhammer speed as she looked at the titles of Brent's folders. There weren't many. Work. Family. Do Not Throw Out. Shopping. When Pigs Fly. Entertainment. Important Stuff. An hour went by as she searched through each mail folder looking for evidence. There certainly didn't seem to be anything incriminating. She logged onto Brent's Facebook page and found nothing out of the ordinary. His status showed married, and he had her listed as his wife. The most recent updates on his news feed pertained to some Coldplay photos he'd recently discovered on his old Nikon camera.

Wanting to be thorough, she viewed the women in his friends folder, and most names were familiar to her. There didn't seem to be much online contact with any of the women. At last, her heartbeat slowed to normal, although her hands were still ice cold.

A recent conversation with a neighbor came to mind, and Amanda decided to check one last place. The computer kept a history file of websites that had been accessed. That was how Amanda's neighbor had discovered her middle school son had been looking at pornography online.

Amanda took a deep breath, anxious to get this task over with. Confident she wouldn't find anything, she double-clicked on the oldest folder deciding to do just a cursory search. She'd just begun reading the name of sites when a bird chirp sounded. A box appeared on the top right-hand side of the screen.

Intruder: DID YOU ENJOY THE MAGAZINES?

Caught off-guard, Amanda stared at the box and the name of the sender, Intruder. *Who was this? Someone from work?*

Telling herself not to be paranoid, she rolled the mouse over to an icon of an envelope which she assumed would send a reply. She would play along. She would pretend to be Brent. Her fingers shook as she placed both hands on the keyboard, but she forced herself to continue. When she hit the reply button, the user name came up as Pawn694, along with a blinking cursor to type her reply.

Amanda guessed that was the screen name Brent had chosen to go by. She answered Intruder's question with a question of her own.

> Pawn694: What magazines?
> Intruder: YOU KNOW.
> THE ONES I SENT TO
> YOUR OFFICE. THE PORN
> MAGAZINES.

Amanda caught her breath.

> Intruder: AND THE
> PACKAGE THAT I SENT TO
> YOUR HOUSE.

Amanda felt her heart turn over. She remembered the package all too well. Amanda got up from the computer and rifled through Brent's office trash can. At the bottom, she found the empty box with the return address torn off. A sob escaped her lips, but she forced herself to return to the computer.

> Pawn694: What if Amanda
> finds out?

106

Several seconds passed while she waited for Intruder to answer. She held her breath, one fist curled tightly against her heart.

```
Intruder: THIS IS
BETWEEN YOU AND ME.
HAVE YOU COME UP WITH
A PLAN?
```

A plan for what? To meet somewhere? To get out of going home at night? To end the marriage? Tears filled Amanda's eyes, but she'd come this far. She had to know. She wiped away the tears and laid her fingers back on the keyboard and repeated the same question.

```
Pawn694: What if Amanda
finds out?
```

Seconds ticked by as she stared at the screen. Waiting.

```
Intruder: DO YOU REALLY
CARE?
```

Sobbing, Amanda blindly jabbed the power button, and the computer instantly powered down. As silence descended, she ran from the room.

Chapter 4

Monday - February 15

Through the familiar twists and turns of downtown Boston, Brent headed for I-93 North and home. It was two thirty in the morning, and he let the racecar rip. Despite his promise to Amanda, he downshifted with abandon flying over the asphalt. His decision to come clean with Amanda had an invigorating effect on him. With a clean conscience, he accelerated to one hundred miles per hour, reducing the few other cars on the road to a blur. He didn't drive this way often, but after all, a racecar deserved to be driven all out every once in a while.

Since it was past midnight, it was already post Valentine's Day, but the day they'd agreed to celebrate. He'd practiced his apology speech, and tonight, instead of just taking his wife out for dinner like he usually did, he'd buy her an amazing gift, a sheath of roses, and the most romantic card he could find. But more importantly, he was making a serious commitment to step up to the plate as a father-to-be. With any luck, she would forgive him one more time. He wasn't going to blow it again.

Adrenalin rushing from the high-speed ride home, Brent turned off the highway, confident of his plan. All of Garnet was asleep as he downshifted to a lower gear and drove quietly at a respectable speed until he turned into his driveway.

His thoughts drifted back to the note he'd found in his jacket pocket. It was unnerving to acknowledge that Intruder must have been somewhere in the club tonight, watching him. That meant Intruder was no longer a harmless email he could simply click and delete. Whoever was behind the screen name, whoever wrote that note was real. And living in or around Boston.

Other than Clive, there were no obvious suspects, and Clive had bought him a beer. Hardly consistent with how you would treat a "worthy adversary." Still, if it did turn out to be Clive, he'd have his job and his head in that order. Brent hadn't recognized anyone else in the bar besides Todd and a few of the guys from Revolution. No one else even knew he planned to go to The Jail tonight except Amanda. *Who was stalking him? And why?* It just didn't make sense.

Brent pulled into the garage and checked his watch. *Twenty-four minutes, a new record from downtown.* That bit of news he wouldn't be sharing with Amanda.

Inside the house, all was quiet. Thankfully, it seemed Amanda has slept through the rattle and bang of the garage door opening. Still wired, he knew he should go to bed, but he also knew he'd never be able to fall asleep. Instead, he tossed his jacket over the banister post at the foot of the stairs and headed into his office.

At the computer, Brent wiggled the mouse but nothing happened. Amanda must have been on the computer checking her email tonight. She was forever hitting the power button instead of just letting the computer go into sleep mode.

Brent booted up the computer, hoping he hadn't received any new emails from DieorDieTrying.com. Another decision he'd made tonight was to get started reestablishing his identity. *Tonight.* If he committed to spending just an hour every night, he could get through it. Maybe it wouldn't be so bad.

He kicked off his shoes and started doing Google searches. Within fifteen minutes, he discovered that Todd, as usual, was right. This was going to take weeks. Brent opened a document and began to read. Less than halfway through, his eyelids began to droop. After a small catnap, he'd get back to it. He closed his eyes.

• • •

The sound of a twittering bird jolted Brent awake. He blinked his eyes and saw an incoming message on his Twitter account. *That was odd.* The sound he'd set for Twitter traffic was a creaking door. *Was this another prank? And who did he know that was sophisticated enough to pull off font changes and hack his Twitter account? Well, other than Todd.*

Determined to get rolling on his identity theft before he lost more than just five grand, Brent clicked the close box, choosing to ignore the tweet.

Almost immediately another chirp sounded and the Twitter box reappeared. Fully awake now, Brent read the single line of text in the box.

Intruder: YOU`RE BACK.

Anger washed over him. He had to convince this asshole to leave him alone.

Brent clicked the direct reply message button. The word Pawn694 immediately popped up in a new box with a flashing cursor. *Pawn694? That wasn't his account name on Twitter. His account had definitely been hacked.*

Brent clenched his teeth as Todd's description of a cracker came to mind: someone who went around causing trouble. By now he knew more than enough about what it felt like to be on the receiving end.

The screen name Intruder had chosen for him, Pawn694, was no doubt a reference to the weakest piece on the chessboard. And designed to annoy him. However, now wasn't the time to contemplate the childish screen name or how Intruder had managed to pull off this latest computer feat.

Brent laid his hands on the keyboard and typed the first question that popped into his head.

```
Pawn694: What do you
mean, you`re back?
Intruder: WE TALKED
EARLIER TONIGHT.
```

Brent thought back to the bar and wondered if Clive was confessing to being Intruder. He felt his heartbeat quicken, and he looked down at the keyboard and began punching letters as fast as he could.

```
Pawn694: Who are you?
Intruder: THAT`S
BESIDE THE POINT.
Pawn694: Why are you
doing this?
Intruder: IT`S A GAME.
Pawn694: Why me?
Intruder: WHY NOT?
Pawn694: I want you to
stop.
Intruder: PLAY THE
GAME.
Pawn694: I don`t even
know what the game is!
Intruder: FIGURE IT
OUT, COLLEGE BOY.
```

Brent started typing another question, but the chirp sounded. Intruder had signed off.

Brent dropped his head into his hands, his brain on overload. It was too late to think rationally.

Dead tired, Brent stood up, ready to head upstairs, and then realized he hadn't checked to see if any email had come through from DieorDieTrying.com.

Each night after Amanda went upstairs, he'd gotten into the habit of deleting any odd messages off the system. He didn't care if the emails were from Intruder, DieorDieTrying.com, or just a name or a site he didn't recognize. Everything and anything that looked even vaguely suspect went into the trash bin on his computer, unopened, and then he went a step further, and selected "Empty Trash" from the dropdown menu and wiped them off his computer for good. He was glad this was the last week he'd have to do this secretive cleanup. In the morning he'd tell Amanda everything that had been going on for the last few months.

Brent double-clicked on the in-box and breathed a sigh of relief. No new mail. He needed sleep. He stood up and flipped off the light at the entrance to the den. At the same instant, from behind him, he heard the chirp of an incoming Twitter message. He had a bad feeling about this. He whirled around and in three strides was back in front of the computer. In the pitch-black room, the Twitter message appeared to be floating in mid-air.

```
Intruder: BY THE WAY...
THAT MUST HAVE BEEN
YOUR WIFE I CHATTED
WITH EARLIER TONIGHT...

Intruder signed off at
3:20:12 A.M.
```

• • •

"What the hell am I going to do?" Brent asked Todd as he paced in front of his office window. It was just after noon on Monday, and the dreary winter sky was spitting snow. The sun hadn't made an appearance all morning, and the gray day matched his mood as he filled Todd in on the disturbing events after he left the bar on Saturday night.

"This guy, whoever he is, knows his stuff," Todd said. "Quite impressive really." He sat perched on Brent's radiator, his flip-flops dangling from his bare feet, ever present drumsticks in one hand.

Brent rolled his eyes, hearing something akin to pride in Todd's voice. "I'm glad you're in awe of this asshole."

"I've got to be. He's using re-mailers, Trojan horses, and remotely accessing your computer. The boy is clever, all right."

"Why would he set up a new Twitter account on my computer?" Brent couldn't hide his frustration. He checked his watch and ran a hand through his hair. He shouldn't be having this conversation right now. He was seriously behind in his February quota.

"Because he can. He's showing off. Intruder wants to communicate with you on his terms." Todd hammered out a soft drumbeat on his thigh.

"But why?" Brent heard the note of panic in his voice. He'd had a pit in his stomach ever since Intruder revealed that he'd communicated online with Amanda.

"He keeps telling you to play the game, and you've been ignoring him."

"Which is exactly what you told me to do!"

"Yes, I did, and I still think it's sound advice. I'm just telling you how Intruder sees it. He wants an opponent; he doesn't want to play solitaire."

"How the hell can you have an opponent in a game where you are waiting for someone to die?"

Todd shrugged. "Good question. Only Intruder can answer that, I suppose. Although I'm betting that every time you log on to your computer, Intruder is now contacting you, right?"

"Yeah. He is clearly being alerted when I log on or when I access my computer. Do you think he really spoke with Amanda last night?"

"Wouldn't she have said something this morning?" Todd asked.

Brent shifted his gaze away from Todd. "She was still asleep when I left for work." What he didn't add was that when he'd finally gone upstairs, the master bedroom had been empty. Amanda had been asleep in the guest bedroom.

Todd let his flip-flops drop to the floor. "You didn't do anything stupid at The Jail on Sunday night, did you?"

"No."

"Or afterwards? Like bang some chick?"

"Don't be stupid." Brent felt Todd's eyes bore into his. "You have no faith in me at all, do you? I swear to God, I went straight home."

"I don't know. You have a guilty look on your face."

"I love my wife. This morning on the way in, I stopped and bought Amanda a killer piece of jewelry. We are celebrating Valentine's Day tonight. I've got a really special night planned."

"Good. Maybe you're not as dumb as I thought." Todd nodded his approval.

"I would never cheat on Amanda. Ever."

"That's right because I'd kick your freaking ass. So what's the plan for tonight?"

"I'm leaving early—"

"For once. That's a good start."

"I'm going to pick up a couple of lobsters and two filets I ordered. I know this is not exactly the perfect day to do it, but I'm actually hoping to show her how much I really love her by coming clean about joining the game. The five grand. The identity theft. I thought it through last night. I had an epiphany of sorts."

"About time. Are you making any progress getting your identity reestablished?" Todd asked.

"That's what I'm working on this morning."

"Here? At the office?" Todd raised his eyebrows. "I'd be careful if I were you." He hopped off the radiator. "Hard to tell how this new regime feels about employees doing personal stuff on company time."

"No one ever cared before." Brent eyed the clock on the monitor. More time had slipped by than he'd realized. "With the hours I put in here and the work I do from home, I can't believe anyone would give me crap about trying to straighten some of this identify stuff out while I'm at the office."

"I'm just saying…there's a new sheriff in town." Todd slid his feet into his flip-flops. "Just FYI, our department has already been asked to implement some changes. This new CEO, Phil, is running a tight ship. Anyway, I gotta get to it." Todd threw his customary salute, touching his drumsticks to his forehead. "Anyway, good luck with everything."

Todd left the office, and Brent listened to the slap of his friend's flip-flops as he disappeared down the hall. With a yank, he pulled open his right-hand desk drawer and reached for the bottle of Tums. *A tighter ship. Great, something else to worry about.*

As he crunched the chalky tablets, Brent winced at his disastrous morning. Late getting into the office after his run to the jewelry store, he'd passed Clive in the hallway, and the guy had a smile on his face like the cat that ate the canary. With a sinking feeling, Brent detoured to the conference room and saw that Ed had posted new sales for Clive.

It was now twelve-fifteen, and he'd let the extra time he'd planned to hone his sales presentation slip away. He wasn't as prepared as he should be for his two client meetings this afternoon, and he knew it. *Too late to do anything about it now.*

Brent shoved aside the identity recovery checklist he'd printed and rose from his chair. He grabbed his briefcase, hit the light, and pulled shut his office door. He sprinted down the hall to the bank of elevators, knowing full well that he would never make it up to Saugus by one.

In the shiny metallic doors of the elevator, he caught his reflection as he reached forward to press the down button. His hair touched his collar, and he had bags under his eyes. About the only thing that looked decent was his suit.

Brent jabbed the elevator button several more times. *Sales. He had to make sales.* It was a constant mantra in his head these days, and it made his stomach churn.

Where was the damn elevator? He needed a big break to get back on track. Or more accurately, he needed to make something happen on his own. *Think. Work smarter, not harder.*

Knowing it was pointless, Brent pushed the elevator button yet again. What he needed to do was overhaul his strategy. *Like he had time for that?* He had to push his smaller accounts into four-color layouts, multiple insertions, and promotional tie-ins. *In the middle of a recession?* His major accounts needed to stop jacking around with radio ads. He needed to insist they go for TV commercials. *Budgets were still being cut.* Everyone needed a video presence on the web. Everyone. Something he needed to do a fair amount of research on before he could sell. It wasn't even midday and patches of sweat soaked through his dress shirt. *Shake it off! Accounts can smell fear a mile away.*

Although not a single source had confirmed Clive's comment about impending layoffs, Brent had a bad feeling that Clive knew something he didn't. The guy was too damn cocky. Brent was at a loss to know how a brand new employee could be so well connected. *Who was his source?*

Brent shifted his briefcase to the other hand. He had to beat Clive. And now it wasn't just about the damn condo. The knot in his stomach tightened.

The reality was, it didn't matter if the rumors were true or not. Salesmen that failed to generate income didn't last long in this company. February was half over, and he was less than a quarter of the way to his monthly quota.

• • •

Brent was on the road headed for home by four p.m. The commute had been a nightmare so far. A nor'easter was predicted to hit this evening, and I-93 was a parking lot. Cars with Massachusetts plates surrounded him with snowboards and skis strapped to roof racks. No doubt they were headed up to any one of a dozen ski resorts in the White Mountains, hoping to get to their destination before the storm hit. By then, he hoped he and Amanda would be in bed together, concentrating on much more personal things.

A massive bouquet of red roses lay on the seat next to him. This morning, he'd noticed an OB-GYN appointment on the refrigerator calendar for late this afternoon. *Perfect.* He'd have the house to himself to prepare dinner and set the stage for the romantic evening ahead. Everything was going according to plan except for the traffic jam.

He reached into his suit coat pocket, and his fingers closed around the jewelry box. He pulled it out and ran his thumb over the smooth black velvet before flipping open the lid. The weak winter sun had finally broken through the clouds, and Brent enjoyed the way the white gold bracelet shimmered in the last vestiges of sunlight coming through the sunroof. He set the open box down on the adjacent seat next to the roses.

The car behind him honked, and he crept forward several inches across the New Hampshire state line. A rustling sounded from the bag on the floor of the passenger seat. As Brent reached over to crimp the bag of live lobsters closed, his cell phone rang. He pulled the phone from the opposite pocket. "Darby."

"I never thought I'd see the day you would leave early. Should I be worried? Did you close some big-ass deal today?"

"What do you want, Clive?" Traffic at dead stop, Brent continued to look over at the bracelet. He pictured himself clasping it around Amanda's slim wrist and how sexy it would look sliding up and down her arm. He couldn't wait to see her reaction when she opened the gift.

"I got my first kill," Clive said.

"What are you talking about?" Brent asked. *Please God, not another major account.*

"The deadpool. Clive's Crypt. My number eight man just bit the dust. Big points."

Relief coursed through Brent. "So who was it?" he asked, not really caring. He edged over into the left-hand lane, forcing his way between a minivan and an SUV. He might as well shoot the shit with Clive; he wasn't going anywhere for a while. The steel snake extended up ahead as far as he could see.

"A guy by the name of Jordan McHenry," Clive said.

"Who the hell is he?"

"1998 Pro Bowl. He was a tight end."

"Sounds like he's about as famous as my mailman."

"Who cares?" Clive laughed. "All I know is that he's officially dead. He died of AIDS."

"How'd you wind up picking him for your roster?"

"The Internet has all kinds of lists naming famous people with life-threatening illnesses. AIDS, Lou Gehrig's disease, cancer. I decided pulling from those lists was about as good a guarantee of death as I was going to get. Half my list is made up of those poor saps."

Brent couldn't believe what he was hearing. Playing the game was bad enough, but to relish in the death of people who had lost their battle with an incurable disease? That was truly appalling. "Congratulations…I guess. See you tomorrow." Brent hit the disconnect button and tossed the phone on the seat next to him. Clive had some serious issues. He needed to cut bait and distance himself from that guy.

• • •

With a critical eye, Brent studied the two place settings on the coffee table in the family room. On top of Amanda's plate, he had placed the bouquet of roses and leaned the black velvet box up against them. When Amanda still wasn't home after he completed the food preparation and set the table, he'd hunted around and found some candles. Unable to find any candleholders, he used shot glasses, but they seemed to work well enough. He placed the candles on the coffee table, further enhancing the romantic mood. Now all he needed was Amanda.

Deciding she had to be home any second, he held a match to the crumpled newspaper beneath the teepee of logs he had built in the fireplace grate. The newsprint caught fire instantly, and soon the bits of kindling began to crackle. He closed the mesh screen but left the glass doors ajar to feed some oxygen to the flames. The fire had been easier to start than he'd thought. Amanda had been a Girl Scout, so she'd been deemed the official fire starter. He'd been worried there was some trick to it, but the fire seemed to be burning just fine. Satisfied, he watched the flames dance.

With the evening perfectly laid out, he grabbed his iPod, scanning the play list for a selection of romantic songs. He so wanted this evening to be a new start for them.

When his watch beeped, he looked down at the face, surprised to see that it was now just past six-thirty. A prickle of fear crossed his mind. *Where was she?* Had something gone wrong at the doctor's office? The OB-GYN appointment had been at four.

The house phone rang, and Brent raced to pick up the extension in the kitchen. *Amanda's Cell* popped up on Caller ID. "Hey, honey. Is everything okay?" Brent asked. Maybe she'd gotten stuck in the tail end of the same traffic jam since she'd been coming home from Boston as well.

The salad he'd prepared sat on the counter, dressed and ready to go. He stole a black olive from the top and popped it in his mouth.

"Brent, we need to talk," Amanda said.

"Are you almost home?" he asked. The French baguette gave off a mouthwatering aroma as he opened the oven door to check the color. *Perfect.*

"I'm at my mom's," Amanda replied in a tight voice.

"Your mom's?" Her parents lived two hours away. *That made no sense.* "Did something happen at your appointment?"

"No."

"So you're okay? The baby is okay?"

"Yes," she answered.

"But it's the night we agreed to celebrate Valentine's Day. Why are you at your folks?"

"I think you know why."

The clipped tone of her voice brought Brent up short, and a cold chill settled over him. *Uh-oh.*

"I know about Intruder."

"About Intruder?" his stomach flip-flopped.

"Were you ever going to tell me?"

"I was going to tell you—"

"When?"

"My plan was…"

"Plan? What part did I play in this little plan of yours?"

Brent slumped down onto a stool at the breakfast bar. He was making a mess of this. "Tonight," he blurted out. "I was going to tell you tonight."

"How romantic."

"I was going to tell you tonight, Amanda. I swear." Brent wracked his brain for a way to convince her.

"I'm hanging up now."

"Amanda, don't! I can explain." She didn't reply, but she didn't hang up either. "I told Todd this morning that I was going to tell you everything. If you don't believe me, call him. I swear it's the truth."

"So you told Todd about your sordid little affair?"

"Affair? What aff-?" A soft click sounded in his ear. Fear raced up Brent's spine. *Just what had Intruder said to Amanda last night? What lies had he told her?* He hit redial. It rang several times, and then he heard his mother-in-law's voice answer. He spoke over her words. "Dolores, may I please speak to my wife?"

"She'd rather not talk to you right now, Brent."

"Please? There's been a misunderstanding. Would you ask her if she'll speak to me?" He waited, pressing the phone hard against his ear, trying to make out the muffled words in the background.

His mother-in-law came back on the line, her voice grim. "She's just not up to it, and I can't say I blame her."

"It's not what you think. I—"

"Goodbye, Brent," Dolores said.

"Wait! Could you please give her a message for me?"

His mother-in-law sniffed in disapproval.

"Tell her..." Brent hesitated. *What? That you didn't have an affair?* He didn't know how much Amanda had confided to her mom. "Tell her I love her." The phone felt slick in his sweaty palm. "Tell her I need her to come back home, and when she does, I'll explain everything. It's not what she thinks." Praying Amanda might actually pick up the phone again, he waited. Instead he heard a click as Dolores hung up on him.

Brent slammed the phone back in the base. For good measure he kicked the refrigerator, leaving a long black scuffmark across the white pebbled surface.

His first thought was to drive to Amanda's parents' house so he could explain everything. *He could be there by eight o'clock.* But then he realized it was just as likely that he'd get all the way up there, and Randy would come out of the house with a damn shotgun pointed at his head.

His entire life was spiraling out of control. Not knowing what else to do, he picked up the phone and called Todd.

• • •

Less than five minutes later, Brent backed the Viper out of the garage. Todd had a couple of hours before his date, and he'd agreed to meet at Revolution. For Todd, coming back in wasn't a big deal since he only lived a short subway hop away.

After parking in his assigned space, Brent used his badge to gain access to the building and took the elevator up to the twenty-sixth floor. The overhead lights were on as were a few lights from various outside offices as he jogged through the empty hallways. He must not be the only one behind in his quota. He zigzagged left and then right through the maze of cubicles until he reached the opposite corner of the building where IT was located.

Up ahead, florescent light spilled from the doorway of Todd's workspace. He slouched against Todd's doorway. "Thanks for coming. I didn't know what else to do."

"Sure. What are friends for? I haven't had such a hot day myself." Todd was sitting on the floor, long legs stretched out in front of him, barefoot as usual. "So what happened between Intruder and Amanda?" He set aside the keyboard and leaned back against the mauve fabric-covered cubicle wall, looking up at Brent.

Brent pulled out Todd's chair only to find it stacked with software boxes and a haphazard tower of CDs. He pushed it back in and squatted down beside Todd on the floor. "Like I told you on the phone, this guy is wreaking havoc on my life—"

"Don't get your panties in a wad. I'm looking into it. What did Intruder say to Amanda?"

"I don't know what he told her last night on Twitter, but it was bad. Bad enough to make her think I'm having an affair." Brent watched as Todd moved the computer mouse across the carpet. "I told Amanda to call you. That you'd verify that I am not involved with anyone and that you knew I was going to tell her about Intruder and the game. Did she call you?"

Todd shook his head no, his eyes still on the screen. "Why would she believe me?"

Brent's heart sank. "What if she doesn't come back?"

"She'll come back."

"How do you know?"

"I don't, but what do you want me to say?" Todd pointed to the screen. "Look, Clive is not the guy. I've done a superficial search of his hard drive, and although he's accessed DieorDieTrying.com from work, I don't see any other suspicious activity. I don't see any evidence on his hard drive. The thing is a mess. Everything on it is totally unorganized. He has files all over his desktop; I don't know how he ever finds anything."

"Maybe that's just a ploy."

"I doubt it. I didn't see any software to skim data or capture user info. The only thing installed on his system is the most basic software package we put in when he was hired. He's added a bunch of documents, but there is nothing to indicate anything out of the ordinary. I think you're barking up the wrong tree."

"So where do we go from here?"

"I started digging around to find information about DieorDieTrying.com. Initially I thought the whole DieorDieTrying.com site was a scam—"

"Is it?"

"No. Just listen for a minute. I researched last year's winner, Frank Miller, and he's a real guy. An insurance salesman who lives in San Diego. It looks like he got the money the deadpool site claims he won. According to a local newspaper article, he donated part of his winnings to charity. He also bought a boat. So it sounds like the game is legitimate."

"Which means what?" Brent rose to his feet and picked up one of a half dozen snow globes from the collection on Todd's shelf. He leaned back against the desk and shook it, watching snowflakes drift down over the tiny replica of New York City.

"If the site was bogus, you could try to get it shut down. But if the game is legit…" Todd shrugged. "Not much you can do."

"Can a game like this be legal? Betting on when people are going to die?"

"Why not? It's not all that different from fantasy football. None of these games would exist if there weren't people willing to bet on them."

"I didn't even know the game existed a couple of months ago. Now, it's clear there are hundreds of them."

"Hundreds?"

"Okay, dozens."

"So you've been looking them up online?"

"No. Intruder, or someone, must have sent my email addresses to all the deadpool sites out there. I get notices of games starting all the time. Yesterday I got an email from BaggednTagged. com," Brent said.

"At work or at home?" Todd asked.

"Work." Brent sighed.

Todd grimaced. "That's what worries me. The folks that run DieorDieTrying.com probably sold your address."

"The BaggednTagged.com game starts on Halloween, and it pays off on October 30th the following year. Devil's night. These guys think they're so clever." He rolled his eyes.

"They are clever. And not just with words. I'm concerned that Intruder or one of these guys from a similar site might start targeting the computer system at Revolution as a way to get to you. If someone succeeds, if someone somehow gets past our security system…"

"But I thought you said everything here was protected."

"I also said, with enough time, hackers can break through any security barrier. It's all a matter of how determined they are to get in and what the prize is on the other side."

"Like what, for example?"

"Here I would think a hacker would want credit card numbers, financial data, account files. Especially if they were a competitor."

"Shit. I didn't even think of any of that."

"There is no way to know their motive. Or why you personally are being targeted."

"I can't think of anyone who would do this to me."

"I don't think our system at work is truly at risk. Still, it doesn't make me sleep well at night, I'll tell you that. Especially since the trail from Intruder leads to you and eventually to me." Todd stood up and balanced the keyboard on top of his terminal. "Needless to say, I haven't shared any of this with my boss."

"So what should I do?"

"I think you better start keeping some of these documents from Intruder as evidence. Just in the event we are forced to explain a breach down the line. IT is all about defense, protecting our system from attack from the outside. But you may have to start playing offense, or this guy is going to make it his mission to destroy you, your marriage, your job, and fuck up pretty much every part of your life. I can't get involved in going after this guy. But you might have to. Make sure you give the file some type of legitimate sounding name and put a password on it."

"Are you serious? Who cares about my files? Do I really have to be so covert?"

Todd shrugged. "Call me paranoid, but when you and I started here, this place was about as laid back as it got."

"Yeah. One step removed from Animal House."

"Those days are gone. Phil just asked my department for flag reports of profanity and trigger words such as games or shopping. A whole lot of people are going to be in a whole lot of trouble."

"Are you kidding me?"

"It's standard practice nowadays to check up on employees. Call it a little black book the corporations keep on every employee. This data is kept on file so in the event they want to get rid of an employee, they have evidence. Lawsuits are expensive. No one gets fired anymore for incompetence because it's impossible to prove. But fire someone for shopping on company time? The employee has virtually no recourse."

"Unreal."

"Everything, including the information inside your head, is owned by Revolution. You try to go to another ad agency with a campaign you thought up here. They will sue your ass for sure. You signed a noncompete contract when you were hired, right?"

"Now that you mention it, yeah, I did." Brent shook the globe again and stared inside it, wishing he could transport himself out of his own nightmare.

"Enough said. So has Intruder tried to contact you by Twitter at work?"

"No." Brent shook his head. "Just at home."

"That's what I thought. He's too smart for that. Okay, when he sends you a tweet at home, try to get him to admit to some of the stuff he's done. Then capture the conversation on your computer."

"Is that it?" Brent set aside the snow globe and crossed his arms thinking Todd's solution didn't sound very promising.

"Listen, I don't need you being a sarcastic asshole. I am trying to help you here."

"Sorry. I just feel so helpless."

"Anonymity is everything to these guys. If a cracker thinks he's busted, he'll disappear. I guarantee it."

"I can try it, but I doubt Intruder will let anything slip."

"The other thing you need to do is to avoid the words Intruder, or deadpool, or anything related to this shit while you are at work. Don't talk about this stuff to anyone. This guy wants a challenge, a game between you two. I don't want him to see Revolution as part of that challenge, or it could be my job on the line. You got that?"

"I'm not saying a word to anyone."

"That includes Clive. Just back off when he tries to wind you up. I've noticed he seems to get under your skin."

"Yeah. I really don't like the guy. Never have."

"So tonight, when you get home, get back online and see if you can make Intruder take your bait. You're a smart guy. Figure out a way to get him to admit something. Anything. The longer this goes on, the more nervous I get. You need to bust this guy." Todd glanced up at the clock.

"Speaking of busted," Brent said, following Todd's gaze to the clock. "Not quite time for your hot date. You said you had a lousy day. What happened?"

"I found out Jordan has been complaining to the other guys in the band about my level of commitment."

"What does that mean?"

"Jordan works at The Guitar Center. Paul doesn't even have a job. Chris works at a sandwich shop, and he's about to quit."

"So?"

"So, they seem to think I'm not committed to the band. That I spend too much time at my real job. They have apparently been discussing that if I had a shitty job, or better yet no job at all, that I would have more time to practice."

"Do you think that's true?"

"Probably, but I also think that if they'd get their lazy asses out of bed earlier on Saturdays and Sundays, we could jam on those days."

"Those guys are hard partiers. I can't see that happening anytime soon."

"Exactly. They are not willing to compromise. It's so frustrating with the demo in the works, and now they bring this shit up." Todd looked back at the clock.

"So who are you taking out on this date tonight? And please tell me it's not that girl that I saw you with at the club on Sunday night."

"Yup. That's who I'm seeing." Todd smiled.

"What is she, the band's first official groupie?"

"Maybe." Todd's eyes slid over to look at the clock again.

"Do I sense more than a casual interest here?" Brent asked.

"Maybe—"

"Hey, what are these things?" Brent picked up an odd-looking pair of metal rods from the pile of junk heaped on Todd's desk. "Another toy to add to your collection?" The steel rods were almost a foot in length and heavy in his hands.

"No. I wouldn't call them toys."

"They look way more expensive than your bendable Gumby and Pokey characters. What are they?"

"Guess."

"Guess? Too heavy to be a pair of drumsticks and too sharp." Brent ran his thumb over the pointed tip.

"It's a pair of Emei piercers. My dad brought them back from the Orient. I went through a whole martial arts phase in high school."

"Too long for chopsticks…"

"I was digging through a box of early recordings from the band for Melody, and I found them in the bottom of the box."

"Her name is Melody?" Brent rolled his eyes. "That's original. And you fell for that?"

"Hey! She's not like that."

"Next she'll be asking to ride the band's tour bus."

"Knock it off," Todd said. "You can be such an asshole sometimes. I know your Valentine's night got fucked up, but don't take it out on me."

"Well I'm sorry, but my wife thinks I cheated on her."

"So stop keeping secrets from her, you idiot."

"I already told you I was going to tell her everything but—"

"But you conveniently never do."

"Shut the fuck up."

"It's true."

"Can you see the living hell my life has become? I'm not the one at fault here."

"Not entirely, but—"

"Fine, don't help me."

"Look, Intruder is messing with Amanda, the same way he messed with you. He found an opportunity, and he exploited it. Hackers rarely know their victims because it makes their crimes more impersonal and, therefore, easier for them to commit. That's another reason I don't think it's Clive. And for the hundredth time, it doesn't matter who it is."

"Still, if I could get my hands on the person responsible…" Brent tapped the heavy rods against the palm of one hand.

"Give me those," Todd said. "I'll show you how they work."

"What do you mean, how they work?" Brent handed Todd the two metal rods.

"Check this out." Todd slipped his middle finger through a ring in the exact center of the slender diamond-shaped shaft. "Any more lame guesses before I explain what these are?"

"I have no freaking idea. Some sort of medieval sex toy?" He heaved himself up onto Todd's desk.

Todd laughed. "Not even close." He slid the ring of the second Emei piercer onto his left hand. "I'd forgotten how cool these are." Todd dropped his arms to his sides. "Any other guesses?"

"What, are you a game show host? Just tell me already."

"Notice how both shafts are now hidden behind my forearms. The only visible piece of the Emei piercers appears to be an ordinary ring on the index finger of each hand. When I approach an opponent, even at close range, I appear completely unarmed."

"Pretty cool," Brent said. "What do you do, bash the guy you want to fight over the head?"

"Watch and learn, young Jedi." Todd held his arms out at length in front of him, palms down, wrists crossed. He began to make slow, fluid movements, first with his hands, and then with his arms. The steel bars began to spin slowly on the inside of his wrists.

"Wow. Very cool." Brent watched fascinated as Todd's deft movements caused the rods to increase in speed, until they both whirled in circles like helicopter blades.

"On guard!" Todd yelled, lunging at him.

Brent jerked backwards, hitting his head hard against the shelf above Todd's desk.

Todd made a stabbing motion just inches in front of his throat.

"Jesus!" Brent said. He shrank as far away from Todd as he could get, bent back at an awkward angle, pinned against the corner of the cubicle wall and the desk.

"You're a dead man," Todd said gleefully.

"Get those damn things outta my face!"

"You have to admit they are quite effective." Todd stepped back and brought the blades together with a metallic clank, stopping their motion.

"Thanks for the up-close and personal demonstration." Brent straightened and rubbed a hand across his throat. "Are you bringing those on the date? If so, Melody has no idea of the fun you've got in store for her. If she did, she'd probably opt for the sex games instead."

"Very funny. I told you she's not like that.

"If you say so…"

• • •

Brent convinced Todd to leave the Emei piercers at the office, telling him that Melody might be expecting something a bit more romantic for their first official date. His best friend sprinted for the elevator, more excited than Brent had seen him in a long time.

Meanwhile, he walked slowly to his car, dreading the thought of returning to the empty house. *Could things possibly get any worse?* Just six months ago, he'd felt invincible.

He decided to try and call Amanda's cell phone, hoping to subvert her mom, and beg her to come home. He realized she would recognize his number on the display, but he hoped she would pick up anyway.

The call went to voicemail. In the seconds before the beep, he tried frantically to find the words to convey what he planned to tell her in person. "Honey, it's me. I want you to know that I have never, ever, cheated on you. You have to believe me. I'll explain who Intruder is and what's been going on as soon as you return home. Please call me, or better yet, just come home. I love you, Amanda."

As he hit the disconnect button, he noticed he had a message waiting. A surge of hope shot through him. Maybe Amanda had already tried to get in touch with him.

"You have twenty messages. Mailbox full."

Brent pulled the phone away from his ear and looked at the screen. *Twenty messages?* Still steering with his left hand, he manipulated the screen with his right thumb, hoping to hear

Amanda's voice. Instead he was caught off guard by the resonance of a deep, unfamiliar male voice.

"Play the game."

His stomach lurched. *The voice of Intruder? Who else could it be? How had that lunatic gotten his cell phone number?* Brent slammed his palm against the steering wheel. "Damn it!" He drove his car into the garage and yanked the key from the ignition. The engine ticked as he sat and listened to all twenty messages, his anger building each time he heard the same command on the recording. There was no message from Amanda. With one keystroke, Brent deleted all the messages.

The minute he opened the car door he heard a shrill piercing sound emanating from the house. *What the hell was that?* He burst through the door, and the noise increased ten-fold, causing him to drop his keys and cover his ears with his hands even as smoke filled his nostrils. *The house was on fire! Shit! The fire in the fireplace!* He tore into the family room, his breath coming in jagged gasps. The smoke alarm continued to shriek, causing every nerve in his body to vibrate.

Thick smoke hung in the air, but there were no visible flames. Through the haze, Brent saw that the fieldstone fireplace had been blackened by a trail of smoke damage that ended in a patch of black soot on the ceiling. The charred remains of several logs lay on the hearth where his teepee of firewood had collapsed and fallen completely out of the firebox. The alarm continued to shriek incessantly.

He ran to the hall closet and grabbed the golf umbrella. Back in the family room, he jumped onto the couch, stabbing at the smoke alarm with the pointed end until he knocked it from the ceiling where it hung from a single white wire. Brent grabbed the unit, breaking off the plastic door in his haste to get to the batteries. Hoisting a chair, he ran from room to room, unscrewing the units from the ceiling and pulling out the batteries until at last the house was silent.

I almost burned down the fucking house! Brent retraced his steps and opened every window downstairs, shivering as the frigid air began to flow on cross-currents through the house. Several times he looked out the window expecting fire trucks, but thankfully the street remained quiet.

Returning once again to the family room, in ominous silence, he stared at the damage. On the coffee table, a large hardened puddle of blue wax was all that remained of the candles he'd set out but had never lit, evidence of just how hot the fire had been. The roses had blackened in the withering heat.

Brent surveyed the sorry remains of his much-anticipated romantic evening. *What an utter disaster*, he thought as he dropped down onto the couch. The smoke was just beginning to clear, and he thanked God that Amanda had been safe at her folks' house.

This fire had nothing to do with Intruder. It was utter stupidity on his part. He wasn't making good decisions. In fact, he was making terrible ones, and they were impacting every area of his life.

On top of that, Intruder was waiting out there somewhere, probably nearby. Waiting and watching. It was unnerving.

He sat there surrounded by the debris completely overwhelmed and dejected. How would he ever explain everything to Amanda now?

Chapter 5

February 16ᵗʰ – Tuesday

It was just after four o'clock, and after a full day Brent was dog-tired but satisfied, at least with his performance at work. He had completed two important client meetings, and one of them he'd knocked out of the park.

He settled back into his office chair, prepared to keep at it. *No reason to go home.* He had plenty to do and working here was better than returning to an empty house. Plus the pile on his desk helped distract him from imaging what a lowlife Amanda thought he was.

"Got a minute?"

Over the top of his terminal, Brent looked up to see his boss, standing outside his office. The width of Ed's shoulders appeared to fill the entire doorway. "Sure," Brent replied, hiding his surprise. Caught multitasking, he quickly minimized both the DieorDieTrying.com site and an email he was typing to one of his credit card companies.

Ed walked over to the metal chair in front of Brent's desk and yanked it back several feet before lowering his enormous bulk down onto the chair.

"What's up?" Brent asked. He could count on one hand the number of times Ed had darkened the door of his office. His boss preferred to call his salesmen on the carpet behind his own desk. Something was up.

Ed pulled out his handkerchief, mopping his dark brow. "I just came down from Phil's office. I thought on my way back to my office I'd walk out to the mound and check on my starting pitcher."

Brent was instantly on guard. "Is there a problem?" It wasn't the walking-out-to-the-mound comment that worried him. Ed was a former football player; everyone was accustomed to his constant use of sports metaphors, but had he been the topic of conversation in Phil's office?

"You tell me."

Brent wasn't touching that one. "No problem that I know of."

"Your numbers are down, and your weekly call report is no longer the first one to hit my desk." Ed paused. "And what was with the porn magazines showing up at the office?"

So word had gotten out. Brent forced out a chuckle. "Practical joke. I've taken care of it, and I apologized to the department secretary."

"Who sent them?" Ed asked, his eyes narrowing.

Brent gave a noncommittal shrug.

"Fine." Ed crossed his substantial arms over his chest and tipped his chair precariously onto the two back legs. "You better get your head back in the game."

In order to get Ed out of his office, Brent realized he was going to have to placate him. "I met with Amazon Athletics this morning." Brent paused for effect, picking up a folder on his desk.

"Let's hear it."

Brent's intention had been to drop the news casually at the weekly sales meetings on Friday, solely for the purpose of seeing firsthand the shock on Clive's face. But now Ed was forcing his hand. "I have the new purchase orders."

"And…"

"They went for the full ride."

"Full boat?" With a bang, Ed's chair came back down on all four legs. The metal creaked under Ed's weight as he reached a hand across Brent's desk to take the folder.

"Three purchase orders." Brent felt a glow of satisfaction as he watched Ed flip through the pages. "Signed." By the time his boss closed the folder and handed it back, both men were grinning at each other.

"Nice save. I was starting to worry," Ed said.

"I had a rough start this month, but now I'm back in the saddle."

"Just in the nick of time, too." Ed dabbed at the perspiration on his brow.

"What do you mean?" He might as well dig for some information.

"Phil is asking for double-digit increases from a number of accounts he considers underperformers. Amazon was on that list."

Brent did a slow burn at the reprimand. "And here I thought congratulations would be in order."

"Phil will be pleased, no doubt about it. But he expects every player to perform. He won't tolerate bench warmers."

"I'm hardly a bench—"

"I'm just saying," Ed cut him off. "Get used to the pressure. It's only going to amp up from here."

"Are you kidding me?" Brent exhaled and shoved his chair back from the desk. "How is that even possible?"

Ed looked him in the eye. "A lot of things are on the table."

"Such as…" *Layoffs?*

Ed ignored his question. "You're the best salesman I've got. If I can't count on you, we might as well both become free agents."

"Right." Brent gritted his teeth, wanting to just let loose on Ed. The last thing he expected was a lecture after the coup he'd pulled off with Amazon.

"Phil has put tremendous pressure on the management team to turn things around in three months or…"

"Or what?"

Ed looked uncomfortable. "Let's just say I need you on top of your game right now." He folded his handkerchief into a neat square and tucked it back into his suit coat pocket. "These POs are a good start."

A good start? Come on! Where was the love? These POs were fucking phenomenal. "Tell Phil not to worry," Brent said, unable to keep a touch of sarcasm out of his voice. "After a short hiatus, I'm back on top of the leaderboard."

"Yes, you are. That ought to light a nice fire under Clive."

"So you heard about the bet between us?" Even with his sorry-ass performance during the first half of February, these three purchase orders would put the lock on winning the month.

Ed nodded. "Everyone on the sales team knows. Clive made sure of that. Since a week ago, he was ahead." Ed strained to rise to his feet.

"Was he, now?"

"You've done a great job bringing Amazon along. I'll make sure Phil is aware of your efforts."

"Thanks, I appreciate that." At least he could count on his name making it upstairs. The phone rang on his desk.

"Answer it," Ed said, waving a meaty hand at Brent, as he lumbered toward the door. "Sell, sell, sell."

Brent picked up the receiver.

"Play the game."

Intruder. Even though the display read unavailable, the deep voice was identical to the voice messages he'd deleted off his cell phone. The happiness he'd enjoyed just a moment ago dissolved into dread. Before he could utter a word, the caller spoke again.

"The game is about to get more interesting."

"What do you mean?" Brent asked.

"You'll know soon enough."

The caller hung up. Brent put the handset back in the cradle. *Was Intruder calling the home phone now as well?* He shuddered to think of Amanda answering one of those calls. The voice was creepy enough to scare anyone.

A check of the clock showed it was four-forty-five. He changed his mind, deciding to call it a day after remembering the mess he still had to clean up at home from the fire.

He locked up and walked down the hall to the elevator, noting that Clive's cubicle was empty. *Was he out selling, or had he gone home for the day?* Still, Brent was confident there was no way Clive could come close to his February sales numbers. Not with Amazon all but in the bank. Today had been one of Brent's best sales days ever. Even with his back up against the wall to make his quota, all the Intruder shit, and his wife convinced he'd had an affair, at least he could still sell.

He checked his phone just in case Amanda had called, but there were no messages from her. The money could be replaced. The practical jokes he could live with. Losing Amanda was simply inconceivable.

As he got into his car, he said a fervent prayer that Amanda had at least listened to the cell phone messages he'd left her this morning. He had made mistakes, lots of them, but being unfaithful wasn't one of them.

Maybe today was going to be a fresh start. With the Amazon purchase orders and Ed's obvious delight in the sales figures, not to mention the boost to his quota, he was going to breathe a lot easier at work. Once he explained to Amanda the reality behind Intruder and how he'd been one hundred percent faithful to their marriage vows, he hoped to get her back in his corner again too.

With hope in his heart and his conscience front and center, Brent stepped on the gas and headed for home.

• • •

At five-thirty p.m., Amanda turned the Jeep into the driveway. Her palms were damp as she pushed the button on the garage door opener. She chided herself for being nervous. The Viper was gone as she had expected. Brent was still at work. *Or somewhere.* Thankful, she let out a shaky breath.

Still, Brent said he would explain everything. But Intruder's words, *Do you really care*, seemed seared into her brain. On the drive home from her folks' house, Amanda vowed to herself that she would listen to Brent objectively, no matter what he confessed. If a decision needed to be made about their marriage, she promised herself she wouldn't do it in the heat of the moment.

Amanda walked through the garage and into the house where the smell of smoke struck her at once. She laid her purse down on the kitchen counter then gasped as she looked over the half wall. Black residue coated the fieldstones and part of the ceiling on the far wall of the family room. She walked toward it in disbelief. *What happened?*

Her eyes were drawn to the two place settings on the coffee table in front of the fireplace. A sheath of roses, blackened and charred, lay across one plate. *So, Brent had planned a special Valentine's Day surprise for her.*

Hand to her throat, she pictured Brent setting up this romantic evening. She replayed the phone call she'd made to him accusing him of infidelity. Had he cheated on her? Or had she gotten it all wrong? She'd gone back and forth so many times now, she honestly had no idea.

"You're home."

Amanda was startled out of her reverie. She turned toward the kitchen and watched Brent walk into the family room. He stopped several feet short of her, his suit coat slung over one shoulder, briefcase still in hand. She read the uncertainty on his face.

"I kept calling you…" he trailed off and then started again. "I'm so glad you came home."

She tried to read his face. *Fear? Guilt?*

Amanda turned back toward the fireplace, staring at the black soot and wondering if it would ever come off. Wondering if it mattered.

"I'm sorry about everything," Brent said. "Whatever other mistakes I've made, I've never cheated on you."

"Who is Intruder?" Amanda asked. Her voice shook.

"Some faceless person on the Internet."

"So you're having Internet sex?"

Brent eyes widened. "No! Is that what he told you?"

"Who are you talking about?"

"Intruder."

"Who is Intruder?"

"I don't know his real name. He's…it's hard to explain."

"Why? Just tell me the truth."

"It's complicated."

"Then explain it. And don't try and pull any of that salesman crap. I want the truth. All of it."

"I'll tell you everything I know." Brent set down his briefcase and dropped his suit coat over the arm of the couch. "I'm still figuring some of it out."

"Don't do this to me, Brent." She stifled a sob. "Have you been faithful to me?"

"Yes."

"Do you swear it?" Amanda asked.

"Yes," Brent replied. "I have never had sex, Internet or otherwise, with anyone other than you since the day we met. I swear on my life."

A shudder ran through her, and she sank down onto the couch. "But you have something to tell me. Something bad."

"Yes. Can I come and sit beside you?"

Amanda held up a hand. "You haven't fallen in love with someone else, have you?"

"No."

"Or met someone else?"

"No. Let me explain. Please?"

"Okay." She nodded. "But it's something really awful isn't it?"

"It's not good." Brent sat on the edge of the couch beside her and took both her hands in his. He cleared his throat and ran his thumb over the back of her knuckles. "I signed up to play an Internet game back in December. I didn't tell you about it because I was trying to get out of it."

Amanda felt only confusion. "Do you mean to tell me this is all about a stupid Internet game?"

"Yes, but there's more."

She watched Brent's face closely. His eyes met hers, and then he shifted his gaze away. "The entry fee for the game was five thousand dollars."

"Oh my God! Five thousand—" Amanda jerked her hands out of his. "Five thousand dollars?" she repeated, staring at him.

"I'm sorry, Amanda. More sorry than you'll ever know. If you'll just let me explain—"

"How could you?" She crossed her arms tightly over her chest, thinking of all the things they still needed to buy for the baby. In spite of her vow to listen and remain objective, she was seething. All she wanted to do was throw a litany into his face: a crib, a bassinet, a stroller, baby clothes. *Wasn't this the Viper all over again?* "When did this happen?"

"On Christmas Eve. Remember when Todd called and tried to get you to join us?"

"We had a fight that night about my parents."

"Yeah. It was also the night Todd's band got the offer to cut a demo record. We started celebrating and—"

"What does this have to do with the Internet game?"

"I'm getting to that. Clive, one of the other salesmen, was at the bar too. You could say he sort of helped me enter a roster for the game." Brent ran a hand through his hair. "Look, the details don't matter."

"The details do matter."

"Suffice it to say I made a lot of bad decisions that night, but the end result is that I ended up signing up for the Internet game. And even though I've tried to get out of it, I can't, so I'm stuck playing."

"And that's supposed to make me feel better? That you tried to get out?"

"No."

"So who is Intruder?"

"According to Todd, he is a cracker—"

"A what?"

"Another player who signed up for the same game, but he gets more enjoyment out of simply causing trouble on the Internet than winning the game. I was ignoring him, but lately he's begun to take things to another level."

"What do you mean?"

"Intruder has begun to contact me at work."

"Oh, Brent…"

"And it's gotten kind of serious…"

Amanda was tired of playing twenty questions. "What do you mean? How serious?"

"It appears that someone from the game, Intruder, may have stolen my identity."

"When? How?" Amanda's anger turned to outright alarm.

"I don't know. Todd is trying to help me figure it out—"

"So how much have we lost?"

"Nothing, so far," Brent admitted.

"But I thought you said—"

"I told you it was complicated."

"So help me understand."

"I don't really understand it myself. I'm not even sure Todd does, and this stuff is his specialty. Somehow our personal information has been compromised. He actually sent me a list of our accounts and even our passwords but—"

"Our passwords? So he can access our bank accounts? Oh, my God, Brent!"

"Hang on a minute. No one has actually touched our credit cards or our bank accounts."

"Brent, that makes absolutely no sense."

"I know. A lot of this doesn't make any sense. Todd thinks the goal of Intruder is just to disrupt my life."

For the next several minutes, Amanda listened to Brent's explanation of the arrival of the pornographic magazines at work,

141

the harassing phone calls, and the voicemail messages, as well as the new Twitter account showing up on their home computer.

"The worst part is that Intruder may also be trying to access the computer system at Revolution. Todd's pretty freaked out about that possibility. The system is his responsibility. If this guy hacks in and steals data from Revolution..."

"What would happen?" Amanda asked. Her hands had turned ice cold. She had a feeling she knew what was coming.

"To be completely honest, the worst-case scenario is that both of our jobs are in jeopardy."

Speechless, Amanda simply stared at her husband. This was far worse than she had imagined after he told her he'd gotten involved in an online computer game. "Did Todd join the game too?"

"No. He's simply trying to help me." He took a breath and then continued. "Todd did a little checking. I thought Intruder was a guy we know from work, but Todd thinks it's just some random guy."

"Why would a random guy—"

"I know. None of it makes sense. Every time Intruder contacts me, he tells me to 'Play the game.'" Brent held up his fingers, indicating quote marks. "But other than the Internet game, I don't know what he's talking about."

"And when you say Todd's done a little checking...is he putting his neck on the line for you?"

Again, Brent nodded. "Yes, because now both of us are involved. If we can't stop this guy, who knows how things are going to escalate? Up until a week ago, before he started contacting me at work, the stuff he's done has been more annoying than scary. I was just ignoring him. Now, it seems the more I ignore him, the worse the consequences."

"Have you changed our credit card numbers?"

"I am in the process of changing everything, but it is time-consuming, and sometimes I wonder if I should even bother. If Intruder was going to rip us off, he would have done it already. He would have gone on a big-time spending spree. This doesn't seem to be about money."

"Except that we've already lost five thousand dollars."

"Yes, that was my fault. Not Intruder's fault. That was the entry fee for the game. On Christmas Eve, I was drunk, and although I don't exactly remember doing it, I apparently signed up to play. I've talked to our credit card company and tried to get the money back, but the bank isn't budging. If I'd filed a report that my card was stolen, maybe, but it appears I gave the credit card of my own free will. We'll just have to pay the balance off little by little. I can't tell you how sorry I am, Amanda. I'll work harder. I promise—"

Amanda held up one hand. "Brent, it's not just about the money you lost and our accounts being compromised." She looked down at her hands and then back up at Brent. "If our marriage is going to last, going to survive tough times, you need to change. We need to change."

"How? Tell me, and I'll do it."

"Marriage is about partnership. One person can't make all the decisions."

"I hope you don't think I—"

"Brent! Please stop talking, and listen to me. You've had your chance to explain. Now, it's my turn to tell you what I need. This isn't up for discussion. You need to change your behavior if you want our marriage to continue."

Brent nodded, although she could see he was biting his lip, still wanting to explain this incident away.

"First of all, you have to stop keeping secrets. Second, you have to stop acting irresponsibly. The decisions in our marriage, the major decisions, need to be discussed. If we don't agree, then we need to hash solutions out until we come to some sort of compromise. You can't go off on your own, half-cocked, making decisions for—"

"The two of us."

143

"The three of us." Amanda paused to regroup. "When you make a decision, like blowing five grand on an Internet game without discussing it with me, it hurts. Even worse, when you hide things from me, it fosters distrust in our marriage. Joining this game was exactly the same as buying the Viper. Don't you see that? Making those decisions on your own is incredibly disrespectful to me."

"I never thought of it that way."

"Clearly," Amanda acknowledged, her temper flaring. "We are in this marriage together. My opinions matter. My wants and my needs matter." They had had similar conversations before, but this time she hoped her words would sink in. "I was so hurt when I told you I was pregnant and you acted like I'd done something wrong."

Brent hung his head.

"You all but implied that I had gotten pregnant on purpose, that I tricked you into conceiving a child. I've never felt so horrible. You ruined what should have been one of the happiest days of our lives."

Silence filled the room, and Amanda looked over again at the blackened fireplace. "The game, the money, the identity theft, all that pales in comparison to your reaction to my news that I was pregnant. And then when I thought you'd had an affair on top of everything, I was devastated."

"Do you believe me? Do you believe that I did not have an affair?"

Amanda nodded.

"I had no idea I'd hurt you so badly. Everything you've brought up is true." Brent captured her hands again. "I won't deny that I'm a selfish bastard and that I need to change. I'm working on it. I really am. Even Todd has called me out recently on some of my behavior."

"But do *you* actually want to change?" Amanda asked.

"I do, and I'm going to try. I really mean it."

Amanda looked at him skeptically. "Those are just words. You've said them before."

"The night I went to see On The Rise was a real wakeup call. After the show, I ended up walking around Boston until who knows what time in the morning, freezing my ass off. I thought about everything. Us. The baby. What was driving my deepest fears."

Amanda waited, not wanting to interrupt.

"You were right to stay away from the club that night. You put the health of our baby first. When I thought about that, I realized I'd never put anyone else's needs before my own. Not once. Not my parents, not you, and certainly not our unborn child."

Amanda wiped away a tear.

"I don't want to be that kind of man anymore. You deserve better. Our child deserves better. It's time I grew up."

"Do you really believe that, or are you just saying what you think I want to hear?" Amanda asked.

Brent shook his head, his face as serious as she'd ever seen it. "The club scene has no appeal for me anymore. Especially without you there. I found that out on Sunday night too."

Brent leaned over to kiss her, but Amanda pulled back. "But those two things are only a part of it."

"I know. I think the word I've struggled with for a long time is control. Some of it probably goes back to my parents' car crash. That's not an excuse, but I think it's been my obsession to control everything, and the consequences when I can't are something I need to learn to manage. Maybe I need counseling, I don't know."

Amanda nodded. "I appreciate you telling me all that. Sharing your feelings with me." She reached over and took his hand. "The last couple of months have been tough for me too. I've done some soul-searching as well. Especially since my business has taken such a dramatic downturn."

"Which is something else I regret, I haven't been supportive of your business. That's another thing I want to change."

145

"Well, by the same token, I don't think I realized all the added pressure you've been under since the new CEO came onboard. And now you have that Clive guy working in your territory."

"It hasn't exactly been a bed of roses. But how did you—"

"Todd called me on my cell on my way here from my folks'. We only talked for a minute, but he gave me the new lay of the land at your office. He also asked me not to give up on you. His exact quote was: 'The guy is an idiot, but he loves you.'"

Brent laughed. "That sounds like Todd. He's called me a lot worse than an idiot during the last few weeks. Did he say anything else?"

"Not really. Oh, he did say, don't kick him to the curb just yet."

"Gee, I'll have to thank him for that glowing recommendation."

"Don't you dare, I swore our phone call to secrecy."

"I can see why," Brent said. "With friends like that, who needs—"

"Todd is your best friend! He was only—"

Brent laughed. "Don't worry, I'm just busting on him."

"He's always had your back, no matter what. That's what we should be doing in tough times, coming together and helping one another, not fighting."

"You're right, although I'm not telling Todd that his witty comments saved our marriage."

"I agree. I don't want us to wind up in the lyrics to some On The Rise song. Ugh." She shuddered.

"What I am going to do is prove to you that I am capable of change. I know I don't have a great track record, but are you willing to give me the benefit of the doubt?" Brent leaned over, and this time his lips found her protruding belly.

"It's a good thing I'm in love with you, otherwise, you wouldn't have a chance."

"Does that mean I'm forgiven?"

"Don't push your luck. Forgiveness is going to take a little longer than an hour."

"How about if I can prove to you that I really did have a change of heart all on my own?"

Amanda looked at him skeptically. "That would be impressive, but that mischievous look in your eyes has me worried."

Brent reached over and picked up a velvet box from the table and held it out to her.

Instead of reaching for it, sadness welled up within her.

"I know what you're thinking. That I'm trying to buy my way out of the doghouse. That is not the case. Open it. You'll see."

"Brent, I don't want a gift."

"Please, just open the box."

Amanda sighed. "Buying me a piece of jewelry is not what I'm talking about."

"If you don't open the box, I'm going to open it for you."

Amanda sighed. "Okay." She took the box. "I hope you have the receipt."

"Ouch! Would it be possible for you to be a little less critical when I do something nice for you?"

"I was trying to make a point."

"We'll see about that."

Amanda slowly opened the lid. At the glint of the white gold inside, she gasped. "Oh, Brent. It's beautiful. It's too much." She reached in and lifted the delicate bracelet from its resting place on the plush satin lining. She ran her finger over the etched pattern.

"That's not the important part." He pointed to the inside of the bracelet.

Amanda tilted the bangle to catch the light. She read the inscription aloud. "Mother and child – All my love, all my life." Emotion overcame her, and tears welled up in her eyes.

"Amanda, this is how I feel about you and our baby."

The tears spilled over and trickled down Amanda's face unabated. "Really?"

"It's taken me a while to come to terms with it, but yes. I want to be a father. There is no place I'd rather be than right here beside you, raising our child together."

Amanda allowed Brent to pull her into his arms. "Nothing could make me happier," she whispered against his dress shirt.

Brent drew her hair to one side and kissed the nape of her neck. "Happy Valentine's Day. A couple of days late."

Amanda looked down at the bracelet, smiling through her tears. Brent reached over and took it from her fingers. He undid the clasp and slid it onto her right wrist.

"The bracelet wasn't that expensive, honest. I just got him to put it in a really nice box."

"Don't lie."

"Okay, you're right. It was expensive."

"I can see that."

"The point is, I want you to wear the bracelet. Don't put it in some jewelry box—"

"…except when I paint."

"Nope." Brent shook his head emphatically. "I especially want you to wear it then."

"But I'll get paint on it."

"Good. That will make it look even better." Brent stood up.

Amanda allowed herself to be pulled to her feet, and when he held out his arms, she stepped into them. It felt so good to be back in his arms. They stood, rocking back and forth, pressed tight against each other. She marveled at how perfectly they fit together, how the top of her head fit just under his chin, like two interlocking puzzle pieces.

Amanda pulled back far enough to look into his eyes. "I love you, Brent. And thank you for this beautiful gift." She held the bracelet out, admiring it at arm's length.

"This is a symbol of my love and commitment to you, and to our baby, and to our family. I'm not saying I'm always going to do it right, but this time my actions will bear out my words."

"Oh, Brent."

"I thought I'd lost you, Amanda."

She heard the catch in his voice.

"I love you, more than you know," he continued. "More than this bracelet can ever convey. I never want to live through the fear of losing you again. Not for a day. Not for an hour." He brushed his fingertips across the intricate pattern of the bracelet. "I've finally figured out my priorities in life. With some men, like your thick-headed husband, it just takes us a little longer to get it."

A single tear slipped down one cheek. "Toss the receipt. I'll wear the bracelet every day."

"Is it time for makeup sex?" Brent asked, pulling her to him.

"Men!" Amanda replied. "You're all alike." She laughed through her tears. "But I have to admit, I was thinking the exact same thing. But first you have to tell me exactly what happened to my beautiful fireplace?"

Brent groaned.

• • •

February 24th - Wednesday

Halfway into the commute to his office, Brent opened the Viper's glove compartment and chucked his cell phone inside with all his might before letting out a Comanche-yell of frustration.

All last night and this morning his cell phone had been ringing like crazy. Every time he'd tried to pick up the messages, the automated voice informed him that his voice mailbox and the text mailbox were full to capacity. Each message was identical: PLAY THE GAME. As soon as he deleted them, the cycle repeated.

He reached over and slammed the glove box shut, and it popped back open as if to mock him. He wondered if he'd broken the latch. *Maybe he'd broken the latch and the damn phone too.* He hoped so. Intruder was getting to him, and he couldn't take much more of this mindless harassment.

Now, as he walked down the hall toward his boss's office. Brent's mood hadn't improved. Why the hell he needed to go to an eight-hour seminar on business ethics was beyond him. He had done everything but beg Ed to let him off the hook, but his boss wouldn't take no for an answer. His numbers were looking sweet due to the mega deal with Amazon Athletics, but he hoped to pad his February sales just a bit more by convincing a couple of his favorite accounts to slide a few of their March P.O.'s to him a couple of days early.

Brent rounded the corner and walked through Ed's open door. "Ready to go?" he said, striving to sound enthusiastic.

"Almost." Ed looked up. "How come you don't look happy about this?" Ed said.

"You know how it is on the downhill side of the month." Brent looked out the window at the morning sun reflecting off the neighboring buildings. "I should be out selling. I'm sure Clive is."

"Yeah, he's kicking butt all right. Everyone is talking about that bet." Ed chuckled. "I've never seen so much interest in the leaderboard. Even the tech heads are coming in to check out the numbers. You can't possibly be worried. Still, I'm glad to see you never stop thinking like a salesman. And I'm also sorry I had to pull you away today without any notice. Phil just gave me the go-ahead yesterday."

"The go-ahead?" Brent asked, turning away from the window. Ed was struggling to button his suit coat jacket. He succeeded, but the strain on the middle button was evident.

"These seminars are required for all management employees."

Brent looked at his boss stunned. "Do you mean…"

"Congratulations, Brent. You've officially been put on the fast track."

"Really?" Brent felt a grin break across his face. He was barely able to restrain himself from dancing a jig right there in Ed's office. He couldn't wait to tell Amanda. Dollars signs danced across his vision. Big ones. He couldn't wait to set up a meeting with Susie Sunshine to go over his new compensation package.

"You had me worried earlier this month," Ed said, coming around his desk. "I thought I was going to have to choose someone else, but the order from Amazon Athletics clinched it."

"Speaking of Amazon, before we leave, I need to run back to my office. I want to key in the tracking number for some promotional materials I had shipped directly from the printer. Just to make sure the first of the packages arrived. Do we have another minute?"

"Sure. I'll meet you in the parking garage. On the drive we can brainstorm about what the future holds for my up-and-coming young sales manager." Ed threw a mock punch at his shoulder. "You're my go-to guy, Brent. Way to bring it home."

Brent held up his hand, and Ed slapped him a high five. Finally, things were falling into place, and the cherry on top would be enjoying a week in Clive's timeshare. The first month had been a squeaker, but he'd blown Clive's doors off in February. *Two months down, one to go.*

• • •

February 25th – Thursday

Amanda sat at the breakfast bar that separated the kitchen from the family room. Her cell phone was propped up against the granite backsplash, and she was talking to her folks on speaker phone.

"Mom, no more baby clothes. I mean it." She studied her latest sketch as she gnawed on the end of a graphite pencil.

"Amanda, let your mother enjoy herself. She's been as giddy as a schoolgirl ever since you told us you were pregnant."

"Dad, you're not any better. Does Mom know about the Tonka truck you brought over the other day? It's practically life-size."

"Randy, is that true?" Dolores asked.

Amanda laughed, tore the page from her sketch pad, and taped it next to the others on the half wall. "Tell the truth, Dad."

He chuckled. "Guilty as charged. Since you kept the news of the pregnancy from us for almost four months, I guess we both felt we had some catching up to do gift-wise. After all, we want to be good grandparents."

Amanda laughed again. "Well, you have no worries on that account. Besides, there won't be anything left for me to pick out if you keep going at this rate."

Amanda said goodbye and disconnected, gazing at all the pages she'd taped to the half wall. Each one had a dozen or more rough sketches of a different puppy. She would never tell Brent, knowing that he'd scoff at the notion, but the puppies had all come from dreams she'd had over the past few weeks. She was now a firm believer that women really did experience a flow of creativity during pregnancy.

Barely able to contain her excitement, Amanda pulled down three of the pages and went in search of art supplies. With a box of colored pencils in hand, she sat back down and goose bumps ran up her arms. A new idea was taking shape within her, and the goose bumps were a sure sign that she was moving in the right direction artistically.

She looked down at the Yorkshire terrier she'd named Corky the Yorkie and selected a pink colored pencil. By placing a tiny pink bow on the top of her furry head and adding a hint of a pink tongue, Corky practically leaped off the page and into her arms. Amanda grinned down at the first character that had literally sprung to life from her dreams. Having always painted from photographs or using animal books as a strict reference, it was so freeing to just draw from her imagination.

She had a feeling Corky was going to be the star of the series: "Corky, the Lovable Yorkie." That was the working name for the children's book series that had popped into her mind this morning. Amanda envisioned toddlers turning the thick cardboard pages with their chubby fingers.

She paused for a minute and rubbed her belly, warmed at the thought of her own child reading about Corky's silly antics. What better way for children to learn how to treat each other than by watching the behavior of dogs? Dogs didn't hold grudges, make fun of each other, or leave someone out of the fun.

She tapped her pencil on the terrier and grinned down at her. "And you might just have enough personality and charisma to pull it off." There was mischief in Corky's black eyes, and the puppy seemed to be practically communicating with her. The dog seemed to be egging her on to draw the rest of her circle of friends.

Amanda drew a few additional sketches of Corky from different angles, and then she scooted Corky's page over and began working on the next dog. Danny was a floppy-eared Dalmatian with giant paws. Unlike Corky, who seemed to be the leader of this little band of pups, Danny was a shy follower. Amanda added a bright orange Monarch butterfly to the tip of the Dalmatian's nose. As she worked, she allowed her mind to create Danny's personality within the pack of puppies. Danny was always ready to go on adventures with his friends, but he had a tendency to wander off, and his curiosity sometimes led to trouble. Amanda envisioned Danny playfully batting an oversized paw at a hornets' nest or splashing in a lily-filled pond dangerously close to a snapping turtle. Without meaning to, this pup often got in over his head, and he simply couldn't get along without the help and support of his pack.

Amanda looked at the clock, aware that she had intended to grocery shop today, pick up the dry cleaning, and do a few other errands as well. Instead, for the first time in a long time, she had been so engaged in her work that she'd completely lost track of time. The refrigerator was empty, but maybe they'd order from that local Thai restaurant tonight. The rest of the errands could wait as well. Brent would understand. On a roll, Amanda moved on to the third puppy.

Picking up her pencil, Amanda gazed down at Pauline, the snow white poodle pup. She added a few more pencil strokes on either side of Pauline's curly tail, indicating furious tail-wagging. Pauline, it seemed to Amanda, was always full of excitement, but she was slightly neurotic about keeping her coat clean. Pauline preferred to stand on the sidelines, watching her friends play, rather than risk muddying her coat or flattening her curls. Amanda gave this puppy a vivid turquoise collar inset with shiny rhinestones of which Pauline was overly proud. Several shiny tags glimmered as they hung from the front of the dog's collar, and Amanda added a bit of gold sparkle.

Her stomach growled. She really needed to stop and eat something, if only for the baby. Amanda opened the refrigerator door and stared at the few items inside, still lost in thought about the antics of the poodle. *What if Pauline accidentally lost her fancy collar?*

Before she knew it, Amanda was perched back on the stool, rough sketching the poodle while munching on an apple. She drew the poodle with and without her pretty collar, and she added in the Yorkie too, bounding off in the lead.

She couldn't wait to show Brent her drawings and tell him her children's book idea when he came home tonight.

• • •

February 26th – Friday

The following day Brent left for the office after nine, aware that a silly grin popped up on his face every time he thought about his imminent move up the rungs of the Revolution corporate ladder.

This morning, he and Amanda had made love and enjoyed a leisurely breakfast together. Eating breakfast at home on a weekday was something he had never done, but after all, they'd each had a reason to celebrate. He'd been on cloud nine dreaming of moving to the thirthieth floor where the big dogs worked. Could he be a VP before he hit thirty? And Amanda was beyond excited about her plans for a children's book series.

Just don't overdo it, he'd warned her. The pregnancy was just into the fourth month, but she said she felt great. The only thing that seemed to have changed was the amount of sleep she needed.

He had gotten into a routine of tucking Amanda into bed each night. It gave them some additional time to catch up with each other, as Brent often had client meetings run late which caused him to miss dinner. Brent liked the opportunity to pamper her a little. He'd plump her pillows and tuck the covers up under her chin, and then they would chat for twenty or thirty minutes until she felt tired and drifted off to sleep.

As Brent merged onto the highway, he breathed a sigh of relief that they had averted a real crisis in their marriage. The only thing that marred his happiness was the eerie fact that Intruder was still on the horizon.

He also felt slightly guilty that he hadn't come one hundred percent clean with Amanda about everything. Somehow the words DieorDieTrying.com never actually made it into his confession. Still, it was guilt by omission and not an out-and-out lie. *Did it really matter if she knew what the game was about? He reminded himself that he had explained the deadpool game to Amanda the very same day he first heard about it from Clive. Way back in December.*

Intruder continued to harass him, just as Todd had predicted. Whenever Brent was online, Intruder would instantly send him a tweet. Brent tried every way he knew to keep the conversation going, but Intruder only stayed on long enough to needle him about the game. He never threatened him, and he ignored Brent's questions, preferring instead to ask his own, usually questions about Amanda.

All his requests to get Darby's Death List removed from the site had gone unanswered. *Straight into cyberspace.* Last night, knowing it was useless, Brent had typed "Last Request before Legal

Action" into the subject line and sent off another email to the only address he had for DieorDieTrying.com.

Winding his way up through the parking garage, Brent pushed away his lingering concern over the game. He had to let it go. His marriage and his career were on the upswing, and those things he could control. Plus, he smiled, morning sex always started the day off right.

As he waited for the elevator, Brent brushed a hand across the back of his neck; the new haircut felt good. In the gleaming elevator doors Brent straightened his tie, confident that today was going to be a great day.

Halfway through the maze of cubicles heading toward the sales department, he literally ran into Ed.

"Brent!" Ed shouted, as he grabbed him by the arm. "Where the hell have you been?"

Brent watched a drop of perspiration roll down the side of his boss's face. "I had a couple things to take care of at home. Is there a problem?" It wasn't even ten o'clock yet, and the guy was breathing as if he'd run a marathon.

"Why haven't you been answering your cell phone?"

Brent brought his left hand up to touch his suit coat pocket. *Empty.* He never took it out of the car last night. This morning, he'd plugged it in to charge while he drove to work, which was where his phone was now, in his car. "Sorry, I—"

Ed rushed on, not waiting for his explanation. "Just after eight this morning, Phil's secretary called me. Phil wants to see us pronto." Still holding Brent's arm, Ed turned toward the elevators.

"Wait a minute," Brent said, shaking him off. "At least let me take off my coat." Ed's heavy breathing followed him as he strode to his office and unlocked the door. "What's this about?" he called over his shoulder as he pushed open his office door and flipped on the light.

"I have no idea," Ed replied.

Brent tossed his coat over the back of the folding chair.

"Come on already."

Brent riffled through some papers on his desk.

"What are you doing?" Ed said. "We need to go."

Brent looked up at the obvious irritation in Ed's voice. "I just want to be prepared."

"Prepared for what? We don't even know what the meeting is about," Ed replied mopping his brow.

"Then why are you so stressed over this?" Brent said. He grabbed two binders of sales data and a blank lined tablet. He reached for a third notebook and then paused. *Should he take his laptop? No, that might make him look worried.* Still, he wanted to be able to answer any question Phil might throw at him. Brent shoved one last three-ring notebook under his arm and followed Ed out the door.

"I've got a bad feeling about this," Ed said. "I've had a dozen meetings with Phil since he came onboard. He's a let's-plan-it-for-a-month-from-Tuesday kind of guy. He doesn't do last minute."

Brent felt a prickle of fear. "You're just paranoid."

"Let's hope so."

He had to hustle to keep up as his boss race-walked toward the elevator. Inside, Ed hit the round number thirty and then jabbed a finger repeatedly at the close door button.

"You sure you don't need to come clean about anything before we walk in there?" Ed asked.

"No."

Ed gave him a hard look.

"What? My accounts are happy. Hell, I've had meetings with just about every one of them in the last ten days. You know that."

Out came Ed's handkerchief again. Brent wondered how it was possible for one individual to sweat twenty-four hours a day.

The doors opened, and they stepped into the corporate lobby of Revolution. "Wow," Brent said looking around. "They've made a few changes here."

"Come on," Ed whispered.

Brent resumed walking while taking in the complete renovation of the space. The red Revolution logo had been turned into an enormous three-dimensional piece of artwork, and it hung suspended over the reception desk.

The last time Brent had been on this floor was many months prior to Phil taking over as CEO. The once standard office space had been transformed. The soft, mauve walls had been repainted stark white. Gone were the cheaply framed ad campaigns from Revolution's early days. In their place hung huge, boldly colored canvases, painted with slashes of red, orange, and black, each lit with a spotlight from above. Modern white vinyl benches, a work of art themselves, stood perfectly aligned under each painting.

"Good morning, Jana," said Ed, approaching the reception desk.

"Good morning, Ed. Good morning, Brent," Jana replied.

"Hello," Brent said, giving the woman his best sales smile.

The reception desk was white and shaped like a teardrop. The surface was completely empty with the exception of a red phone. Jana lifted the handset, punched several buttons, listened, and then returned the receiver to the base.

"Mr. Anderson is waiting for you. You may go right in."

Brent read the surprised look on Ed's face. Perhaps Phil enjoyed making people cool their heels in his little art studio before being invited into the inner sanctum. He'd have to remember to ask Ed about that later.

"Thank you," Ed replied.

Brent shifted his gaze back to Jana, studying her. This was the first time he'd seen Phil's personal assistant, and she was every bit as gorgeous as rumor had it.

Ed took off down the hall to the left of the reception desk. "Maybe this is a good sign," Brent commented.

"I doubt it," Ed growled.

Brent followed his boss down the hall. In contrast to his floor, with discordant phones going off, laughter, conversation, and people scurrying in every direction, here on the thirtieth floor the only sound was barely audible classical music drifting down from somewhere high above them. There didn't appear to be many offices on this floor. And with the exception of the double doors which stood ajar at the end of the hall, every door was shut tight.

Brent watched Ed's shoulders rise and fall as his boss took a deep, calming breath before entering Phil's office.

Phil's back was to them as they crossed the threshold, and Brent took a quick glance around. The room was huge and felt very masculine. The dominant color in the room was a deep rich brown with tan accents. A built-in unit filled one wall, and on the opposite wall were three Eames chairs that encircled a brushed nickel coffee table. *Very elegant*, Brent thought, nodding his head in approval. *Very expensive.*

Phil's massive desk and a towering executive chair sat in front of a wall of windows which overlooked a spectacular view of the Charles River. Brent mentally filed away the view and the room amenities. His long-term goal was to have this very office along with the CEO title before he hit forty.

Phil turned to face them, and Brent could see he held a manila folder in his hands. The moment Brent caught a glimpse of Phil's florid face he knew that they had not been called to the thirtieth floor for a congratulatory handshake. *Shit!*

His heart thudded in his chest and his mind cart-wheeled at the realization that he was about to be called on the carpet by his CEO. *Expense reports? Couldn't be. That clothing account he'd lost? Unlikely.* He felt his stomach drop as Phil's booming voice filled the room.

"Gentlemen. Sit."

Brent followed Ed toward the oval mahogany conference table surrounded by eight black swivel chairs. As Brent pulled out his chair, Ed shot him a dagger-filled look. Brent raised his shoulders in a barely perceptible shrug. He had no idea what was about to come down. Aware that his hands were shaking just the tiniest bit, Brent set his stack of information on the table and purposely dropped his hands into his lap. Ed sat to his right. Phil remained standing.

"I received a call this morning from Amazon Athletics," Phil said.

The way he tapped the folder against his open palm only served to further unnerve Brent.

"What they told me—" Phil said.

"The flyers arrived on time," Brent said, unable to contain himself. "I personally checked the tracking numbers—" He abruptly closed his mouth at the hostile expression on Phil's face.

A hush enveloped the room. After several moments of uncomfortable silence, Phil resumed speaking. "Amazon Athletics has just terminated their relationship with Revolution."

Brent froze, unable to believe what he'd just heard.

"Not only have we lost the account," Phil continued, "they are considering legal action against us."

The saliva in Brent's mouth turned to sandpaper, and he swallowed with difficulty. *Legal action?* Determined not to interrupt again, Brent clamped his lips shut, holding back any number of unasked questions.

"Have either of you seen this?" Phil asked.

The CEO tossed a glossy, full-page full-color ad onto the table. Brent reached for it, and out of the corner of his eye saw Ed nod in his direction. Confidently, Brent spoke up. "Yes. Amazon changed the ad at the last minute. It was a rush job, but I pulled out all the stops and got it done. The headline was changed to—"

The rest of the sentence evaporated, and Brent struggled to catch his breath. The headline under the company name read, "First Fool of the Jungle."

No. It couldn't say fool. It was supposed to say rule. First Rule of the Jungle. The words seemed to waver in front of his eyes.

"First Fool of the Jungle," Phil read the words aloud. "Ed? Brent? Would either of you like to comment?"

Ed remained silent.

Brent felt two sets of eyes shift in his direction. He dropped his gaze to the glossy print, still unable to believe what he was seeing. His voice rose an octave in panic. "I checked the proofs myself. This has got to be a printing error."

"Is it?" Phil asked, his eyes dark and mocking.

"I have the PO and the latest proof on my desk." Brent had begun to rise from his chair when Phil suddenly sent another item sliding across the polished surface of the table. Instinctively Brent reached out a hand to stop the document before it slid off the table.

Eyes fixed on the document, he slowly sank back down onto the chair. The purchase order revision was filled out in its entirety. The tagline read: "First Fool of the Jungle." When he saw his signature on the bottom of the form, he felt lightheaded.

"Frankly, gentlemen, I'm at a loss," Phil spoke in a deadly quiet voice. "Thousands of these posters were put up last night in multiple cities by overnight crews hired by Amazon at great expense. The purpose was to promote their inner city tournaments this weekend. In one day, Revolution turned Amazon Athletics into a laughingstock in each and every tournament city. The damage to their reputation, and to ours, is untold."

Brent's head was reeling.

"To further complicate the matter, the printer informed me that they were unable to reach you all last night, Brent," Phil continued. "I tried to reach you myself this morning, but the existence of this signed PO makes that fact a moot point."

Brent felt impaled by Phil's eyes, and when he turned to look at Ed, his boss' eyes were no less fierce. It was clear that both men held him fully responsible.

"Let me—" Brent said.

Phil held up his hand, and Brent froze in mid-sentence.

"Ed, I don't know what happened here," Phil said. "But I demand that you salvage this account. Handle it however you need to. Do whatever needs to be done to get our client back and to make our client happy." Phil shot a meaningful glance toward

Brent, his unspoken threat heavy in the air. "I expect a status report from you" he pointed at Ed, "first thing Monday morning."

Brent felt the full force of Phil's eyes return to his own. "Get out."

Brent slunk out of the room after Ed, wondering if he had worked his last day at Revolution.

Chapter 6

Brent leaned up against the inside of his office door, his body trembling, acid burning in his gut from what had gone down in Phil's office. There was no doubt in his mind that this was the work of Intruder.

The initial pranks Brent had attributed to Intruder had been more annoying than anything: the '***BRENT WILL DIE***' font being added to his computer, someone hacking into his Twitter account, the porn magazine subscription delivered to him at work. Those he could deal with. The stolen identity had seemed much more serious until he'd realized that Intruder hadn't charged anything to his account. The contact, via Twitter, between Intruder and his wife had escalated Brent's fear factor to another level entirely and damn near cost him his marriage. But this outright desire to ruin Brent's career…and for what? *What did Intruder get out of any of this?*

Brent walked to his desk and sat down. The news about the Amazon implosion was probably already making its way around the office. There was nothing to be gained from staying at Revolution today. His fellow salesmen would be licking their chops, especially Clive. Clive was the newest golden boy at Revolution.

Office phone in hand, he called Todd. The call went directly to voicemail. He hung up and opened a new email. Still rattled from the dressing down in Phil's office, Brent banged out a thirty-second note to Todd and hit send. The more difficult task lay ahead.

His next thought was of Amanda. Since they had talked everything through, there was an ease between the two of them now that he attributed to his new vow to be one hundred percent upfront with Amanda. In short, no more secrets between them. Each night, after he tucked her into bed, they would talk through the day's events, the good, the bad, and the ugly. When Amanda was drowsy enough to fall asleep, he would return to the den to work for a couple of hours.

He sighed, wishing he had his cell phone and again picked up the handset to call Amanda. No doubt, this was going to be in the bad and the ugly category. Brent had to tell her now. He dialed her cell phone number.

Amanda picked up on the first ring. "Brent, I can't b-believe this is h-happening." Her voice wobbled and then a sob broke free.

Brent's heart rate jumped at the sound his wife crying. "Honey! What's wrong? What happened?"

"Dad. He's gone, Brent."

"Gone? Gone where?"

More sobs. "He...he...had a heart at-attack. It must have happened last night, after Mom went to bed. She found him downstairs this morning. It was too late. Oh, Brent! How could this have happened?"

Brent was truly shocked. His father-in-law was dead? *He wasn't that old.* Brent added the years up, remembering that Randy and Dolores had had Amanda late in life. Still, he was somewhere in the sixties. "Oh, honey, I am so sorry." Images flashed through Brent's mind. His baby had one surviving grandparent.

"Can you c-come to my mom's?"

Brent was already on his feet. "I'm walking out of the office now."

Amanda's only reply was another heartbreaking sob.

"I'm on my way."

"How could this have happened, Brent?"

Brent didn't know what to say, remembering the useless platitudes people had said to him after the car accident that killed

164

his parents. No one wanted to admit it, but seemingly healthy people dropped dead every day. A woman in finance had died last year from pancreatic cancer. She'd been a vegan and a triathlete who weighed maybe one hundred and twenty pounds. On Facebook just a few months ago, Brent had been shocked to read that one of his high school classmates, a nerdy guy who'd ended up going to MIT, had died of a brain aneurism, leaving behind a wife and twin daughters under the age of four. *How did you explain that?* All he knew was that his father had been gone five years, and he still missed him every single day.

"I'm so sorry, Amanda. I'll be there as soon as I can."

Brent typed a quick email to Ed, telling him that Amanda's father had passed away unexpectedly and that he was taking the afternoon off.

• • •

March 1st – Tuesday

The last few days had been rough, to say the least. Amanda had been all but inconsolable in the days following the death of her father. Dolores had been surprisingly strong through it all, and it was she who had pulled Amanda through. Together Dolores and Amanda made all the decisions and funeral arrangements, which left Brent little to do but play doorman to the assorted family members, friends, and more than a few bank employees. It was a revolving door of people dropping by the house with covered dishes, bouquets of flowers, and sympathy cards. Left on his own much of the time, Brent had plenty of time to think as he reorganized the freezer to hold all the extra lasagna pans and Pyrex dishes of pulled pork. He also had time to think on the drive home when he went to pick up the clothes they both needed for the funeral. In the three days since Randy's death, he and Amanda hadn't had time for the two of them to talk.

After the funeral and the calling hours which were back at the house, Amanda had convinced Dolores to come home with them and spend a few days in Garnet. They hadn't been home an hour when Dolores pulled out the vacuum cleaner and began a thorough cleaning of the entire downstairs.

Brent sat back against the headboard of the queen-size bed, his arms wrapped around Amanda as she lay against his chest. For a long time neither spoke. Instead they lay listening to the hum of the vacuum below.

"Why is she doing that, Brent?"

"You mean your mom?"

"Why is she vacuuming?"

"It's just a coping mechanism." Brent had his eyes closed, and he was just drifting off when Amanda spoke.

"I feel so guilty."

"Guilty? Why? You were the apple of your dad's eye."

"I know, but..."

"But what?"

"I wasn't going to tell you."

"Tell me what?" Brent asked in a soft voice, reaching up to stroke her hair. "You can tell me anything. We made a pact to tell each other everything, remember?" He felt a twinge of guilt as the words left this mouth. With the funeral, he hadn't yet told her about the Amazon debacle.

"I know, but this is really hard."

Brent waited.

"All I keep remembering is the last argument my dad and I had."

"When was that?"

"The day after Valentine's Day."

Brent groaned silently. He knew what was coming next.

"I was looking for sympathy, but my mom wasn't exactly crying a river for me."

Dolores had actually been on his side? "Did you tell her what the fight was about?"

"Not specifically, just that you'd done something really hurtful."

"So I'm guessing your dad didn't exactly jump on the bandwagon to support his son-in-law?"

Amanda gave him a soft elbow in the ribs. "Dad was just concerned for me, like he always is…was."

"You and your dad were thinking the worst."

Amanda nodded, but she didn't speak.

Brent squeezed her hand as she took a steadying breath. "How bad was it?" Brent asked. He watched Amanda wipe away a tear.

"He called you no-good."

Ouch.

"I started defending you, but at the same time I was so angry at you. I said some terrible things to my dad."

"Those were just words spoken in anger."

"But that fight was one of the last conversations I remember having with my dad. For a variety of stupid reasons, I was still mad at him. The night I was home, I never even told my Dad I loved him. And now I never can."

Brent held Amanda tightly as her body shook with sobs. He pressed his lips against her hair. "For the first time, with my own child on the way, I think I finally understand your father." Brent took a moment to pull his thoughts together. "You were his precious little girl since the day you were born. His whole life revolved around loving you and protecting you and providing for you."

"Then I got married."

Brent chuckled. "Right. Your dad and I never saw eye to eye. When you returned home badly hurt by something I'd done, I imagine your father probably hated me."

Amanda reached over to the bedside table for a tissue and blew her nose noisily. "My dad never hated you."

"No, maybe not hated, but I don't think I ever measured up to the man he envisioned his daughter marrying either."

"Could anyone?" Amanda asked in a soft voice.

Brent exhaled, feeling for the first time that he and Amanda were talking honestly about Randy. "Still, I wish I'd figured this out sooner so that I could have held out an olive branch. I'm not sure we would have ever been buddies, but all my anger at him over the years seems so stupid and pointless now." Amanda squeezed his hand. "The scary thing is, if we have a girl, I can see myself acting exactly the same way."

Amanda blew her nose again and then twisted around in Brent's arms and kissed him full on the mouth.

"Hmmm. Nice. What was that for?"

"For trying to understand my father."

"But it's too late."

"I know. I guess we both have regrets."

Brent looked down at her and saw tears fill her eyes. They lay quietly for a long time until he heard Amanda's breathing settle into a rhythm. He wished he could sleep, but he was wired.

He slipped out from beneath her and out of bed, taking a minute to pull up the comforter at the end of the bed and tuck it around her. Then he loosened his tie, shrugged off his suit coat, and tossed them over a straight-backed chair in the corner of the bedroom.

The house was silent as he walked downstairs. He found Dolores curled up asleep on the couch. He turned off the TV and covered her with the multicolored afghan that lay across the back of the couch before he headed into his office. A stack of bills needed his attention.

When the desktop finally appeared, Brent logged onto his online banking site and checked the balance in his checking account. He groaned before setting the automatic payments to be paid on the due dates. He had enough to cover the bills, but not by a lot.

The amount due on his MasterCard irked him. The fee for the deadpool now meant he couldn't pay off the balance. It was all he could do to pay the minimum.

Brent dropped his head in his hands, trying to remember his last interaction with Intruder. So much had happened since then. Suddenly Intruder's words popped into his mind. *The game is about to get more interesting.*

Fear brushed the back of his neck as he remembered not only the threat, but Intruder's distinctive voice on the phone as Ed stood in his office, grinning at him after he closed the Amazon sale.

But what exactly had Intruder meant? Was he foreshadowing tampering with the flyer from Amazon? Or could he have meant something far more sinister?

Tapping the credit card bill on the edge of the desk Brent pondered once again his inability to contact Intruder. Suddenly he had an idea. He set aside the February bill and began to leaf through several piles of paper on his desk. It took him a few minutes, but eventually he found the previous month's bill. He unfolded the January bill. *There it was.* Transaction date - 12/25. Post Date – 12/25. Gamerboys#10267 Brooklyn, NY. $5000.00. That dollar figure still made him wince.

Whoever the Gamerboys were, they had Brent's credit card number. Which must mean they had Intruder's credit card too. Credit card information was tied to a phone number, an address, and most importantly, whoever the sick individual was who was turning his life upside down. If Brent could find Intruder's physical location, he could end this nightmare once and for all, or at any rate, the police could.

Brent looked at the time and decided it wasn't too late to call Todd.

"Hey, man. Where the hell have you been?" Todd asked. "It's not like you to blow off work two days in a row. Either you've been fired or contracted the black plague. Which is it? People are starting to take bets."

"Clive?"

"How did you guess?"

"So Ed didn't say anything?"

"About what?"

"Amanda's dad passed away on Friday."

"Hey, I'm sorry, man. And here I am making jokes."

"It's okay. Amanda's pretty devastated. The funeral was today. We got back to Garnet a couple of hours ago."

"Please pass my condolences on to Amanda. Was it unexpected?"

"Yeah. Big time. He was only sixty-two. I sent Ed an email when I left the office after I found out on Friday. I'm kind of surprised he didn't say anything. So what's the chatter been around the office?"

"I'm sure you know."

"My spectacular flame out with Amazon?"

"Correct. Well, at least you haven't been fired."

"Not that I know of."

"That's a relief. I have a feeling if you get the boot, I will too. At least if they find any system irregularities."

"Right. What happened with Amazon on Friday has Intruder's fingerprints all over it."

"Yeah. All hell broke loose this weekend with systems issues, too. It was not a fun weekend."

"Do you think…"

"That Intruder has compromised the system? I honestly don't know."

"That's a scary thought."

"I don't want to give this guy too much credit."

"But?"

"But I haven't been able to do a thorough check of the system because my boss has been literally breathing over my shoulder. He's been more hands-on with this last batch of problems. Maybe they put two and two together and he's been told to keep me on a short leash due to our friendship. I am being very careful."

"Right. On that same note, I have a question for you."

"Shoot."

"I was looking at my credit card statement, and it listed Gamerboys as the name the fee went to for DieorDieTrying.com. That company now has all my credit card information and, therefore, all my personal data. Right?"

"Right."

"Which also means they must have Intruder's information as well."

"Right. So?"

"Well, I was wondering if there was a way, a legal way, to find out where Gamerboys is located?"

"Sure. If I have a few pieces of data, it's easy enough to reverse engineer it."

"How long would it take?"

"Probably just a few minutes. Why? Is this a test?"

"The statement lists Brooklyn, New York for the address." Brent smiled when he heard Todd clicking away on his keyboard.

"Crap. I'm getting another call."

"Look, I've kept you on the phone long enough already, but if you can just get me something, I—"

"Hang on one sec."

Brent heard more typing. He looked up at the clock. It was almost ten o'clock.

"Got it."

Damn, Todd was good. Brent grabbed a pen. He scribbled the address Todd rattled off, writing sideways across the bottom of the credit card statement. "Thanks, man."

"I won't even ask what you're going to do with that information."

"Good, because I wasn't planning on telling you."

"Are you coming in tomorrow?"

"No, I think I'll spend at least another day at home with Amanda. I should be in on Thursday, though."

"Got it. I'm really sorry about your father-in-law. Let me know if there is anything I can do."

"Thanks." Brent disconnected and then sent Ed a text that he planned to take off one more day. Maybe he needed to take a little road trip.

• • •

March 3rd - Thursday

"I can't believe you did something so hare-brained," Todd said. He spun in a lazy half-circle in his office chair, lobbing paperclips through his cubicle doorway into the recycling bin located opposite his office.

"I was this close to getting the information I needed to find Intruder," Brent replied, holding his thumb and finger a millimeter apart.

"You drove how many hours to find what, exactly?"

"I made it to New York in four hours, in the Jeep no less. It was just a boarded up storefront."

"I could have told you that."

"Well, I had to do something."

"Going after the company really wasn't going to get you anywhere. Plus, legally, the information they have is covered under the privacy acts."

"But if I get Intruder's address and phone number, I could turn that over to the police."

"Don't start on that shit again."

"Come on! It would be so easy for you to get."

"How do you know? Asking me to hack the site and download a file is like me asking you to rob a bank. Would you do that?"

"This is different. It's—"

"No, it's not."

"You wouldn't be stealing credit card numbers. You'd just be getting one address and one phone number."

"That is just as illegal!"

"I haven't even been to my office since the funeral. I'm scared shitless that I may get fired."

"It's always all about you, isn't it?"

"No! I'm just asking for a little help, that's all."

"You have no right to even ask me for anything else. I've already helped you way more than I should have."

"How can you say that? It's my life that's falling apart, not yours."

"Oh, really? When was the last time you even asked about my life?"

"Well, I'm sorry. I've been a little busy going to a funeral and trying to save both my marriage and my job." Todd stared right back at him. "What? Did something happen to you too?"

"Yeah, as a matter of fact. Thanks for asking." He stood up.

Brent placed himself in the doorway of the cubicle, blocking Todd's exit. "What happened?"

"The band gave me an ultimatum. Either I make all the practices with the band, or they are kicking me out."

"They wouldn't—"

"They put it in writing."

"They can't—"

"They can, and they did. So stop bitching that your life is the only one going down the toilet. Except I have you to thank for screwing up mine."

"Me? What did I do?"

"My life was going just fine until you joined that damn game."

"How many times do I have to tell you—"

"Oh, right. Clive signed you up. You are completely innocent."

"He did!"

"Well, here is a reality check on my life lately: suddenly my job requires me to be here basically round the clock. And that is entirely your fault!"

"My fault?"

"Yeah. I think Intruder has gotten into the system." Todd's cell phone rang. "Be right there." He stood up.

"You said Revolution had fail-safe protection."

"You really don't listen."

"But are you sure? I mean—"

"And guess who missed practice on Saturday night. Guess who was here. Again."

"The band can't kick you out. You write half the damn songs."

"Apparently that didn't weigh as heavily as a drummer who can't make practices."

"I don't think—"

"Of course you don't. Thinking has never been your strong suit. And another of your failings is that you seem to have no filter between your brain and your mouth. I don't know if I can trust you anymore, Brent. You are starting to sound like a lunatic. I'd rather you just leave me alone. Frankly, with all the trouble you've caused at Revolution…"

"Now, wait a minute…"

"Maybe you should get fired. Now, get out of my office. In fact, get the hell out of my life."

Todd pushed past him and strode down the hall.

• • •

A headache pounded at the edge of Brent's temples as he sat in the den in front of his computer. He'd had the headache all day, and he hoped once he got home it would go away but no such luck. He wished he could just go to sleep and put this day behind him, but he knew he'd toss and turn so it was pointless to even try. Voices emanated from the family room where Dolores was watching the eleven o'clock news. Amanda was upstairs reading.

He intended to catch up with some email, but instead he relived the huge blowout he and Todd had earlier in the day. The things Todd had said weighed heavily on his mind. Todd had placed the blame squarely on Brent. And it hurt. His best friend's dream of getting a recording contract had seemed within his grasp a little over two months ago. Now, On The Rise was effectively moving on without Todd. *Was he really to blame for that too?*

Brent turned back to the computer. The screen was filled with unread messages. He worked his way from the bottom up. About to double click on the next email, he saw that there was no header information. His blood ran cold.

The email had been sent on Friday, in the late afternoon. Brent's hand hovered above the mouse only a moment before he double-clicked.

As expected, the email was written all in capital letters.

BRENT,

CONGRATULATIONS ON YOUR POINTS. YOU ARE MAKING THIS ALMOST TOO EASY FOR ME.

DIEORDIETRYING.COM/ DARBY'SDEATHLIST/ ROSTER

INTRUDER

The embedded link was hot, and Brent steeled himself before he clicked on the link, knowing that whatever was coming wasn't going to be pleasant.

On the DieorDieTrying.com site, Brent inserted the required password and the home screen opened. The alphabetical list of rosters was displayed on the left side of the screen. Brent noticed that three were highlighted in red. It wasn't hard to guess what that meant. Points had been awarded to Darby's Death list, Intruder's Chalk Outlines, and a roster entitled Deceive 'em and Cleave 'em.

His first points of the game. Distaste filled his mouth, but he forced himself to click on his roster to see which one of his nominees had died.

A full screen graphic of a skeleton dancing on a grave popped up with the word congratulations below it. *Lovely.* When the graphic dissolved, Brent saw the first nominee on his list had been crossed out with a blood red line. It was hard to read the name beneath the thick red line, but Brent knew his first pick was Fadhl Sharma. Brent leaned forward. The name beneath the red line didn't start with "F." It started with "R."

Randy. Brent sat back in horror. The thirty-eight points he had won had been for the death of his father-in-law.

Heart palpitating, Brent used the arrow keys to go back to the home page. He clicked on Intruder's roster and saw that Intruder has gotten points for his father-in-law as well. "You bastard," Brent spoke aloud as his eyes scanned the remaining names on the list.

"Brent?" came a concerned voice from behind him.

Brent jumped and quickly closed the browser window before turning to see his mother-in-law standing in the doorway.

"Is everything all right?"

"Yes, fine. Just a few computer issues."

"I'm sorry, dear. You work so hard. Well, then, I'm off to bed. Thank you for cooking another wonderful meal tonight."

"You're quite welcome. Sleep well." Brent's voice cracked on the last word. He listened to his mother-in-law's footsteps ascend the stairs to the guest room.

With the computer closed, an unsettling silence filled the room. Brent stared out the window into the dark night. His anger had morphed into blatant fear, and he realized he was trembling. Intruder was out there. Waiting.

The sixth nominee he'd seen on Intruder's list would be worth seventy-six points. The math was simple. Brent was twenty-four years old.

• • •

March 4th – Friday

Brent pulled into his parking space and sat motionless in the Viper, keys in hand, listening to the engine tick. His eyes stung with tiredness and grit from a sleepless night. All night he had spooned against Amanda's warm body, holding desperately onto the only two things in his life that he was sure of, Amanda and baby.

Piece by piece, Intruder was touching, and summarily ruining, everything in his life. Now his best friend had abandoned him as well. He had no one in his corner that could help him fight Intruder.

Despite Todd's warning that he wanted Brent out of his life, he had to make one last effort to make Todd understand. If he could do that, maybe he could save their friendship.

Head down, as if on a mission, Brent entered the building and headed for Todd's office. It was empty, as was the server room. He swung by marketing and made a pass along the wall with the three conference rooms, looking through the window for Todd's blonde ponytail. No luck. Out of ideas, he was about to head to his own office when Todd popped out of a cubicle. Their eyes met, and then Todd turned in the opposite direction and darted off.

"Todd," Brent called out, sprinting after him. Turning the corner, he spotted Todd through the glass door of the break room. He halted in mid-stride, yanked open the door, and stormed inside. "Hey!"

Todd refused to look up. He had his drumsticks out, and he was banging away on the countertop next to the microwave.

"So, that's it? You're tossing our friendship, just like that?"

"I think I made it pretty clear. You go your way, and I'll go mine."

"Fine, but just let me explain a few things in detail. Okay?"

"No thanks."

"I'm not asking for your help. I just want to warn you, all right?"

"Warn me? I think it's a little late for that."

"Just listen. Last night I got another email from Intruder. He congratulated me on winning points in the game."

"Yeah, so?"

"I won thirty-eight points for my father-in-law."

"You are a sick bastard, aren't you?" Todd moved to step past him.

Brent put out a hand to stop him.

Todd whirled around, knocking away his hand. "Don't touch me. You got that?"

Brent sighed. "Would you just listen? I never had Randy on my list. Intruder got points for Randy as well. Don't you see? Intruder killed him."

"That is bullshit. There has been no investigation. You are the only one who finds this suspicious. Brent, your father-in-law died, and Intruder hacked both lists and added Randy's name to the rosters."

"Listen to me! Intruder is murdering people and collecting points for their deaths. Why don't you believe me? I'm in mortal danger."

Todd let loose a laugh. "Mortal danger? Please." He rolled his eyes. "Brent, listen. Intruder is probably some computer whiz-kid who lives in Oklahoma. My guess is that he is a high school geek with no friends who enjoys messing with people's lives when he's not studying for his SATs."

"Then how would you explain the note that was put in my coat pocket at The Jail that night in February?"

"Okay, maybe the kid lives in Massachusetts, not Oklahoma.

It doesn't matter. This was a hack job. No one was murdered."

"You're wrong."

"And you're an idiot." Todd swung his drumstick at a soda can, and it rolled off the counter onto the floor, leaking brown liquid into the carpet. "And I'm not the only one that thinks so." Todd slid his sticks into his pocket, then he yanked open the door to the fridge and peered inside.

"Will you just listen to me and stop being such an asshole?" Brent asked.

"You're the asshole," Todd said. "Intruder did compromise the Revolution system. Worse than I thought a couple of weeks ago. No one knows what is going on except me. I'm the one stuck cleaning up and hiding your mess. At this point, the rest of the IT team probably thinks I'm completely incompetent." Todd slammed the refrigerator door shut. "When we are finally in the clear here, I'll be the first one to tell them that you're the one responsible." He pointed his finger in Brent's face. "You."

"I'm responsible?"

"You signed up to play the game."

"Oh come on! This isn't my fault—"

"It is!"

"That's bullshit," Brent replied. "And you know it. You should be angry with Intruder, not me. I've said I'm sorry. And I am. I'm sorry about everything."

"Are you? Or are you just sorry Intruder screwed up your precious sales for the month? And that you're out a free vacation to Bermuda?"

"The trip was to the Bahamas, and do you even know what happened with Amazon? You haven't gotten the story from me, so you must prefer to listen to the rumors. Going off to the Bahamas is hardly my biggest problem."

"Yeah? Well, there are no free trips in my future either, so cry me a river."

"I'm going to the cops."

"Don't."

"I'm going. In fact, I'm heading there now."

"Don't do it."

"Maybe this is the scare Intruder needs. A lesson that there are more ways than one to play his little game."

"Oh, that's just perfect." Todd shook his head. "I'm working my ass off day and night to mitigate the damage, trying to save your job, my job, and all the while, you're looking to teach Intruder a fucking lesson."

"Going to the cops is the only way I can think of to stop him."

"Are you kidding me? You have no idea who or what you are dealing with. Don't do it, man. Don't call the cops."

"At this point, I don't have any other choice."

"Listen to me. If you go to the cops, you're putting my job on the line—"

"Your job's already on the line," Brent argued. "You said so yourself—" He broke off when a lanky intern he recognized from the marketing department entered the break room. He was wearing a Mickey Mouse tie and sneakers.

"I still don't have a handle on the extent of the damage," Todd hissed. "Let me do that first."

Brent glanced over his shoulder as the young man fed bills into side-by-side vending machines. He lowered his voice. "We can't hide this stuff forever."

"When I've got some answers and gotten my ass out of the sling that you got me into, then you're free to go sing your heart out to Phil or Ed or Jana or whoever gives a fuck. I don't give a rat's ass. I'm out of the band, by the way. Thanks for asking."

"Thanks for your support," Brent said, his voice thick with sarcasm. "I think I'm Intruder's next victim."

"Oh, please. You are delusional. Calling in the National Guard right this second won't help either of us keep our jobs."

"Will you keep it down?" Brent whispered.

The intern gave them a glance over his shoulder, juggling

an uneven tower of Swiss Rolls, Cheetos, and M&Ms stacked on top of two cans of Mountain Dew.

Brent walked over and held open the door for the intern. "Breakfast of champions, my friend" he said, nodding at the array of snacks. When the door closed, he turned around and saw Todd leaning casually against the counter. Todd's pose was relaxed, but his face was dark with fury.

"What is it you think the cops are going to do?" Todd asked. He stalked over to the door through which the intern had just left. He was right in Brent's face, his hand resting on the doorknob.

"Arrest Intruder."

"Why? For what? On your say-so alone?"

"Come on, Todd. You know what he's done! Altering the purchase orders has to be a crime. The police must be able to arrest him for that."

"Even if Intruder's broken some kind of law, they've got to find him before they can arrest him. You think the cops are going to miraculously locate this guy in twenty-four hours?"

"He's broken into the Revolution computer system. He's compromised our data. That has to be illegal," Brent argued.

"Hell, what do you think I've been doing here at all hours of the night? I'm in damage control mode."

"But if we go to the cops, they must have resources you don't have. Ways to prove this stuff…"

"Maybe, but along the way they'll ask a whole lot of questions. Do you honestly think you can be one hundred percent truthful and still keep your job?"

"They'll be after him, not us."

"You can't really be that naïve." Todd yanked open the break room door. "If the cops start an investigation, we are goners."

Brent flinched as Todd slammed the door behind him. *Was his life in danger, or was he just being paranoid?*

Worse still, he hadn't told Amanda about losing the Amazon account, and he certainly hadn't shared his fears that Intruder was somehow connected to her dad's death. Secrets were beginning to mount between them once again, and he only had himself to blame.

• • •

March 11th – Friday

The puppies were calling Amanda. Since her mom had returned to her own home the day before, it was time to get back to work. A character had nosed into her imagination during the last two weeks, and this little guy wouldn't leave her alone until he secured his place in the pack.

Perched on a stool at the breakfast bar, Amanda ripped a fresh sheet of drawing paper off the pad. Before she picked up her pencil, she closed her eyes for a moment envisioning the pup, and then she began to draw.

George the Great Dane took shape quickly, flowing from the end of her pencil. The puppy had a brindle coat, a boisterous personality, and a set of fiercely bushy eyebrows. He also had a ferocious bark, and he jumped up on everyone, causing chaos because he weighed well over a hundred and forty pounds, which belied the fact that he wouldn't hurt a flea.

Amanda added a hunter green vest to the last drawing, which said Therapy Dog in Training. She grinned down at George and felt the warmth of her father wash over her. It was as if he were looking over her shoulder, watching her as she drew. She could even feel him itching to debate the qualities she'd given the Dane. George was much too hyper to ever qualify as a therapy dog, but he didn't seem to know that. He wore his green vest everywhere; after all, it contained business cards with his height, weight, and how much dog food he ate, along with a color photo. He was the only dog in the group who had been inside the mall, the grocery store, and the pharmacy, which gave him a rather high opinion of himself. He tended to give too much advice to the rest of the pack yet failed to take his own.

Amanda included the vest on all the remaining drawings of George, which filled three enormous sheets. She drew the Dane sitting, standing, digging, as well as carrying a long branch in his mouth, easily as thick as her wrist. She did a series of close-ups of his face, concentrating on capturing both sweetness and the pride in his enormous chocolate brown eyes. Finally, Amanda put aside the mocha-colored pencil and taped the pages of the four puppies to the half-wall.

Brent had made chicken parmesan the night before, and she heated a piece up for lunch. Still hungry, she grabbed a banana from the fruit bowl and sat back down to study the drawings while she peeled and ate it.

The pack, so far, consisted of two males and two females. Each looked up at her, tails wagging, seeming to almost ask permission to jump from one page to the next.

Amanda clapped her hands together in pure joy. Without the pressure to make the drawing of each dog come out as perfect as the photographs she usually worked from, or a cantankerous dog owner's expectations, the whole experience was freeing. And in the process, she'd fallen head over heels in love with all four pups.

It was time to start painting. *But should it be acrylic or oil?* Maybe she'd let Brent decide. He'd been quiet of late, and she was a little worried things weren't going well at work, although she'd managed to refrain from asking too many questions. Things were good between them, and she didn't want to rock the boat.

Maybe she could do something special for him tonight. She grinned at the drawings, thinking all six of them could eat dinner together tonight.

She walked back over to the refrigerator and poked her head inside. It didn't look like Brent had taken anything out of the freezer. A pasta dish was something she could pull off.

Unearthing a half package of mushrooms, a stick of pepperoni, an onion, and a jar of Ragu that Brent kept on hand for emergencies, Amanda put everything down on the counter. Pulling out a cutting board, Amanda chose one of the smaller, less lethal-looking knifes from Brent's vast array that hung on a magnetic strip on the wall next to the sink. Not wanting to lose the tip of a finger, Amanda chopped the vegetables carefully.

An hour later, with the sauce bubbling on the stove and her head full of book-signing opportunities, Amanda heard the garage door open. "Hey, honey," she called, when she heard the garage door slam. "How was your day?"

Brent walked in, set his briefcase down, and shrugged out of his coat. "Lousy." He made a show of sniffing the air. "Did you make dinner?" he asked with a surprised expression.

"I did," Amanda said.

"It smells great. Thanks. Before we eat, though, can we talk for a few minutes?"

Amanda nodded and felt a twinge of alarm. "Is everything okay?"

Brent took her hand and led her into the family room. "I just had an incident at work that I wanted to tell you about. I would have told you sooner, but with the funeral and your mom staying here, we haven't had much time alone."

Amanda nodded. Still, she didn't like the sound of this.

Twenty minutes later, she was aghast. "Brent, you have to explain things to Ed," she replied when he'd finally finished. "You have to tell the truth," Amanda pleaded. "You didn't make the mistake that caused Amazon to break with Revolution. Ed will understand your situation once you explain it to him."

"Why would Ed believe me? None of this stuff with Intruder makes any sense. You said so yourself."

"Maybe that's true, but hiding a forged purchase order and the knowledge that a hacker has broken into your company is certainly grounds for dismissal."

Brent sighed.

"You can't just sit around hoping Todd will save the day."

"I would rather go to the police, but Todd has asked me not to."

"Why?"

"He thinks going to the cops will blow everything wide open and that one or both of us will be fired for sure."

"You're the victim here. If anyone is breaking the law, it's Todd."

"But everything he did was to try and help me."

"Why are you allowing him to call all the shots on all this anyway?"

"Because he happens to be a computer genius, and as ripping mad as he is at me, he continues to try and help me."

"Are you sure about that?"

"Amanda! How can you even say that?"

"He's trying to save his job. I don't see how he's helping you."

"Are you seriously asking me to throw Todd under the bus?" He all but shouted at her.

"Brent, from what you've said, your job is in serious jeopardy because Ed and Phil blame you for losing the Amazon account due to incompetence. You have to come clean. You can't worry about Todd right now."

"I have to trust that Todd will figure this out."

"Why are you putting all your trust in him? What if he fails? What if he's wrong?"

"Then we'll both go down together."

"No, Brent! That is not the answer. We need to make decisions with this family's best interest in mind. How does losing your job to protect Todd help us?"

"I have to trust him. I can't do this on my own. Maybe he's close to figuring everything out, to scaring Intruder off. If he succeeds, everything will go back to normal."

"Back to normal? We lost five thousand dollars. You lost a major account and all the commission that went along with that. You might lose your job. You have to stop hiding this!"

"I can't do that to Todd."

"Can't or won't? He is not your responsibility!"

"You want me to save myself at Todd's expense?"

"If it comes to that, yes."

"He's my best friend. He's never let me down. Not once."

"Is his friendship worth more to you than our marriage?"

Brent let out a strangled cry and dropped his head back against the couch.

Amanda went into the kitchen and dumped the pasta sauce down the drain.

Chapter 7

March 31ˢᵗ – Thursday

"Hey, buddy," Brent said, strolling into Todd's cubicle still wearing his overcoat. Todd was leaning over a computer, his back to Brent. He looked over his shoulder and gave a dismissive snort before he returned his attention to his computer.

"I'm here to make peace. Did you read the email I sent you yesterday?"

"No," Todd said, keeping his back to Brent and inserting a cable into the back of a laptop on his desk. "I delete all your emails unread, you ungrateful piece of crap. And by the way, I'm still not speaking to you."

"Oh, really? Well, neither is my wife."

"Smart woman."

Brent sighed. "Amanda and I were doing great. Then all this mess happened with Amazon. She knows how close I came to getting fired."

"Don't expect any sympathy from me."

"I wouldn't dream of it. So did you get my email?"

"Did you think I was kidding when I said I delete your emails unread? The last few weeks have been a pleasure."

"Come on."

"I wasn't kidding."

"I've never known you to hold a grudge."

"I've never had a so-called friend ask me to put my job on the line for him and then ignore my advice."

"Look, can we just change the subject for one second? If I don't put a singular happy thought into my overloaded brain, it is going to explode. Please?"

"No."

"You really didn't read my email?"

"Are you deaf?"

"Amanda sent me a couple of baby names she is considering, and I was asking your opinion. Which name do you prefer, Walter or Lucas?"

"No way," Todd replied.

"Okay, you don't like either one. I can respect that. Let's move on to the girls' names. Samantha or Jessica?" Brent asked.

"No comment. I'm not getting in the middle of a baby name debate. Which works perfectly within my new rule of never speaking to you again."

"Chicken," Brent grinned.

Todd nodded. "You got that right. Now, get out of my office. You are my sworn enemy."

"You don't mean that. Okay, forget the baby names. In five minutes, you'll be begging to be my friend."

Todd pushed a CD into a slot in the side of the laptop. "That is not going to happen. I'm on Amanda's side. I'm not getting any deeper into your shit."

"Well, this particular shit is very close to your heart."

"What are you talking about?"

"On The Rise."

"My former band? The last thing I want to talk about are those traitors."

"Just listen, will you?"

Todd began typing away on his keyboard. "Go away. I have work to do."

"Then work away, but will you at least listen while I talk?"

"You should be working too. Last I heard, you were actually still employed here."

"Shut up and just listen, will you? You're right. I have Intruder to thank for tanking my career. Still, on the plus side, I haven't been fired yet. So today I took a break from my desperate groveling to get back into the good graces of my accounts to have a little talk with Chris."

"Chris? The lead singer of On the Rise?" Todd turned around and leaned back against the desk, arms folded.

"Yup."

"The last thing I need is you speaking on my behalf. I can just imagine how that conversation went."

"Actually, if there is one thing I am good at, it's sales. I am a damn good salesman."

"What's your point? What were you selling him?" Todd's eyes narrowed.

"You."

Todd raised his eyebrows. "Me?"

"Yeah."

"Just spill it, will you? What did you say?"

Brent had Todd's full attention. "I just explained that all the time you've been working overtime at Revolution and missing practices was my fault. I didn't go into details, but I explained that you were trying to get my ass out of some very serious trouble."

"And…"

"He knows we're best friends and how loyal you are. I also reminded them that you had written a good portion of the original songs for the band. Including Glamour Girl, which got the band the demo track."

"I've already reminded Chris of all that. He didn't give a shit."

"Yeah, but you probably didn't close the deal."

"Meaning what?"

"I gave him a little added incentive to keep you in the band."

"What?"

"I told him you had written a few new songs. Good songs, in fact, great songs. I may have even hinted that the Executive Producer knew about them."

"Are you shitting me?" Todd stood up and ran both hands down the legs of his jeans. "And what did Chris say? About these nonexistent songs?"

"Suffice it to say that by the end of the conversation, he agreed that maybe the band members had been a bit too hasty in their decision to look for a replacement drummer. He is very anxious to hear what you've come up with."

"You're serious?"

"Completely."

"All I have to do is come up with a couple of great songs?"

"Yup. Can you do that?"

"I sure as hell can! Thanks, man."

Brent reached into the pocket of his overcoat and pulled out a couple of ripped sheets of paper. "I made him tear up the termination contract he wrote. Not that it would stand up in a court of law anyway." He laughed. "At least that's the opinion of my old Business Law professor. I gave him a quick call."

"He is one slimy bastard."

"Hey, don't call my professor that."

"I was talking about—"

"I know who you were talking about, chill out. So, are we friends again?"

"I guess so. Until the next stupid-ass thing you do."

"Then I guess I don't need to sweeten the deal with these." Brent pulled two tickets from the other pocket of his overcoat. "Guess what these are?"

"Probably Celtics tickets. Basketball players are a bunch of crybabies."

"Nope. For your information, Mr. Die-Hard-Boston-Bruins-Fan, these two beauties are for the Bruins-Islanders game in one week. On the blue line."

Todd spun around eyeballing the tickets. "No way. Playoff tickets?"

Brent nodded. He did a little strut around Todd's cubicle, enjoying the look of longing on Todd's face.

"Let me see those." Todd made a grab for the tickets, but Brent pulled them just out of reach. "Where did you get them?"

"I still have one or two clients that like me. I got a call on my way back to the office. A Senior Vice President I know in the financial industry can't go to the game, and he offered me the tickets. I saw no reason to let them go to waste. I was thinking of asking Clive."

Todd plucked one of the tickets from Brent's fingers. "Clive? Yeah, right. You wouldn't invite Clive to your own funeral." He studied the ticket. "Bruins' side. Three rows from the glass. Unbelievable."

"One more thing…" Brent lowered his voice. "I want to be straight with you. I did make a call to the police a couple of hours ago."

Todd closed his eyes and held the ticket back out toward Brent. "On second thought, never mind. Enjoy the game."

Brent spoke in a soft voice. "Listen, I told you I didn't know what else to do. I didn't mention Revolution, and I called from the one working payphone in this whole damn city. And I gave them a fake name."

Todd rolled his eyes. "Brilliant. I'm sure no one's ever tried that ruse on the cops before."

Brent ignored the barb and tossed his coat over the side of the cubicle. "I was kind of hoping that the Amazon thing was Intruder's big finale, but then Randy died, and I know you don't believe me, but I think Intruder had something to do with his death."

"You're crazy."

"Yeah, so you've said. So when you didn't believe me, going to the police was my last resort. I spoke to a cop and gave him a few examples of what Intruder had done, and he said the local police don't even deal with Internet crimes."

"Who does?"

"The cop threw a bunch of alphabet agencies at me." Brent pulled a scrap of paper from his pants pocket. "Two of them, MCCTF, Maine Computer Crimes Task Force; and HTCCD, High Technical Computer Crime Division, both work in the New England area. Of course, he also told me that these guys are underfunded and understaffed," Brent continued. "The officer said, unless the perpetrator had made an actual threat, my complaint would be considered low priority."

"Let me guess, Intruder telling you to 'play the game' isn't considered a threat."

"Exactly."

"Is now a good time to say I told you so?" Todd had a sour expression on his face.

"I guess." Brent pocketed the note.

"Is Intruder still in contact with you?"

"Constantly. Twitter, email, cell phone messages. I don't even use my computer at home anymore, but since everything goes to my phone anyway, I can't get away from him."

"What happens when you reply back to him?"

"I've stopped even bothering, but I used to get an auto message from the system administrator that the address is undeliverable. Something about domain missing or malformed."

"He's set up a sock puppet," Todd said.

"What the heck is that?" Brent asked.

"A bogus address hackers set up so they don't have to deal with return emails."

"Great." Brent sighed. "Another dead end."

"See?" Todd asked. "Let it go. This is completely out of your control."

"Still, thoughts of Intruder wake me up in the middle of the night."

"You need to get yourself some Prozac."

"Brent, I finally found you." Claire, the department secretary, popped her head into Todd's cubicle. "Suzette from personnel needs you in her office."

Brent's stomach dipped, and he exchanged a look with Todd. "Sure. I'll stop by."

Claire remained in the doorway. "She said right away."

Brent swallowed and turned back around to face her. "You bet. Tell her I'm on my way." He leaned over toward Todd. "Personnel?" he whispered. "What could this be about?"

"You made it through the Amazon catastrophe with your job intact," Todd answered. "How I'll never know. It must be that you've still got some shine on you from winning that Rookie of the Year award."

"That feels like a lifetime ago. Maybe that stupid metal bra is cursed."

"You better get going." Todd handed him his coat and inclined his head toward Claire who still hovered, looking nervous, just outside Todd's cubicle. "Apparently, Mary Sunshine expects a command performance."

"I'm sorry," Claire said, poking her head back in. "Suzette told me to escort you if necessary."

"Escort me?" Brent felt a chill pass through him. "Okay, I'm going." He stepped into the hallway and headed for the elevator, hoping that Claire would not follow him. He refused to allow her to accompany him to personnel as if he were an errant school boy.

Brent stepped off the elevator and saw Ed standing inside the personnel director's office. *This couldn't be good.* He swallowed the unease in his throat and walked inside Suzette's spacious office. The personnel director was standing behind her desk, and Ed stood near the file cabinet, just inside the door.

"Have a seat." Suzette motioned toward a white wicker couch with green cushions.

Brent sat down and brought his right ankle up until it rested on his knee, pretending an ease he didn't feel. He folded his coat and set it on the couch beside him before looking around, pretending to study the office decor. It was impossible not to notice the peach paint on the walls and the overabundance of live plants. The place reminded him of a sunroom in a Florida retirement community. "Nice office," he said, hoping his tone sounded genuine. Suzette didn't reply.

The door clicked shut, and Ed leaned his bulk back against it, his arms crossed over his chest, his brow beaded with sweat. Suzette sat down and gave Brent one of her patented, everything-is-just-fine smiles as she picked up a bright red folder on her desk.

His heartbeat increased. The shit was about to hit the fan. For what, he could only begin to imagine.

"Something came up yesterday that we need to discuss," Suzette said. Brent's internal warning device went up another notch. She slid on a pair of reading glasses and peered at Brent over the top of the rims. She lifted a single sheet out of the file and reached across the desk, handing it to Brent. "If you would please read this email, we would like to discuss the contents." Her eyes slid over to Ed.

Brent took the paper gingerly, aware that two sets of eyes were examining him while he read. He scanned the one page document, zeroing in on a single sentence: "Jana is one hot babe." *Shit!* A sinking sensation went through him. Taking his time, Brent read the document in full, conscious of the heat that crept into his cheeks at his supposed desire to perform several sexually explicit acts on Jana, the CEO's receptionist. As it turned out, the first line in the email was the only one he'd actually written. Intruder was at it again.

Brent's gaze jumped back to the top of the page. His name was listed as the sender, the recipient was Todd. Despite his best efforts, both he and Todd were going to go up in flames thanks to Intruder. *That bastard!* Brent closed his eyes for a brief moment, hoping to marshal his thoughts. "I didn't write this."

"You deny being the author of this email?" Suzette asked, making a notation on the legal pad in front of her.

"Yes," Brent said, "absolutely." He tried to quell the voice in his head that told him to own up to the five relatively innocuous words he had written. *Jana is one hot babe.* Neither Suzette nor Ed spoke. The only sound in the room was a clock ticking just above his head. He began to sweat.

"Just so that I'm absolutely clear," Suzette said, "you disavow any knowledge of this email?"

"I did not write this filth."

Ed's ever-present handkerchief appeared, and he dabbed at his forehead. "You're sure?"

Brent nodded his head, watching Suzette and Ed exchange glances.

"You would agree then that this email contains inappropriate content?" Suzette asked.

"Absolutely," Brent replied.

"An email of this nature is a clear violation of our sexual harassment policy. Not to mention improper use of the corporation's assets."

"So what are you accusing me of?" Brent said, rattling the paper in his hand for emphasis. "And what exactly is improper use of the corporate assets?" He repeated one word for emphasis. "Exactly."

"Capital equipment such as phones, fax machines, and computers," Suzette answered smoothly. "Any use of this equipment for any non-work-related purpose is a violation of the employment contract you signed when you were hired. Excessive personal phone calls and online shopping would be two additional examples."

Brent watched Suzette's gleaming smile reappear, as if she had found her last comment to be particularly witty. He gritted his teeth before giving her a strained smile in return. Why hadn't he heeded Todd's warning?

At a seemingly invisible signal from Suzette, Ed pulled himself away from the door. He spoke slowly and clearly, "Brent, we can prove the email was sent from your computer."

Brent's heart skipped a beat.

"What we don't know—" Ed said.

The intercom on Suzette's phone buzzed.

"Suzette, please pick up," an authoritative female voice demanded.

Suzette sniffed in annoyance and placed the receiver to her ear. "I asked not to be interrupted. I see. Yes. I'll be right there." She replaced the receiver. "I am afraid a situation has arisen that I must handle immediately. Let me get straight to the point." Suzette removed her glasses and placed them on the desk in front of her.

"As Ed mentioned, the offensive email was generated from your computer. It goes without saying that Ed and I are both concerned about this matter, and we will find the culpable party." She gave Brent a level stare. "It has come to our attention that you have been involved in several, shall we say, questionable incidents, all of which have occurred in recent weeks. Therefore, your computer files and personnel record will be reviewed."

Brent felt the blood rush to his face. His heart was hammering so hard he imagined Suzette could count each visible beat through his shirt.

"Have I made myself clear?" Suzette asked.

Brent blinked, still in shock. They would find plenty of evidence on his hard drive of inappropriate use of corporate assets, given Suzette's broad definition of the word. He'd made stock trades, checked game scores, and purchased innumerable gifts, as no doubt, had every other employee in the company. That didn't even take into account all the work he'd done on company time to clean up his credit report, the endless emails from Intruder, etc. Before he could respond, Suzette continued.

"The most severe consequence for the aforementioned infractions would be the termination of your employment with this corporation. For the moment, while this matter is under investigation, you are being put on unpaid leave. Do you have any questions?"

Brent was jolted back to the present. "Unpaid leave?" he spat out. *This was outrageous.* "When do I go on trial?"

Suzette frowned. "I do not appreciate your sarcasm, Mr. Darby."

"It sounds like you've already found me guilty," Brent said, striving to keep his tone neutral.

"Quite to the contrary, it is our obligation to provide all employees of this company a safe working environment as required by law. In doing so, we also protect Revolution from potentially damaging lawsuits."

"I'm sure." He nodded sagely as if she had made a valid point. He had half a mind to call a freaking lawyer the minute he got back to his office.

Suzette replaced her glasses. "Brent, I need you to initial and date this letter."

"You've got to be kidding me? I told you I didn't write that stuff."

"Your signature acknowledges only that you were informed of these allegations. It does not constitute guilt or innocence. It is, however, standard practice. If you refuse to sign it, we will have no choice but to terminate you."

"This is unbelievable." Brent grabbed the proffered pen and scribbled his name on the bottom of the letter. The last paragraph contained the most sexually explicit comments, and Brent circled that paragraph and wrote in capital letters, "I DID NOT WRITE THIS." With a withering look at Suzette, he slammed the pen down on the edge of the desk and thrust the paper back at her.

With pursed lips, Suzette slid the signed paper back inside the red folder and crossed her arms on top of it. "Brent, I will schedule a phone meeting as soon as possible so you and I can communicate further about this matter. Now if you'll both excuse me…" She stood up, indicating the end of the meeting.

Ed opened the door and motioned for Brent to leave the office ahead of him. With his heart still thudding in his chest, Brent grabbed his coat and walked out into the hall. *Was Ed his enemy or ally?* He paused, hoping to have a private word with him.

Suzette brushed past, leaving a trail of expensive perfume in her wake. Ed followed on her heels as if Brent were a ghost. He had the answer to his question. *Enemy.*

Deep in thought, Brent turned the corner and decided to take the stairs back to the sales department. His shirt was damp with perspiration by the time he pushed open the fire door on the sales floor. When he walked into his office, he was startled to find Clive with his back to Brent, holding his Rookie of the Year award in his meaty hands. "What the hell are you doing?" Brent snatched his plaque out of Clive's hands. "How did you get into my office?"

"Ah, matey," Clive said in a thick brogue, turning to face him. "I've come to collect me spoils."

"What are you talking about?" Brent returned the trophy to his bookshelf.

"Today is the thirty-first. Time to hand over the Viper. What happened to that famous Midas touch?"

"I never agreed to hand the Viper over today." Brent said. *Was it possible that Clive knew what had just transpired in personnel? Had Ed sold him out?*

"Ed and I talked yesterday. It's pretty clear to me that you're going down. He mentioned something about an ethics course he wants me to take. Would you happen to know anything about that?"

"Fuck you." The corner office on the thirtieth floor materialized in Brent's mind. Except Clive was sitting behind the massive desk, and Ed was patting his nemesis on the back. The image evaporated, but the sick feeling in his stomach remained.

"Come on, toss me those keys," Clive said. He rubbed his hands together with glee. "You lost the bet fair and square."

"Even if I was going to give you the Viper today, which I'm not, I'd need some way to get home, asshole."

Clive's eyes glittered. "I'll drive you."

"Not a chance," Brent said. "We need to agree on a date."

"Fine, as long as it's sometime this week." Clive paused in Brent's doorway. "My girlfriend found an amazing deal on The Cape for this coming weekend. I'll tell her to go ahead and make our reservations." Clive smiled. "I can't wait to see how the Viper handles the curves along the ocean road." He strolled out.

Brent clenched his teeth, still seeing the smirk on Clive's face in his mind's eye. It took all his willpower to close rather than slam the door on Revolution's newly crowned golden boy. He couldn't pretend it didn't hurt.

Brent dropped down into the chair behind his desk, and, out of habit, checked the bottom right-hand corner of his monitor for new email. Apparently, they hadn't locked him out of his computer yet. He supposed that was only a matter of time. Or maybe Todd had been told to do it, but he hadn't gotten around to it yet. He hoped his buddy still had his back.

In any case, the writing was on the wall. *How much time did he have?* He needed to pull his contact information and phone numbers, emails, etc. Next he could look forward to hunting for a job. Brent sighed. He scanned the two new pieces of mail in his inbox. One was from Amanda, the second had no header information. *Intruder.* Brent closed his eyes. At least when he left Revolution, he would leave Intruder behind. Or would he? Despite his weariness and desire not to care, his heart rate jumped back up.

Brent moved the cursor over the envelope from Amanda and double-clicked.

> *Brent,*
>
> *Don't forget, tonight we have our first childbirth class at seven o'clock. Maddie from across the street is dropping me off since her shift at the hospital starts at seven. That way we'll*

*have only one car downtown, and we
can drive home together afterward.*

I'm so excited. Hope you are, too.

*Love,
Amanda*

Brent typed a quick response.

Amanda,

I'll meet you inside the hospital lobby
tonight. Seven sharp.

Can't wait.

Love,
Brent

Brent sent the message to Amanda and paused a moment, contemplating the remaining email. If it was the last thing he did, literally, he wanted to find a way to trap Intruder. As his stomach continued to churn, he wondered briefly if maybe he'd gotten an ulcer. If he had, he could thank Intruder for that, too. He clicked on the blank email.

A box came up requesting receipt confirmation. In order to see the email, Brent had no choice but to click okay.

**THE GAME IS RAMPING UP.
ARE YOU GOING TO PLAY?
WHAT DO YOU HAVE LEFT
TO LOSE?**

Did Intruder know he was about to get fired? Probably. Intruder wanted blood. He wouldn't stop until he succeeded.

There was no alternative. Brent had to somehow go on the offensive and make Intruder think he was playing the game. And he had to start now. *Think like a game player. You need a strategy.* Brent stood up from his desk and began to pace in front of the window.

A chirp sounded, and Brent turned back to his computer. A Twitter message had appeared on the screen.

Intruder: HELLO BRENT

Brent leaned over his desk, staring at the screen. Intruder was no doubt monitoring everything Brent did and knew the second he touched his keyboard, both at work and at home. He was no longer surprised, just incredulous at the guy's skills and his nerve. Intruder was clearly able to access the Revolution system at will.

He jammed the receiver between his ear and shoulder and called Todd's extension. Then he used the mouse to click the direct message button on the incoming tweet. The response box came up.

```
Pawn694: What do you
want from me?
Intruder: I AGREE WITH
AMANDA. WALTER WOULD
BE MY CHOICE FOR THE
BABY`S NAME, IF IT`S
A BOY, OF COURSE.
```

The hair on the back of Brent's neck stood up and then Todd spoke in his ear. "What did Mary Sunshine have to say?"

"It wasn't good. Can you come up? Plus I'm tweeting with Intruder on my Revolution laptop as we speak."

"Be right there."

The phone went dead in Brent's ear, and he slammed the receiver back in the cradle.

> Pawn694: Leave my wife
> out of this.
> Intruder: I`VE ALWAYS
> BEEN PARTIAL TO
> BLONDES.

The words made Brent want to jump through the screen. *He's guessing,* he told himself, even as his skin began to crawl.

> Pawn694: This is between
> you and me. If you want
> me to play, I`ll play.
> Intruder: EXCELLENT.

Brent pushed his fear aside. It was time to see how good a poker player Intruder was. He began to hunt for letters on the keyboard.

> Pawn694: I`ve already
> started my offense. I
> called the cops.
> Intruder: WHAT A
> SHAME. NOW YOU`VE
> SPOILED EVERYTHING.
> Pawn694: How so?
> Intruder: CALLING THE
> COPS IS NOT PLAYING
> THE GAME.
> Pawn694: Here`s my
> game. I have you
> arrested and sent to

```
prison. I win.
Intruder: FAIR ENOUGH,
BUT HOW WILL YOU KNOW
IF I WIN?
Pawn694: Why don`t you
tell me.
Intruder: WHEN YOUR
NAME IS RED-LINED.
```

Todd burst through the doorway of Brent's office, caught the door and slammed it shut behind him. "Move," Todd ordered. He tore around the side of the desk and grabbed the back of Brent's chair.

Brent jumped up. "Hurry, type something, or he'll log off."

"Let me just set the file to copy so I can grab the code."

"We'll lose him. Let me just type a reply first." Brent yanked the keyboard back.

```
Pawn694: What do you
mean, red-lined?
```

Todd had his hand on the mouse, waiting to take control. As soon as Brent typed the last letter, he moved the cursor over to one of the dropdown menus.

Brent stood over his shoulder, watching the screen waiting for Intruder's reply.

```
Intruder: LET`S
REVIEW. I KNOW
EVERYTHING ABOUT YOU
AND YOUR WIFE. WHAT DO
YOU KNOW ABOUT ME? LET
THE REAL GAME BEGIN.
GOOD LUCK.
```

"Did you get what you wanted?" Brent asked.

"I think so," Todd replied, flipping his ponytail back over his shoulder.

Brent's door swung open again, and they both looked up. A Revolution security guard planted himself in Brent's doorway, feet apart, massive arms folded over his chest. "Step away from the computer. I'm here to escort you from the building."

"Yes, sir," Brent said, letting go of the mouse and catching the stunned look on Todd's face.

"If you'll be so kind as to hand me your badge," the guard said, walking toward the desk.

"I've been told an examination of my computer files is pending," Brent said, looking straight at Todd. "Is that right?"

Todd held up both hands in a gesture of innocence. "I was sent over here from IT to take the computer." He looked up at the officer and touched the Revolution badge hanging around his neck. "Is it okay if I continue?"

"I don't know anything about that." The officer turned back to Brent. "I need your badge and the key to the door. My job is to lock the office and escort this individual out of the building."

Todd nodded, his eyes on the screen. "You do your job, and I'll do mine."

Brent unclipped his Revolution badge and handed it to the guard along with the key to his office.

"Cell phone too," said the guard.

"Can you give me a few minutes to pack up my personal items?" Brent asked, handing over his phone.

"I'm afraid not," the guard said. "Let's go. Now!"

Brent watched Todd unplug the laptop and tuck it under his arm. The guard followed them through the door. It looked like Todd once again had his back.

• • •

"I learned so much from our first childbirth class, didn't you?" Amanda asked.

Brent nodded, although in truth, he'd barely heard a word the child birth instructor said. Instead, he tried to stay in the moment, enjoying the feeling of Amanda's mitten-covered hand gently linked with his over the Viper's center console as they drove home.

"Now that I know what to expect, I feel so much more confident that I'll be ready when the time comes."

"You're going to do great."

She turned in the seat to face him. "I am going to do great, aren't I? Suddenly I feel like this is the most important thing I'll ever do in my life."

"You may just be right. Our son could be President of the United States or a CEO of a Fortune 500 company or a world-renowned inventor."

"Or our daughter…" Amanda leaned over and poked him, "could be President of the United States or a prima ballerina or a brilliant surgeon."

Amanda radiated happiness. She'd looked breathtakingly beautiful in class tonight as she sat listening intently to the instructor, even scribbling notes into a spiral bound journal she'd bought just for the occasion. Twice during class, she'd reached over to squeeze his hand, jarring his thoughts away from Intruder. Not wanting to disappoint her, he pretended to be as caught up in the lecture as she was.

"I love you," Amanda said, out of the blue, smoothing the folds of her cape over her protruding stomach.

"I love you too," Brent replied. They were almost home, yet he continued to procrastinate, not wanting to spoil the joy within her and the closeness between them these last few weeks. He didn't want to admit that he'd failed her. Instead, he rubbed her mitten-covered fingers with his thumb.

"So if it's a boy, it's Jerome?" Brent said. "Is that what you've decided?" He'd tell her tonight, he vowed, when they were lying in bed.

"I don't know. I'm having second thoughts," Amanda replied. "If it's a boy, I want our son to have a cool name. Do you think Jerome sounds cool?"

"No." Brent laughed. "But it's better than Walter."

"Walter is still one of my top five."

Brent groaned. "Me and my big mouth. How about girl names? Have we agreed upon—"

Something struck the car from behind, and the rest of Brent's words vanished in a sickening crunch of metal. Amanda screamed.

"What the hell?" Brent instinctively hit the brakes and snatched his hand out of Amanda's, grabbing the wheel with both hands. The car went into a stomach-churning skid, and Brent pulled the wheel to the left as he fought to steer out of it. "Are you okay?"

"I'm fine, but what happened?"

"I'm not sure." With the car back under control, Brent shot a quick glance into the rearview mirror and then another at Amanda.

She reached down and adjusted the seatbelt so that it lay underneath her protruding belly. "I hate this car. We should have taken the Jeep."

Brent let the comment go, again checking the rearview mirror. Behind him everything was pitch black. It was a moonless night, and the road they were on cut through the Garnet Forest Reserve. No houses, no street lights, just acres of trees on either side.

"Will you promise me next winter you'll put this car up on blocks and not drive it?"

Before he could answer, something struck the Viper a second time from the rear. Brent was thrown forward by the impact before the seatbelt locked in place, causing him to be whipped back against his seat. Amanda's high-pitched scream filled his ears, and he felt the front tires leave the pavement. For a brief second the car was airborne, and then the Viper careened down a steep embankment. The jolting headlights illuminated a pristine field of snow beyond which lay a dark line of trees.

"Oh my God!" Brent yelled. "Amanda, hold on!" He threw his right arm across Amanda in a pointless gesture of protection even as he braced for the impact. Suddenly the Viper spun, and a blur of trees raced past Brent's vision. The car smashed up against a tree and a whoosh sounded as both airbags burst open and pain blossomed in Brent's chest. The car tipped sideways and seemed to hang precariously for a moment before it slammed back down to earth. The headlights illuminated the sharp angle of the car, sunk unevenly deep into the snow.

"Amanda?" Brent shook his head once to clear it before he turned to look at Amanda, who was silhouetted against the window in the faint glow of the dashboard lights. "Honey? Talk to me. Are you hurt?"

Fear raced along Brent's spine when she didn't answer. Reaching overhead, he fumbled until he was able to switch on the interior dome light. Bathed in sudden light, he saw a small amount of blood on her face. Her head was down as she cradled her pregnant belly in both hands beneath the deflated airbag.

"I don't feel the baby kicking." Her voice was filled with panic.

Brent reached over and turned her face toward him. "Everything is going to be okay." Using his fingers, he brushed a mixture of blood and tears off her face, running his hand over her face, ears and neck. His breathing slowed somewhat when he'd concluded the blood was coming only from her nose. "I'll call 911."

"Hurry."

Brent reached for his phone and felt the empty holster. He relived being escorted from the building at the same time a torrent of panic threatened to overtake him.

"Why aren't you calling?" Amanda asked, her eyes wide.

"I left it at work. Hand me yours."

"I can't find it," Amanda said, continuing to dig through her purse. "It must be at home; I was charging it."

"It's okay," Brent said. She forgot her phone all the time. On the other hand, his cell phone was a permanent appendage except when he was asleep. But now was not the time to explain.

"It's okay, baby," he repeated. "I'll go for help." Pulse racing, Brent unbuckled his seatbelt as he assessed the situation. He could see the ghostly outline of the tree the car had struck between the headlights. His breath caught as he stared at the mangled door frame just above Amanda's head. Six inches lower and she would have been killed. The only way out of the vehicle was through the driver's side door. Desperate to free himself from the racecar, Brent slammed his shoulder against the door, ignoring the wave of pain that radiated across his upper body. He had to free himself so he could go for help. He took a deep breath and then tried again, slamming his body against the door with all his might. Then he tried a third time. And a fourth.

"Stop it!" Amanda cried. "The car is buried in the snow. Look at the headlights. You'll never get the doors open. We're trapped."

She was right. Brent reached over and tried to push open her door anyway, before he slumped back, defeated in the driver's seat. "Have you felt the baby move yet?"

Amanda shook her head, and tears once again began to stream down her face. "What are we going to do?"

"It's going to be okay."

"How can you say that? It's not okay."

"I know you're scared, but we are alive."

"But the baby—"

"The baby is in the best possible place he could be right now, protected inside your body." The overhead dome light faded to black.

"Brent," Amanda called out in the darkness.

"I've got you." He linked his arm through hers and rested his hand on her belly. Now the only light source came from the dim glow of the dashboard lights and the faint illumination of the headlights buried deep beneath the snow. *Which way were they facing? How far off the road was the car?*

"Brent, my baby needs help."

"All three of us are going to be fine. Just fine. I'll get us out of here. I just have to think." Brent realized he was babbling, but he couldn't help himself.

"No one is going to find us out here." Amanda whimpered.

On the heels of her comment, another even more horrific thought crept into Brent's mind. *What if the gas tank was leaking? Could the car catch fire? Could it explode?* He had no idea. He pulled his hand back and punched off the headlights. Then he yanked the key out of the ignition. Now, in complete darkness, silence pressed down upon his ears.

He needed Amanda to stay calm. He turned in his seat and a fresh bolt of pain shot through his chest. He clenched his teeth and reached back over, groping to find his wife's hand. He'd either cracked or broken a rib. Fighting the pain, he struggled to think. He had to stay strong for Amanda. He rubbed her fingers through the mitten, and he felt her body shaking.

"Brent, you have to do something." Urgency filled Amanda's voice.

"I'll think of something." In his mind, Brent methodically went through every inch of the Viper. The trunk was empty, even if he could get to it. The only other storage area was under the front seat. Brent yanked the drawer open and felt around. He came up with a jumble of business cards, pens, and an assortment of loose change. He tossed everything to the floor and reached under the seat, grasping for anything useful. *Nothing.* He didn't have a first aid kit. He didn't have as much as a candy bar, a bottle of water, or a blanket. He cursed his own stupidity.

In growing desperation, Brent wondered if it was possible the Viper wasn't visible from the road. He clicked on the headlights, putting on the high beams. He pushed aside all the news reports that flooded his mind of searches that had gone on

Deadly Intruder

for weeks. Bodies uncovered. Distraught families weeping in front of television cameras.

"You have to save our baby. Don't let her die out here."

Amanda's words stopped Brent cold. *He couldn't fail her. Not again.* Determination surged through him. His fingers found the cup holder, and he retrieved the key and inserted it back into the ignition. Although the engine remained silent, he fumbled for the driver's side window button. Relief filled him as snow tumbled, wet and cold, onto his lap.

"Brent, what are you doing?" Amanda asked.

"Going for help." Brent put his left hand on the window ledge and awkwardly lifted first one heel and then the other until he was crouched on the seat, head now outside the window. He bit his lip at the stabbing pain each movement caused and the additional pain he knew was coming. "Trust me, Amanda. I'll be back with help as soon as I can."

"Brent, I'm really scared."

"I know. Me too." Brent squeezed Amanda's hand once, trying to wordlessly reassure her, and then he tumbled out the window.

210

Chapter 8

April 7ᵗʰ – Thursday

Brent drained the last sip of coffee from his mug and took a moment to just breathe before he headed into work.

It had been a week since the car accident, and slowly the nightmare was fading from his consciousness. He'd managed to wade through thigh-high snow back to the road, and finally a long-haul trucker had spotted him and slowed down, grinding his gears until he managed to get the big rig stopped. Brent ran to the driver's side window and waited until the trucker made contact with the police. Then he fought his way back through the snow to Amanda. He kicked a path through the snow to the passenger side of the car. Amanda lowered her window, and he leaned in, hugging her and keeping her warm with his own body heat until help finally arrived.

"Good thing I was on my way to visit my sister, I guess," the trucker had said nonchalantly about the odds of him being on the little-used back road.

They'd been forced to use the Jaws-of-Life to get Amanda out of the shattered vehicle. By that time, she was frantic about the baby. The medics had put her on a backboard, and the ambulance had whisked her away. One of the cops had dropped Brent off minutes behind her.

After several hours of monitoring in the hospital, the doctor had told them the baby had shown no ill effects from the traumatic car accident. Both Amanda and Brent had broken down into tears, their long night of stress finally eased by the one piece of news that made everything else meaningless.

"Bye, hon," Brent called out, still grateful for yet another stroke of almost impossible-to-believe good fortune. Brent was being allowed to return to work.

Stepping into the garage and hitting the automatic garage door opener, Brent looked with distaste at the rental car.

The Hertz agent had called the color Sunburst Metallic Orange, but Brent thought it looked more like burnt pumpkin pie. He slid into the driver's seat, experiencing a twinge of discomfort as he clicked his seatbelt in place. The pain in his ribs, unnecessarily confirmed by an x-ray at the hospital as being due to a cracked rib, had subsided for the most part. Initially the simple act of moving had been agony. Something he had not experienced since his days on the high school football team.

Now, as Brent merged onto I-93 and into commuter traffic, he thought about the brief call from Suzette yesterday. She had informed him, in an I'm-not-buying-this-for-a-second voice, that he could return to work and that full pay would be reinstated for the week the matter had been under investigation. No disciplinary action had been filed.

Brent had been shocked and more relieved than he'd been willing to admit. He had been convinced that his career with Revolution was over, but he wasn't going to look a gift horse in the mouth. He hated job hunting, and now that he'd been given a second chance, he was going in to kick some serious sales ass. A fighter and a winner, he'd make his way to the top of the heap yet again.

He shifted into the passing lane and stomped on the accelerator. The Chevy's four-cylinder engine strained, barely making headway against the eighteen-wheeler he was trying to pass. Talk about torture. Maybe he'd call the rental car company back and upgrade.

Yesterday afternoon, after Suzette's call, he'd gone car shopping online. Due to the crash safety rating, Amanda had finally sanctioned the four-door Beemer he'd chosen. After working out the financing and placing the order, he realized he could have gotten a better deal if he'd been willing to drive one off the lot of a local car dealer, but somehow he couldn't resist the combination of Monaco blue with the birch trim and the special order split seat. The custom features increased the arrival date of the new car six weeks, but then again, the baby wasn't due to arrive until August. The new BMW would be here long before then.

Several long moments later, Brent finally won his highway battle with the oil truck and settled unhappily back into the right-hand lane for the rest of the commute, badly missing the power of the Viper and his cell phone.

Forty-five minutes later, he crossed the Zakim Bridge and zigged and zagged through the turns to the office. He pulled into his parking space and hurried across the oil-stained cement. He hadn't bothered with a coat, but now wished he had, chilled by an unusually cold wind for April.

It was only at the glass door to the building that Brent remembered that his badge had been confiscated. He would not be able to enter the building except through the ground floor lobby.

With a sigh, and nerves jangling from apprehension about how he would be received by his coworkers, Brent rode the garage elevator down to the ground floor. He entered the glass doors, glad to finally be inside the building, and paused to pull off his leather gloves. He used the lobby phone and dialed Todd's extension. He had a nine a.m. meeting with Suzette to get his cell phone back, and it was only eight-thirty. As the phone rang, he turned to look out the window at the temperature displayed on the electronic bank sign across the street. Twenty-four degrees. *Global warming, my ass,* he thought.

"Hello?" Todd said.

"Hey, buddy," Brent replied, happy to hear Todd's voice. "I'm downstairs in the lobby. I don't know if it's common knowledge, but I've been reinstated."

"Is that so?" Todd answered. He broke into a chuckle.

"Any chance you can meet me down here and give me the lay of the land before I go upstairs into the lion's den?"

"Sure," Todd said. "I've got a few minutes."

Brent hung up and headed over to the most secluded of three seating areas that decorated the enormous lobby. He sat down, noting that the stiff leather was designed for appearance's sake rather than comfort.

With nothing electronic to occupy him, Brent watched people hustle in and out of the building, most talking or typing away on cell phones. The last six days at home he'd been unable to log into the office from home since his password had been locked out, and he'd had no cell phone. It had made the last six days at home bizarrely quiet.

"Welcome back," Todd said, striding over from the elevator, flip-flops slapping his heels. "The last time I saw you, all hell was breaking loose in your office. Now the suspect has returned to the scene of the crime."

"Not funny," Brent replied. "How was your week-long conference?"

"Boring as hell." Todd plopped down on the couch next to him.

"How are things upstairs?" Brent asked.

"The gossip was flying that you were getting canned, but I can see the rumors of your demise have been greatly exaggerated." He grinned. "Anyway, who gives a shit about that? It's just a job, right? Priorities, man. How's Amanda doing? How's the baby?"

"Amanda is fine. The baby's fine too."

"And the Viper?"

"It disintegrated."

"Disintegrated? Really?"

"Yeah, but that's probably also what saved our lives. The snow was littered with hundreds of bits of red composite. The exterior shell just shattered."

"Wow. Someone this morning said it was a deer."

"I don't think so," Brent answered.

"No? Bigger? What did you hit, a damn moose?" Todd kicked off his flip-flops and propped his feet up on the coffee table. "I've seen those signs up near the White Mountains, 'Brake for Moose. It could save your life.'"

"Except I live in the suburbs, and I don't think a whole lot of moose live just over the Massachusetts state line. I think someone tried to run me off the road."

"What? Are you serious?" Todd leaned forward. "What do the cops think?"

"The cops disagree. They claim I was driving over the speed limit and that I lost control of my car." He shook his head in disgust. "That is such bullshit."

"Because…" Todd prompted.

"Would you speed late at night, on a back country road with your pregnant wife in the car?"

"No, but I've seen the way you drive—"

"Amanda screamed not once, but twice," Brent continued, talking over Todd's interruption. "I distinctly remember that. The Viper was hit from behind. By something or someone. I'm sure of it." It felt good just to voice his fears out loud for the first time.

"Don't tell me you mean…"

"Yes. I think it was Intruder."

"Come on, Brent. Not this bullshit again."

"I'm telling you, he killed Randy, and now he's after me." Brent ran a hand through his hair.

Todd shook his head.

"I know you still don't believe me, but until you come up with some other explanation…" Brent replied.

Todd looked up at the clock. "Didn't you say you had a meeting with Suzette?"

"At nine. I got a couple of minutes. So do you know why I'm still employed? If Suzette really went through my hard drive, she would have found plenty of evidence of inappropriate use of company assets."

"She'd need more than that to fire you. I think she threw that at you during your meeting to try and get you to confess to something on the record. There's not a person in this company that's not guilty of using Revolution computers for personal reasons."

"Yeah, but what about the sexual harassment charge?"

"Impossible to prove. Besides, the actual email you wrote stated, 'Jana is one hot babe.' I grabbed the copy off the backup. You don't deserve to be fired for saying that. It's not like you grabbed her ass or anything."

"Still, Suzette looked like she was licking her chops for my blood that day."

"That's probably true, but your computer wasn't the only one I ran a check on." Todd grinned.

Brent stared at him. "Meaning, what?"

"Let's just say it's part of my job to make sure Mary Sunshine is aware of inappropriate computer activities. As it turned out, Suzette would have had to fire the entire executive team if she's holding everyone to the gold standard she set that day for you."

"Ahhh. Touché." Brent couldn't help chuckling. "Still, I hope you didn't do anything—"

Todd brushed off his concern with a wave of his hand. "I did my job. Nothing more, nothing less."

Brent nodded although he wondered if Todd had done more than he was admitting. "I was convinced I was a goner. I even spent some time while I was home floating my resume."

"Probably a good call. Just make sure your new employer has a position for me too when you jump. I don't think I'm Mary Sunshine's favorite employee any longer."

Brent grinned. "So we're a package deal?"

"You know it. Until then, forget about Intruder. I'm close to sending him packing. Shopping and stock trades weren't all I found on the executives computers."

"Oh, really? I found out a couple things too."

"Such as?"

"While I was home, I started looking for clues to Intruder's identity, and it appears that he uses multiple names. Maggot Meal is one of them."

"Now there's a lovely image," Todd replied.

"Clever, I guess, depending on your perspective. It appears that he's playing multiple deadpools."

"How did you figure that out?"

"Three of his same nominees come up on different deadpool games: James Smith, Juan Garcia, and Mary Jo Frizione."

"Frizione? Who the heck is that?"

"Why? You never heard of her?"

"No. Who is she?"

"No one famous. How about the other two, James Smith and Juan Garcia. Have you heard of those guys?"

"No, but come on. Those names are about as common as dirt."

"Exactly. And that's what didn't make sense to me. The nominees on my original list were actors, politicians, athletes, and supermodels, right?" Brent said.

"True," Todd replied. "From what I remember, you picked famous or at least infamous people. Didn't you put a serial killer on your list?"

"Yeah, I did, or rather Clive did. That seems to be another popular category. Famous murderers or convicted criminals."

"That makes sense."

"But there is a third category too."

"What's that?"

"Lesser-known famous people. In other words, famous people you've never heard of. Nobel prize winners, award-winning poets, chefs, local TV anchors—"

"So the question is, what constitutes fame? Just how famous do you have to be to get your name on a deadpool list."

"Exactly. I never gave those unfamiliar names on the rosters a second thought. Then yesterday I did some checking."

"And…"

"Every name on the deadpool rosters that I checked out could arguably be considered famous in some regard except…"

"Except who?"

"Me and Mary Jo Frizione. Neither of us is famous, and yet we're on Intruder's deadpool list."

"I'm not following you," Todd said.

"Remember Intruder's last message? He said he wanted me red-lined?"

"Yeah."

"If a nominee on a deadpool list is red-lined, it means they died."

"Would you spit out this grand theory already?"

"Intruder is stalking me. And probably stalking Mary Jo Frizione, whoever the hell she is. He's planning to kill both of us for the points. Just like he killed Randy for those points and then added him to his roster."

"No way." Todd dropped his feet to the floor, shaking his head. "Impossible."

"Intruder is playing two games. Kill someone and add them to the list. Add someone to the list and then kill them."

"That's ridiculous."

"Listen, I didn't believe it either at first. But think about it. It's also impossible that my car went over an embankment on a perfectly dry night. I was driving the speed limit, Todd, on a back country road which had no lights, no houses, no witnesses…"

"I can't even wrap my brain around what you're implying," Todd said, shaking his head. "Why would Intruder want to murder you? He doesn't even know you."

Brent shrugged. "Help me out then. Can you draw any other conclusion?"

Todd just stared at him.

"That's the game. Intruder is encouraging me to go after him. To kill him before he kills me."

Todd's cell phone rang, and he pulled the phone from the front pocket of his khaki pants. "What's up?"

Brent stood up, realizing he had five minutes before his meeting with Suzette.

Todd stood up as well, still holding the phone to his ear.

At the elevator, Todd said a few words, then dropped the phone back into his pocket. "Intruder messing with you is one thing, thinking he is out to kill you is quite another. That, I'm not buying."

"Still, just think about it. I'm open to other theories, but I can't think of any."

"You're obsessed."

"Maybe. You might be too if someone was out to kill you."

"Maybe you should go see a shrink. After all you've been through with the stuff at work and your father-in-law passing and now the car accident. Maybe—"

"I don't need a shrink, and I'm very appreciative of what you did to save my job," Brent said. "I mean it. I owe you." He pushed the up button.

"No, you don't." Todd pulled his drumsticks out of his pocket. This pair was wrapped in red metallic tape. He did a soft drum roll on the edge of the gilt mirror above the buttons. "How are things with the band?"

"A little tense, but okay."

"Are you still up for the Bruins game tomorrow night?"

"Third game of the playoffs, tied one game each. Do you really need to ask?"

"Excellent." Brent grinned as they entered the elevator.

"Even if it does mean going to the game with a delusional coworker."

"Now that I'm getting a salary again, I'll even buy us dinner. We can grab a bite at one of the sports bars. Anything's better than stadium food."

"I like stadium food," Todd said, pressing the button for the twenty-sixth floor.

"That figures." Brent laughed and jabbed the button to go to Human Resources.

• • •

April 8th – Friday

It was the end of Brent's second full day back at work after his reinstatement, and both had gone smoother than Brent had anticipated. The guys in the sales department had somehow, for once in their lives, managed to restrain themselves and not give him shit about his second unplanned vacation in just over a month, and his complete fall to the bottom of the sales ladder. *Nowhere to go but up.*

Brent had his badge, his cell phone back, and his laptop back. Best of all, it seemed to Brent like he'd gotten his life back. Miracle of miracles, Intruder had disappeared.

Going through the dozens of emails he'd received from the previous week, not a single one was from Intruder. Not a voicemail on his office phone. Not a computer tweet. Not a word. *Thank God.* Going to the police had scared Intruder off. Todd agreed that Intruder had left the game unfinished rather than risk getting caught. Obviously Brent's theory that Intruder planned to murder him for points had been fueled by paranoia and overwhelming stress. *Still, what caused the car accident?*

Brent shook his head. *Stop thinking about that!* The three of them had survived, that was all that mattered. With a solid marriage, a healthy baby on the way, and commission checks once again headed into his bank account, rebuilding his sales reputation was a manageable task. *Did Randy really just have a heart attack out of the blue?*

Brent felt his own heart rate bump up. *Don't think that way. Randy's death was untimely and tragic, but not suspicious.*

Brent still hated Intruder with every fiber of his being, and he'd never forget what he'd done to him. But he was trying like hell to be grateful for what he had instead of wasting time on his many regrets of the last three months. His part in the game was over and done with. He was never responding to anything from Intruder or DieorDieTrying.com as long as he lived.

Tonight was the Bruins playoff game, and Brent was more than ready to kick back and spend a relaxing evening with Todd, thankful their friendship had survived. It had been dicey there for quite a few weeks.

As he packed up for the night, ready to grab Todd and head for the game, he heard a knock on his closed office door.

"Come on in."

Clive stepped through the door, and Brent groaned inwardly. His nemesis looked more dapper than usual, which irritated Brent further still. "New suit?" Brent asked. Amanda's daily warning to be on his best behavior at all times at work flashed through his mind.

"Yup." Clive smiled and brought both hands up to tug on the lapels of the black worsted wool suit. "Not custom, but let's just say I bought from the better end of the rack this time."

Brent spotted a bright yellow mustard stain on the underside of one sleeve, and he didn't even attempt to cover the smirk that escaped. *Typical.* "What do you need?"

"You know why I'm here," Clive said.

Brent nodded. "Where are you having this high-powered meeting with Regency?" There was no need to get personal and insult the man, but no need to roll over and die for him either. "The account you stole from me, if I recall."

"I won them fair and square on a cold call, and you know it." Clive eased down onto a folding chair. "I've got an eight-thirty reservation at the Top of the Hub. That rotating restaurant at the top of the Prudential Build—"

"I know where it is," Brent snapped. "Good luck getting your expense account approved for that meal."

"I'm not worried. When they sign the contract, I'll have officially replaced you on the fast track." He chuckled. "Come to think of it, I already have."

Brent didn't bother to respond.

"Let's get to it," Clive walked over to Brent's desk. "Let me have the boards."

"What boards?"

"Don't dick around with me on this, Brent. When your precious racecar got reduced to a pile of paint chips, we agreed that you would hand over your original storyboards for Regency."

Brent gritted his teeth, wondering which weasel in the art department had told Clive about the Regency storyboards. He had made them months back, anticipating a meeting exactly like the one Clive had set up. Brent knew the CEO would be blown away by the concept. While Brent had waited patiently for the CEO to return his repeated calls, Clive had walked in off the street and snatched up the company that should have been the crown jewel on Brent's account list.

Cornered and bound to his promise, Brent reached behind his desk and picked up several oversized advertising mockups. There was no doubt in his mind this was the best concept he'd come up with in his career at Revolution. With certain termination hanging over his head, he'd agreed to give them up. Now that he had been reinstated, he hated like hell to hand them over to Clive.

Instead, he stalled. "What's your estimate on Regency's second quarter budget?"

"Seven figures, easily," Clive said rubbing his hands together. "How sweet it is."

Brent felt a stab of out-and-out jealousy.

"I'm proposing a seventh inning ad at Fenway Park on the Jumbotron," Clive continued.

"With a seven-figure budget, they can easily afford it. What else are you proposing?"

"Enough digging for scraps of information. Come on. Come on," Clive snapped his fingers. "Hand over the boards."

Brent propped the large foam-core-backed drawings up against his computer facing Clive but held onto them with a proprietary hand. "These are the final sketches, but the dialogue hasn't been incorporated. Do you want me to walk you through the concept?"

Brent watched Clive narrow his eyes and then shrug.

"Sure, but make it fast. I've only got a couple hours to finalize this dog-and-pony show for tonight."

Brent picked up the retractable pointer in his pencil jar and came around the front of the desk. He gave the presentation his all.

• • •

"Great game," Brent said as he and Todd moved with the crowd en masse down the exit ramps of the TD Garden and finally out onto the city street.

"Outstanding," Todd agreed.

Brent was swinging a plastic bag that contained a miniature Boston Bruins hockey stick, as well as a tiny sleeper with the Bruins logo. The perfect gift for Lucas. Lucas Darby was the latest name Brent had latched onto in the event Amanda gave birth to a boy. He liked the sound of it, and Lucas was a good name for a sports player. He just had to convince Amanda to let go of the name Drew. Drew, he would never forget, was the name of the youngest nominee on the DieorDieTrying.com list. It caused a shudder to run down his spine each time he heard it. Of course, if the baby was a girl, her name would be Jessica. And Jessica could still be a sports star, softball, basketball, tennis. He would be an equal rights father, boy or girl.

Everyone on the crowded sidewalk was in good spirits after the win. The majority headed for the subway station. At the top of the stairs, leading down to the North Station T stop, one of the city's trash can drummers was plying his trade. Todd was already digging in his pocket for a donation.

"He's better than you, man," Brent joked, poking his buddy in the ribs.

Todd stuffed a couple of ones into the man's tip jar. The drummer in the tattered army jacket nodded his thanks, without missing a beat.

Brent descended the stairs, and Todd swiped his subway ticket and motioned for him to go through the turnstile. As they headed toward the Orange Line, Brent's gaze was drawn to a tousle-headed boy carried by his father. The boy was wearing red sneakers, and he clenched a Bruins' pennant. The boy's eyes drooped as he rested his head on his dad's shoulder. Brent smiled, noticing the little boy's mouth was rimmed with chocolate ice cream. It reminded him that, one day soon, he'd be taking his boy to a game here too.

Anxious to make the first train and get home to Amanda, Brent motioned for Todd to follow him. He worked his way to the front of the crowded platform, ignoring the occasional dirty look, telling himself that these people didn't have a forty-five-minute drive once they got off the train. Todd was more laid back; he would have patiently waited, but Brent was a man on a mission.

He checked his watch, realizing he didn't miss this part of living in the city, waiting on trains, waiting on pedestrian crossing signals, waiting on traffic lights. He peered down the dark tunnel, and a shrill whistle sounded. He sensed the crowd behind him surge forward, anxious to board.

Brent felt a hand in the middle of his back, and he was pushed hard from behind. He gasped and threw out his arms for balance, throwing a frantic look over his shoulder to see who had pushed him. He teetered on the edge of the platform and panic rose within him as he stared into a sea of unfamiliar faces. His arms windmilled, and the plastic bag flew from Brent's grasp. Todd emerged from the crowd even as white noise filled his ears and a guttural scream escaped his lips. He clawed at empty air and then miraculously Brent found his fingers gripping the cracked leather of Todd's Red Sox jacket.

The second train whistle blew, shrieking in intensity, announcing the arrival of the train at the platform. Brent's fingers clutched Todd's jacket in a death grip, and he used every bit of strength he possessed fighting for his life.

Horror surged through Brent. He was going to die. He could see the strain on Todd's face as he fought to counterbalance their shifting weight. Todd wasn't strong enough. A split second later he found himself sprawled safely on the concrete platform as hands reached for him and bystanders came to his aid. In the crush, Brent lost sight of Todd. Then he heard a scream.

Brent scrambled toward the edge of the platform on hands and knees. "Todd!" The wind sucked at him from the oncoming train. He saw a flash of Todd's jacket before it disappeared and a splash of bright blood shot out from beneath the rails of the hissing metal car. The train came to a screeching halt and with a whoosh, the hydraulic doors of the car opened. Brent bent over the edge. The tip of a splintered drumstick spun in a lazy circle next to a widening pool of blood. He put his hands over his ears and curled up in a tight ball, Todd's scream echoing in his ears.

• • •

In the emergency waiting room of Massachusetts General Hospital, Brent sat with his elbows on his knees, his head buried in his hands. It was all he could do to remain sitting in a semblance of an upright position on the orange plastic chair. What he wanted to do was run down the hallway of the hospital, howling at the top of his lungs. He jumped when he felt a hand on his shoulder. He looked up into Amanda's face and got to his feet, sliding into her arms. He wrapped himself around her, sobbing, feeling the dam of emotions burst.

The chaos of the emergency room swarmed around them. When his sobs finally quieted and his body was no longer quaking, Amanda eased him back down onto the chair. Her hand rhythmically rubbed his back as he tried to wipe away his tears with the back of his hand.

"Is Todd in surgery?" Amanda asked.

"I don't know."

"Have you heard anything?"

Brent shook his head. Amanda kissed him gently on the lips and gave his arm a squeeze before she stood up and walked toward the nurses' station. Brent was afraid to watch. Instead, he slid down low on the seat and shut his eyes, but that only made the horrific images running around his head come into sharp focus. Clutching at empty air. Todd reaching out to help him. Blood spurting onto the wall. His eyes flew open and he started to shake. *It was his fault Todd was dead. His fault.*

Sometime later Amanda returned, touching his knee and inclining her head toward a stocky Boston transit cop making his way down the long hallway toward them. His face looked youthful, but he carried himself with authority. Brent pushed himself upright in the chair and waited for the man to speak.

The officer stopped in front of them and touched his hat, "Ma'am. Sir. Does this belong to you?" A small bag with a Bruin's logo dangled from one thick finger.

Brent nodded, feeling a fresh wave of emotion come over him.

Amanda reached up, took the bag, and set it down on the adjoining chair.

"Mr. Darby, can you tell me what happened tonight?" The officer pulled a pen and a pad of paper from his jacket pocket and flipped back the cover.

Brent cleared his throat once and then again. It didn't seem to do much good. He felt like he had a golf ball lodged inside his throat. Amanda reached over and interlaced her fingers with his.

At that moment a female doctor with red frizzy hair turned the corner and came through the double doors. "Darby? Brent Darby?"

"Yes." Brent's voice came out in a croak. He rose from his chair, a bit unsteady. Amanda stood as well and put her arm around his waist. Out of his peripheral vision, Brent noticed the police officer walk to the other side of the waiting room and remove his hat.

"If you'll follow me, please," the redheaded doctor said.

Brent felt a surge of hope. They were being taken to see Todd. *He was okay.*

The woman took them back through the set of swinging doors and then motioned for them to proceed into a tiny room. Amanda held his hand in a tight grip. "How is he…" Brent asked. The woman motioned for them to sit down, but Brent shook his head.

"I am the emergency room doctor who cared for Mr. Tanklefsky when he was brought in. I understand he has no living relatives?"

"No," Brent said. *These questions were just routine formalities. Once he answered them, he would be brought to Todd's bedside.* "He was brought up by a foster family. An older couple. They passed away a few years ago."

"No brothers or sisters?"

"No. He is an only child."

The doctor nodded. "You are listed as the emergency contact in his wallet. Are you sure you wouldn't like to sit down?"

Brent shook his head. Everything seemed surreal. "When can I see him?"

The doctor shook her head, meeting his gaze.

All at once he read the answer in the doctor's eyes, in her body language. What he'd known before he left the subway station. What he'd known as soon as he peered over the wall. He couldn't breathe.

"I'm sorry to tell you that Mr. Tanklefsky was pronounced dead at the scene due to massive internal injuries." She spoke so softly that Brent had to lean forward to catch her words. "Every protocol was followed, but given the extent of the injuries, we were unable to save your friend."

A strangled sound escaped Brent's lips, and he felt lightheaded. His knees buckled, and he felt the doctor reach out and grab his arm. He collapsed into a chair, and Amanda knelt down on the floor beside him.

He heard the doctor speak somewhere above him, her voice distant. "I'm terribly sorry for your loss."

Chapter 9

April 25th – Monday

Brent sat in his office chair, watching the sun glint off the windows of the skyscrapers across the city. It was his second day back in the office, and he would be the first to admit he hadn't accomplished a single thing at Revolution since he'd been back. But aside from physically sitting in his office, he wasn't willing to ask too much more of himself. Two weeks ago purchase orders, client meetings, and design jobs requiring twenty-four-hour turnaround had seemed critical. Now everything was pointless. Todd's death had left him rudderless and incapable of making even the smallest of decisions.

He'd taken a week of personal time and then called in sick every day for a week. Only an internal job posting online for a new systems administrator had propelled him back into the office. Mary Sunshine certainly wasn't wasting any time trying to find Todd's replacement. He looked at his watch, not surprised to see that he had once again idled away most of the morning staring out the window.

Yesterday he'd hid out in his office with the door shut and the light off. No one even knew he was in the building. Today, however, word had gotten out, and people had been dropping by his office, offering their condolences. Finally, just to get a moment's relief, he had escaped to Todd's cubicle. A stack of empty boxes were piled haphazardly on Todd's chair. Someone was preparing to clean house. The thought of someone going through Todd's personal effects made Brent uncomfortable.

He picked up an eraser and read the lame knock-knock joke in Todd's familiar looping cursive on the whiteboard before wiping it clean. Gingerly stepping between Ethernet cards, hard drives, and over a mountain of shrink-wrapped computer manuals, he picked up the smallest empty box. With one arm he swept Todd's stash of toys and personal items off the cubicle shelf and into the box. Next, Brent riffled through the desk drawers, unearthing two pairs of drumsticks and Todd's favorite Scooby-Doo coffee mug. About to switch off the desk light, he caught a glimpse of the bulletin board. A calendar, Twelve Ugly Cats, hung from a mangled paperclip, beside a dozen or so photographs. He unhooked the calendar and removed the photos, chucking each colored pushpin into Todd's wastebasket, breathing through the guilt that threatened to overwhelm him from all sides.

It took only minutes, and Todd's office, stripped of personal belongings, became just another sterile workspace. Brent vowed never to enter this particular cubicle ever again.

Back in his own office, Brent stood picking through the box he'd just carried down the hall. He pulled out Todd's glow-in-the-dark football, remembering a late night game of cubicle football they'd played. Picking up the dead ivy plant that was sitting inside his Golden Bra Award, he stuck the football in its place.

Next he pawed through the top layer of toys in the box and pulled out Todd's favorite Barney Rubble Pez dispenser and his Magic 8 Ball. He set them both on the shelf and continued to rummage through the remaining items. There were simply too many to keep in his office. The rest would have to go home: the Rubik's Cube, the bendable rubber Gumby toy, and of course, his entire collection of snow globes. The guy was a classic; there was no doubt about it.

At the very bottom of the box was the pair of Emei piercers Todd had waved around like a crazed samurai just two months ago. Brent remembered Todd saying they were valuable, a gift from Todd's foster father, but they were also dangerous. Amanda wouldn't want them at home with a baby in the house, but not knowing what else to do with them, he left them in the box and threw a purple Barney dinosaur and an Etch A Sketch on top until the weapons were hidden from view.

"Morning."

Brent looked up as Clive walked through his office door.

"I wanted to stop by and pass on my sympathy about Todd's passing." Clive turned and swung shut Brent's office door. "He was a good guy. Julia and I were real sorry we couldn't make the funeral."

Brent nodded once. "Thanks."

"He was a standup guy," Clive said.

For some reason, that simple honest statement coming from a slimeball like Clive disturbed him. "Yes, Todd was a standup guy, not that you'd know what that feels like. And now that you've said your heartfelt condolences, you can get out. And tomorrow, I better not find your piece-of-shit car in my parking space." Brent sat down in his chair and began fiddling with his computer mouse, ignoring Clive.

Clive chuckled. "It's only a matter of time, my friend, until that parking space is reassigned to me. But obviously we're through with the pleasantries, so let's get down to business, shall we?" Clive dropped down onto the chair in front of Brent's desk.

"And what business could that possibly be?" He watched a muscle tick in Clive's cheek.

"I may not be a standup guy, but don't pretend that you are either." He tipped his chair back. "You set me up," Clive responded.

A glimmer of amusement made its way through Brent's sadness. He knew exactly what Clive meant, but it was more fun to play along. "Set you up? I'm afraid I don't follow. Please, enlighten me."

"Regency."

"What about them?" Brent bit back a smile. Todd would be proud that Mr. Game Player Extraordinaire was back.

"You know exactly what I mean." A deep, red flush crept up Clive's neck.

"You're right. You were outplayed." It was nice to know he'd finally found a way to get under Clive's skin.

"Nice trick, giving me the Regency storyboards but feeding me total bullshit about the concept."

"Yup. Did you really think I was going to let you just screw me over like that?"

Clive stood up and walked to the edge of Brent's desk. "You made me look like an ass in front of Regency's board of directors."

"Yeah? Well, I'm sure it's not the first time."

"Fuck you."

"You tried that, and it didn't work. Now, I'll tell you how this is going to play out." Brent felt emotion course through him for the first time since Todd's death. Selling was selling, and whether it was diamonds, ad space, or bullshit, you had to close the deal in order to get the sale.

"I sent Ed a memo, and I copied Phil," Brent continued. "The two of them know that we worked hand in hand on this deal. So, you've got two choices. Either you run to Ed and admit you stole the storyboards, knowing I've got stacks of proof it was my original idea and the word of the guys in the art department, or we split the account fifty-fifty. Your call." Brent watched splotches of color creep further up Clive's neck until even his ears had turned dark crimson.

"You conniving bastard," Clive said, leaning toward him.

"Takes one to know one." Brent pushed back in his chair and interlaced his fingers behind his head. He was through being screwed. By Clive. By Mary Sunshine. By Intruder. By everyone.

"It's not going to do you a hell of a lot of good to get half the account if you're no longer employed by Revolution," Clive shot back. "Somehow you've managed to bullshit your way through so far, but your luck cannot last, especially now that your buddy, Todd, isn't here to watch your back. I know a few of your secrets, and I'm sure personnel would love to hear about them. I'm confident I can provide the final nail in your coffin."

Brent swallowed, wondering who was bullshitting whom. "I already came clean with personnel," he bluffed, thinking back to when he'd asked Todd to check out Clive's system to see if he could possibly be Intruder. *But how would Clive know about that?* "I'm totally in the clear."

"If you say so," Clive leaned over the desk. "Still, I'll just confirm it with Suzette all the same."

"Suit yourself." Brent snapped forward in his chair, getting right into Clive's face.

"Mark my words, you're going down."

"If so, then you're going down right alongside me."

Clive laughed. "Well, I'd say the odds are in my favor. You're going to wind up DOA, just like your buddy. If I'd had Todd on my deadpool list, I would've gotten enough points—"

Before Clive finished the sentence, Brent was on his feet. He stepped around the desk and slammed his fist into Clive's face. Blood spurted from Clive's nose. "You son-of-a-bitch!"

Clive held both hands over his nose, trying to stem the flow of bright red blood leaking through his fingers.

"Get out!" Brent shouted. He grabbed the doorknob, wrenched it open, and shoved Clive into the hall with both hands.

Clive dropped his hands, allowing blood to drip onto the carpet. "Game, set, and match," he whispered to Brent. "You just sealed your own fate."

Employees began to stream out of their cubicles to see what was going on. Brent kicked his office door shut on the shocked faces of the employees gathered around Clive.

• • •

Amanda put the piece of charcoal down on the table next to the easel and sighed. She was really worried about Brent, and whenever she had something weighing on her mind, she couldn't draw. Since Todd's death, her husband had changed into someone she barely recognized.

Amanda slipped off the stool in front of the easel and brushed the charcoal dust from her hands. She knelt down next to the couch and felt underneath with her fingers until she found what she was looking for: a thin book entitled, *The Grieving Process.* She settled onto the couch and flipped it open to the bookmarked page, a chapter entitled "Stages of Loss."

It was clear that Brent blamed himself for Todd's accident. Amanda had suggested counseling, but Brent had simply shaken his head. According to the book, Brent had moved from the anger phase into the guilt phase. This second step was often the hardest part, and the best thing for friends and family to do was to listen and be supportive.

The phone rang, and Amanda replaced the bookmark and picked up the receiver.

"Hello?"

"Is Brent Darby available?"

"No. May I ask who's calling, please?"

"Mike Corrigan. I'm an old college friend. I tried him at the office, but I got voicemail."

"No surprise there. So you and Brent went to college together?"

"Yes. Although I haven't seen him since I took a job on the West Coast after graduation. I've heard through the grapevine that he's done quite well for himself in Beantown."

"Yes. That's true." Amanda felt a quick rush of pride.

"Anyway, I didn't mean to trouble you. I knew it was a pretty slim shot to find him at home."

"I'd be happy to tell him you called. Mike, right?"

"Mike Corrigan. We were fraternity brothers. Alpha Pi. The stories I could tell…" He let out a warm laugh. "We had some good times. Anyway, my conference ends this afternoon. I can't wait to get home to my wife. I fly back tonight on the redeye. I was just at loose ends this evening, and I thought the two of us could grab a bite."

Fraternity brothers. Amanda turned the book over in her hands. "I've got an idea. Is there any chance you could join us for a home-cooked meal?"

"I wouldn't want to impose..."

"I don't think inviting a fraternity brother for dinner would be imposing. You guys probably took a sacred oath to each other, right?"

"Something like that, although I think it had more to do with beer than religion. We do have a secret handshake through."

"You're kidding, right?" Amanda asked.

"Nope. If you're sure about the invitation, I'd be happy to accept."

"Great. Say, six-thirty?

"Sounds wonderful. Hey, how about we keep my visit a surprise? Fraternities are all about pulling a good prank. It'll be fun to pull one over on Brent. I can guarantee he'll be surprised when I walk in the door and don't forget to keep an eye out for the handshake."

Amanda proceeded to give Mike directions, and then she hung up with a smile, looking forward to the evening ahead. *A secret handshake? Was he kidding?* She liked the idea of meeting an old college friend of Brent's, and Mike had been so easy to talk to on the phone.

She walked into the den to pull out Brent's senior yearbook from college and look up Mike, but when she stepped into the hall, she remembered all their hardback books were still packed in boxes in the basement. The baby kicked in her belly, and all at once it seemed silly to go to all the trouble of dragging out a dusty college yearbook. Instead, she returned to the couch and placed both hands on her belly, trying to determine which bumps might be knees and which might be elbows.

When the baby quieted down, Amanda opened the book to the page with her bookmark, and a sidebar caught her eye. The first bullet point was that the grieving process was different for each person. The second indicated that the process simply could not be rushed.

Amanda hoped that maybe an old friend was just what Brent needed. She was glad she'd impulsively invited Brent's fraternity brother to the house for dinner. She didn't want to get her hopes up, but even if Mike could get Brent to laugh a couple times tonight, she would consider the evening a raging success.

The mantle clock struck the half hour, and Amanda set aside the book and headed into the hall to grab her purse. She was excited to be past the halfway point of her pregnancy. She felt good, not quite so tired anymore. Checking the clock, Amanda realized she had just enough time to hit the grocery store before her OB-GYN appointment that afternoon. Tonight she'd make a real guy's dinner: steak, baked potatoes, and Caesar salad. Just to make it a celebration, she'd stop at the bakery and get a cherry pie for dessert.

• • •

As the red haze of his anger dissipated, Brent leaned against the wall, feeling shaky. He was holding his right hand, which still hurt like hell from the blow he'd delivered to Clive's face. He didn't regret punching Clive. The weasel deserved far worse than just a bloody nose for disrespecting Todd less than two weeks after the funeral.

Brent stood up, knowing that security guards would barge into his office any minute. He'd assaulted a fellow employee, and he wasn't foolish enough to think that he'd be given another chance. This time he knew he was out for good. Fired.

He surveyed the contents of his office and gave himself thirty seconds to get out of the building. He yanked open his top desk drawer and flung a set of backup disks into his briefcase. Next he tossed in his favorite framed photograph of Amanda, where it landed with a clank on top of the jewel cases. He slammed the lid and latched it, then tossed the briefcase on top of the box of Todd's personal effects sitting on the corner of his desk.

He cracked open his office door, looking both right and left, surprised to see the halls were empty except for a lone secretary crossing the aisle between the cubicles and carrying a vase of yellow daffodils. Brent glanced at the clock on the wall; he'd caught a break. The entire department was in Ed's mandatory eleven o'clock sales meeting.

A knot formed in Brent's stomach as he hurried down the hall, feeling like a fugitive. The realization of what he'd done struck him. He could wind up in jail for what he'd done. *Oh my God!* Head down, Brent wound his way through a series of cubicles, forcing himself to walk, even though he desperately wanted to break into an outright sprint.

Both armpits were drenched by the time Brent got through cube city. He headed for the stairwell door and the fire exit. Just a few feet shy of the stairs, he heard his name. He stopped short before passing the open doorway.

"No, I haven't seen him," a male voice replied.

The nape of his neck tingled, and he ducked down so that his head was lower than the partition wall.

"Sure. I'll keep an eye out."

Brent forced himself to move. *Ten steps to go. Nine.* Barely breathing, Brent ran past the open cubicle and pressed his back up against the aluminum bar on the fire door, opening it only as wide as necessary to slip through. Inside the stairwell, he caught the door with his foot to prevent the heavy door from clanging shut.

His arms ached from carrying the box, but he refused to leave behind Todd's treasures. Instead, Brent set off down twenty-six flights of stairs.

On the landing, three flights down, Brent was breathing hard, and his calves burned from trying to dash down the stairs on the balls of his feet to prevent his escape from being broadcast throughout the stairwell of the entire building. By the time he made it all the way down to the ground level of the parking garage, perspiration was dripping from his face, and he felt like he'd been carrying a pallet of bricks.

In the parking garage, Brent crept around the corner, expecting a barrage of security officers to have his car surrounded. Then he realized no one would tie him to the illegally parked orange rental car. Throwing caution aside, Brent ran full out to the Chevy, opened the driver's door, and heaved the box across the interior onto the passenger seat. Shoving the key in the ignition, Brent revved the engine and backed out, tires squealing.

• • •

Dressed and waiting for the doctor to return after her exam, Amanda studied the birthing poster on the wall, wondering what was taking so long. She'd dropped off groceries at the house prior to the OB-GYN appointment, and she hadn't had time to put them all away. She stood second-guessing whether she'd left the ice cream out on the counter.

Dr. Shelby returned, but this time, his expression was all business. Amanda's mouth went dry. Something was wrong. She couldn't draw her eyes away from the doctor's serious expression. "What is it?" she asked, her heart pounding. "Is something wrong?" Instinctively her hands came to rest on her protruding belly.

"Amanda, you've developed a condition called preeclampsia," Dr. Shelby said. "Your blood pressure is elevated, although not alarmingly so, and your urine came back with protein in it."

"And the baby? What does it mean for the baby?"

"Preeclampsia occurs in about six percent of all pregnancies, however, no cure exists," Dr. Shelby replied. "But there are measures you can take to reduce the risks."

"What does that entail?" Amanda asked. She felt chilled, and a shiver ran through her body.

"First off, I'm going to put you on a blood pressure reducing medication. Second, I would like you to decrease your salt intake and increase your fluids, especially water. Third, and most important, I would like to put you on bed rest."

"Bed rest?" Amanda repeated, surprised. "I thought that was an old wives' tale."

"No. A number of studies have concluded that bed rest might prevent your condition from becoming more serious. I'd like you to lie down as many hours during the day as is practical, on your left side especially. This position will help reduce edema, or swelling, and also help to lower your blood pressure by increasing urinary output."

"How long?" Amanda asked, knowing that it didn't matter and she'd do anything to protect her baby. "I'm not even in my third trimester yet."

"That's the difficulty. I'd suggest bed rest for the remainder of your pregnancy.

"Will this condition harm my baby?" Amanda asked. She nervously chewed on her lower lip.

"Not if we can keep the symptoms mild. You should be able to have a perfectly normal, full-term birth."

"And if not?" Amanda couldn't help from blurting out her greatest fear.

"If your blood pressure continues to climb and the protein in the urine increases, I would consider hospitalization, but that is quite uncommon. I expect things to stabilize at home within a fairly short time. This booklet will give you more information." He handed a pamphlet to Amanda. "Again, complications are rare."

Amanda looked at the cover, which was entitled "High Risk Pregnancies." She flipped the first few pages and paused on a list of possible symptoms: spots in front of the eyes, bleeding gums, severe abdominal pain, seizures. She let out a small gasp. By the time she read the last item on the list, decreased movement of the fetus, a lump was wedged in her throat, making speech impossible.

"I know this is upsetting, Amanda," Dr. Shelby said. "But remember, you have a very mild case."

Amanda blinked back tears.

The doctor scribbled on his prescription pad, then ripped off the top sheet and handed it to her. "Do you have any questions?"

Amanda shook her head.

"Studies have indicated that stress may be a mitigating factor in this disease. I know it's difficult, but try not to get too overwrought. The best thing for you and your baby may be to maintain a positive attitude and give full consideration to the bed rest I'm recommending."

Amanda nodded.

"Feel free to call the office with any questions," the doctor said. "I'll see you next week."

The minute the door closed, Amanda burst into tears.

• • •

On the entrance ramp to the highway, the rental car almost spun out as the wheels hydroplaned on the rain-slick road. Brent regained control and struggled to come up with the words to explain to Amanda that he was out of a job, this time for good. Tomorrow was Amanda's birthday, not a great time for a confession. Would she stand by him? He honestly didn't know.

Brent hit the button for the garage door, surprised to see the Jeep was gone. He grabbed his briefcase and the box of personal items he'd taken from Todd's office and headed inside.

He deposited his briefcase on the kitchen counter before opening the basement door and heading down the steps. In the center of the unfinished basement, near the alcove under the stairs, Brent set the heavy box down and shoved it up against a half dozen other unpacked moving boxes.

As he jogged back upstairs, the garage door rumbled, and Brent felt his stomach flip-flop. It was time to face Amanda. He swallowed as he opened the door between the kitchen and the garage. The next thing he knew, Amanda had flung herself—sobbing—into his arms.

"Amanda, what's wrong?" he said. He wrapped her in his arms, her tear-stained face eclipsed all thoughts from his head.

Brent led her to the couch and listened as Amanda recounted what the doctor had said. He held her hand and stroked her back, trying to comfort her even as his own fears mounted as she described the possible risks.

The words Amanda repeated verbatim from the doctor, "stress may be a mitigating factor," reverberated through Brent's head. How ironic that her newly diagnosed medical condition now dictated that he keep silent about losing his job.

The enormity of his situation made Brent feel as if a vice were clamped around his airway. He felt light-headed, and he tried to use the breathing exercises he and Amanda had practiced together in their childbirth class. It didn't help. Two more lives, that of Amanda and the baby, now hung in the balance. Their survival possibly dependent on his ability to keep up a charade that all was well. Brent felt as though all the oxygen had been sucked from the room. Amanda sagged against him, taking shaky breaths, while he leaned his head back against the couch and stared up at the ceiling.

His thoughts churned in a hundred different directions. It took him a long time to realize she'd fallen asleep. Being almost six months pregnant and overwrought with fear for her unborn child had no doubt drained all of Amanda's reserves.

He eased out from beneath her and gently slid her down until her head was resting on a pillow on the arm of the couch. He covered Amanda with the throw and headed for the den.

Maybe he couldn't come clean with Amanda, but it was time to confess everything to the cops. Intruder had killed Todd. This time, he'd bring evidence.

He walked into the den and wiggled the mouse. After printing out everything he had about Intruder, a rather meager stack of pages, Brent turned to leave when he heard a familiar sound from the computer. He turned slowly around and stared at the Twitter box on the screen.

> Intruder: BRENT, GOOD
> AFTERNOON.

Rage blossomed in his chest. Brent fell into his desk chair; the pages he'd just printed fluttered to the floor. He typed as fast as he could.

> Pawn694: You murdering
> bastard!
> Intruder: IT WAS AN
> ACCIDENT.

Brent felt the blood rush to his face as he fantasized about using his bare hands to rip chunks of flesh from his faceless tormentor and reduce him to a bloody mass. Todd's voice suddenly rang out in Brent's mind as clear as if his best friend were standing in the room: "The worst sin for a hacker is to leave fingerprints."

If he could capture the conversation and force Intruder to admit what he'd done, the police would have a double murder investigation on their hands. In his mind, Brent heard Todd remind him to ask open-ended questions. He typed the first thing that came into his head.

> Pawn694: Who`s next on
> your list?
> Intruder: I THINK WE
> BOTH KNOW THE ANSWER
> TO THAT.
> Pawn694: How many
> people have you

```
murdered?
Intruder: YOU`RE THE
ONE THAT SENT TODD
OVER THE EDGE. NOT ME.
```

Brent read the words and steeled himself not to lose focus. That was what Intruder wanted. Instead, he clenched his teeth and typed his response.

```
Pawn694: Only after
your attempt to push
me onto the tracks
failed.
Intruder: IF I DON`T
TALK TO YOU AGAIN
BEFORE TOMORROW,
PLEASE WISH AMANDA
HAPPY BIRTHDAY FOR ME.
OH, BY THE WAY…YOU`VE
GOT MAIL.
```

Brent silently squeezed his hands into fists. Intruder had been online less than a minute. He hadn't gotten much, but he hoped it would be enough. Still shaking with rage, Brent printed out the conversation and picked up the scattered pages.

In the course of just a few months, Intruder and DieorDieTrying.com had robbed Brent of just about everything in his life. He closed his eyes, going over the staggering list: his best friend, his father-in-law, his job, the Viper. On top of that, he had lost his confidence, his pride, and his ethics. He'd lost it all. Or almost. The only exception was Amanda, their unborn child, and their marriage. Now, all three seemed they might just as easily slip away.

Brent opened his eyes and forced himself to look back at

the screen. The last sentence seemed to vibrate in front of his eyes.

YOU`VE GOT MAIL.

He pressed his fingers to the sides of his temple forcing himself to concentrate. Intruder was back in his life, and it was game on again. If the cops had any chance at finding this guy, Brent needed to provide them with as much information as he could. With a sigh of despair, Brent set aside the pile of papers and opened Intruder's newest email. It contained a link to a site named MaggotMeal.com.

Brent typed in the address as he wondered just how many different deadpools were on the Internet and how many players were reading the obituaries every day with glee. It gave him a sick feeling in his stomach, but he clenched his teeth and clicked on the link.

On the home page, a bony skeleton hand held a large serrated hunting knife and stabbed a lifelike human heart repeatedly as blood spurted in all directions.

This deadpool obviously catered to hardcore violence lovers. Brent shook his head in revulsion. This site seemed to have everything: grisly crime scene photos, close-ups of actual corpses, plus a graphic account of seemingly every famous murder in history. Everything about it made Brent's skin crawl.

Brent found the nominees by clicking on the button Hope You Die Today. The game seemed almost identical in structure to the other deadpools Intruder was playing. Brent knew they included BaggednTagged.com and CadaversCrypt.com.

With immense distaste, Brent began scrolling through the list, trying to avoid looking too closely at the endless QuickTime movies that popped up, claiming to show actual murders caught on tape.

Anxious to be off the site, Brent used the find feature to look for Darby. Sure enough, the search came back immediately, with his name highlighted. He'd read his name on three deadpools already, so he felt no additional sense of panic. *Three deadpools or four, did another one really matter?*

Uncomfortable with the fact that Intruder had mentioned Amanda's birthday tomorrow, Brent clicked back on the Twitter feed, hoping for a clue. The few sentences weren't much to go on, but as he reread the tweets, another thought struck him. In a previous tweet, Intruder had listed one of the baby names he and Amanda were considering. *How was that possible?*

Brent stared at his outdated computer system, and suddenly all the pieces seemed to fall into place. Intruder had accessed Brent's electronic mail to get into the Revolution computer system. His computer system, which had no firewall, had been Intruder's access point. And because Brent used this computer to log into Revolution, Intruder too had been able to overtake Brent's unsecured home terminal and tap into Revolution undetected anytime. Goosebumps ran up his arms.

Brent logged off the Internet, shut down the computer, and grabbed the stack of printouts. He had to act now.

In the family room, he checked on Amanda. She was still asleep. He wrote her a quick note and then unplugged every phone in the house, even going as far as to power off Amanda's cell phone and put it upstairs in their bedroom. He would only be gone thirty minutes at the very most.

Car keys in hand and clutching the sheath of papers, Brent headed into the garage. He would explain everything to the police and turn over the evidence. Then he would get Amanda someplace safe tonight. He'd tell her that they were spending her birthday at her mom's.

It was time to put this nightmare behind them.

• • •

The doorbell rang, and Amanda jolted out of a deep sleep. She sat up and rubbed her stiff neck, noticing a Post-It note stuck to the coffee table.

Brent had gone out to grab takeout. The doorbell rang again. She was halfway down the hall before she remembered her newly diagnosed preeclampsia. In a hurry to return to the couch, Amanda twisted the deadbolt at the same time she glanced through the sidelight.

A man holding a bottle of wine and a wrapped package smiled at her. Belatedly, she remembered inviting Mike, Brent's college fraternity brother, for dinner. Amanda sighed and opened the door, an apology for having to cancel dinner on her lips.

• • •

Brent sat in disbelief, having just been dismissed by the young Garnet police officer. "What do you mean, you'll call me?"

"The department will review the information. We'll be in touch." The officer stood up and held out his hand.

"This Internet hacker is getting away with murder!" Brent said, aware that he was shouting. "I want you to do something!" He stood up so suddenly that his chair toppled over.

The officer dropped his hand. "Mr. Darby, I know you want an immediate arrest, but you said yourself you don't know the identity of this person you call Intruder, where he lives, or even what he looks like. Rest assured that we will contact the Boston authorities and follow up on the information you've given us. As far as tonight, we've agreed to have an officer do a few extra patrols by your house—"

"I told you, I'm taking my wife up to her mother's for a while. I don't think you understand the seriousness of this."

"I will personally speak to the chief about this the first thing tomorrow," the policeman said.

Brent bent over and righted the folding chair, feeling the fight go out of him. "I'm sorry. It's been a hell of a month."

"Perfectly understandable."

"You can reach me on my cell phone." As the words left his mouth, he wondered when Revolution would deactivate the phone. It was a company phone, after all. "Please don't call my home phone. My wife…" he trailed off, realizing how complicated it would be to explain his wife's recent medical diagnosis. "It's complicated," he finished, knowing how lame that excuse sounded.

The officer nodded. "I understand. Rest assured, I am taking your allegations very seriously. Thank you for coming in."

Brent drove home, holding the cell phone in his hand. No doubt they would cut off his service tonight or tomorrow. He was a couple streets from home when the phone vibrated, signaling the receipt of a text message. He flipped it open with one hand.

BRENT, GOOD AFTERNOON.

Brent almost drove off the road, wishing he was still at the police station. He read the second line.

THE GAME HAS CHANGED.

· · ·

"You must be Mike," Amanda said to the man standing on the porch. Her mind was still a bit fuzzy with sleep. "I'm afraid—"

"Nice to meet you, Amanda," the man interrupted. He stepped over the threshold and leaned toward her, brushing her check with a kiss.

Now wide awake, Amanda took a step back, shocked by the man's familiarity, not to mention the fact that he had just walked into her house before she'd invited him inside.

He turned away from her and closed the front door. "I can't tell you how much I've been looking forward to tonight." He turned back around to face her. "Thank you for saving me from another fast-food meal."

The cancellation of tonight's dinner plans stuck in Amanda's throat. "I'm glad you could come." Once Brent got home, she would plead a headache and slip off to bed. That would give the two of them the opportunity to eat and talk, and she would do as the doctor ordered and lie back down.

He extended the bottle of wine. "I hope red is all right. Shall we open the bottle and let it breathe?"

Her upbringing kicked in, and Amanda accepted the bottle. "How nice of you." She turned and led the way into the kitchen, wishing Brent would get home. Pulling a corkscrew from the drawer, Amanda turned around and barely suppressed a gasp. Mike stood inches from her.

"A 2002 Hewitt Vineyard Rutherford Cabernet Sauvignon." He held out his hand for the corkscrew. "A very good year."

Amanda relinquished the corkscrew and backed away from her guest, following the curve of the counter until she stood with the width of the granite counter between them. She pushed one wineglass toward him with a slightly shaky hand. *Hadn't he said on the phone that he was married?*

"No wine for you?"

She shook her head, then seeking to reassure herself, gazed at his left hand. No wedding band. He was tall and broad shouldered, with rimless glasses that balanced out a cherubic smile and very white teeth.

"Thank you again for the wine," Amanda said in an attempt to push aside her unease. *Men with ulterior motives did not come bearing expensive wine and wrapped packages.* "Brent should be home any minute."

"Indeed." With his index finger, Mike pushed his glasses up on his nose. "I spend so much time in hotels that a home-cooked meal is a rare treat."

"Brent is the cook in this house. He'll fire up the grill as soon as he gets home." *Not all married men wore wedding rings.* She pulled the steaks from the refrigerator and set the package on the breakfast bar next to the bottle of wine. As she drew back her hand, Mike grasped her fingers.

"Hopefully his taste in food is as splendid as his taste in women." He kissed her fingers.

Amanda snatched her hand away. "Stop it, Mike. You're making me uncomfortable."

"Oh, really? And I haven't even yet begun."

Amanda's hands began to shake in earnest. She prayed for the rumble of the garage door.

• • •

Brent was so unnerved by the words on the screen that he pulled off the side of the road and shoved the Chevy into park. Immediately, his phone vibrated again. This time it wasn't a text message, or even a voicemail. Intruder had sent him a video.

Brent sat in stunned silence, eyes glued to the tiny screen.

Brent watched the jerky movements as the sender held the phone in front of a computer. A skeleton hand began stabbing a heart with the razor knife. Brent instantly recognized the MaggotMeal.com deadpool site. The video then zoomed in on the payout date. April 30th. Five days away. Next the camera zoomed in on the nominee list, and he saw the name Darby. "I know, I know," he said out loud in the car, impatient for whatever clue Intruder was willing to provide him. "What's the point of putting me on yet another deadpool list?"

The camera panned over to the next column. First name… "Oh my God! No!"

Brent stared in utter disbelief. The newest addition to the MaggotMeal.com deadpool list was Amanda.

• • •

Amanda was pushed down onto the couch, none too gently, by the man she'd invited to dinner.

"When are you due?" he asked pleasantly.

"Less than four months." Amanda was barely able to get the words out between her chattering of her teeth. She sat rigid, as close to the arm of the couch as she could, but Mike's thigh brushed her own, and she suppressed a moan. There was no other way to interpret this man's actions. He was vile and horrible. Amanda cast a glance toward the front door. *Could she make a run for it?*

Mike handed her the wrapped package he'd brought. "For the baby," he said.

Amanda tried to hide her growing panic. "How did you know I was pregnant?" Mike patted her knee, sending a wave of revulsion through her.

"I know everything about you and your husband."

"But why…" she left the sentence unfinished. So many questions were racing around her head that she wasn't even sure which one to ask. Or if she really wanted to know the answers.

Mike nodded toward the box on her lap. It was a typical department store gift box for a shirt or a sweater. "Open it." Mike pushed his glasses up again.

Alarm bells clanged in her head. His black hair, slick with gel, stuck up all over his head in sharp, little tufts. A bracelet poked out from underneath the cuff of his shirt. This man was too young to be in Brent's class at college.

"Open it," he demanded. The friendly tone he'd used earlier had disappeared.

Amanda tried to stall for time. "Shouldn't we wait for Brent?"

"We need to get started," Mike replied.

Amanda's mouth turned to sawdust, and her heart hammered in her chest. She nodded her head, pretending she hadn't heard the threat behind his words. Mike rested one hand casually on the back of the couch behind her head. Close enough, Amanda realized, to grab her if she tried to leap off the couch.

"Do it," Mike said, tapping on the box on her lap with his right hand. This time it was a command.

Her gaze was drawn to his bicep which seemed to bulge from beneath his shirt.

"The next time you need a reminder, you won't like the consequences."

With trembling fingers, Amanda removed the gift wrap and lifted the top off the box. The contents were concealed beneath a layer of white tissue paper.

"Any guesses?" Mike asked.

Amanda shook her head, staring at him.

"Oh, by the way, you can call me Intruder. That's my official name in this capacity." Mike took the box top from Amanda's hands and set it on the coffee table. He dropped his left hand down onto her shoulder. A warning. The danger was now palpable.

"What is it you want?" Amanda asked as she pulled back the white tissue. "We can give you money and—" The rest of the sentence died in her throat as she stared at the items nestled together inside the box: a gun, a coil of rope, duct tape, a pair of scissors, and a Ziploc bag full of medical supplies.

• • •

Brent floored the rental car, and the back wheels spun in gravel before they gained traction and the car bumped up onto the pavement of the narrow two-lane road. Only a few streets from home, Brent made a right-hand turn. The tires squealed, and he glanced over at the passenger seat just in time to see his phone slide off the seat and disappear between the passenger door and seat. "Damn it!" Brent yelled, smacking the steering wheel. He had to stop making mistakes. The last one had cost Todd his life.

With the accelerator jammed to the floor, Brent knew he had to get his wife to safety. *Just one more day of secrets.* Tomorrow, once both the New Hampshire and Massachusetts police were involved in the manhunt for Intruder, he could confess all, but only under a doctor's supervision, where Amanda and the baby would be safe.

Brent overshot his own driveway and drove up over the lawn, barely missing a row of hedges. He hit the garage door opener and began driving inside the garage before the double-wide door was even half open.

Brent threw the car into park before the car had stopped its forward motion, and it lurched forward. He threw himself across the seat and retrieved the phone before he flung open the door and sprinted across the garage. His dress shoes skidded on a winter's worth of road salt and sand. He said a prayer as he grasped the cold metal doorknob and bolted into the house.

"Amanda?" he bellowed, as he tore from the hallway into the kitchen. He anticipated sweeping her up into his arms and never letting her go. "Amanda?" he yelled again. "I've got a surprise!" He had to play this cool. He headed into the family room "We're going to your mom's for—" Brent froze in his tracks. The words on his lips evaporated.

Chapter 10

"Brent, it's nice to see you again," Intruder said.

Brent came to a dead stop just inside the family room. He stared at the young man wearing surgical gloves and pointing a gun at him from across the room.

Intruder walked toward him and plucked the cell phone from Brent's hand. "Remember? Your friend Clive introduced us at the club, and we spoke, albeit briefly."

"So Clive is involved in your sick game too?"

"Clive has a bit of a gambling problem which I used to my advantage. Let's just say in exchange for certain information, I agreed to boost Clive's points in the game."

"Where's Amanda?" Brent tore his eyes away from Intruder long enough to make a sweeping glance around the kitchen and family room. Both were empty. Fear constricted his throat.

"You'll have to guess," Intruder said. "After all, it is a game. By the way, Amanda is under the impression that my name is Mike Corrigan."

"As in the Mike Corrigan, I went to college with?" Brent asked.

"Right. That's how I introduced myself on the phone. She wouldn't have invited a complete stranger to dinner now, would she?" Intruder winked.

It took a minute for Intruder's words to sink in. "Amanda thought you were a college friend of mine."

"Yes. We agreed to keep my visit a surprise. And I see she kept her end of the bargain. I used the Internet to locate one of your fraternity brothers. I had to be careful, just in case she actually checked the name. It had to be a friend, but not a close friend."

Brent was speechless. Just then Brent's cell phone rang in Intruder's hand.

"Interesting," Intruder said, staring at the display. He cocked the gun in his hand and walked toward Brent, keeping it pointed directly at Brent's chest. "Don't say a word."

"Hello?" Intruder said. "Yes. We're about to leave. Thank you again for calling." Intruder snapped the cell phone shut and dropped it into his pocket. "How nice of the Garnet police to keep an eye on the house."

"Your name. It's Joe something, right?" Brent swallowed, staring at the gun.

"Impressive memory. No harm in telling you my real name. Not now. It's Joe Kalaris. Intruder is my online alias."

Face to face, Intruder didn't look like the psychopath Brent had envisioned. Except for the surgical gloves and the gun, this well-dressed man standing in front of him could have been a coworker or a neighbor.

"Anything else you want to ask?" Intruder took several steps backwards, picked up a wineglass from the mantle, and brought the glass to his lips. He seemed to savor the taste, rolling the liquid around in his mouth before he swallowed. "What's the matter, cat got your tongue?" Intruder chuckled. "You were never proficient at this game."

Brent's tongue felt thick inside his mouth. He felt completely helpless and stupid for not screaming when Intruder had answered his phone. *He had to think.*

"Until you recover your power of speech, I'll do the talking. The cops look for means, motive, and opportunity when investigating a murder scene," Intruder said. "We have all three. Let me explain. Tonight, Brent, you simply snapped. Fresh on the heels of your impending termination from Revolution, along with the horrible accident that claimed the life of your best friend, life suddenly became unbearable. If you add in Amanda's diagnosis of preeclampsia," Intruder paused, holding up the brochure, "which was an unexpected bonus, it only bolsters the fact that your life hit rock bottom." He took another sip of wine.

"That's not true."

"Right. Well, reality isn't exactly what I'm after here, and the police only want to wrap things up nice and tidy. Your suicide note, signed in your own hand, will neatly tie up all the loose ends. What do you think? Air tight? Even with the cops alerted?"

Brent clenched and unclenched his fists in fury. He couldn't let Amanda down again. He had to think of a way to beat this man. This monster. He looked around furtively for a weapon. There was nothing. When he looked up, he saw Intruder watching him with amusement. Brent stared back at Intruder defiantly, refusing to cower.

"There are plenty of witnesses to say that you've been under immense pressure," Intruder said. "You're known as a hothead, especially after the beating you gave Clive. People will shake their heads and say they should have seen it coming." Intruder clucked his tongue. "They'll say it was a tragedy. A beautiful couple. So young, so—"

"Where. Is. Amanda?" Brent spit out each word.

Intruder paused at the interruption and set his wine glass back on the mantle. "You'll know in due time."

"Is she alive?"

"Yes, at the moment."

"Thank God." Brent felt relief sweep over him, and he put a hand on the back of the couch to steady himself. Amanda was alive. He still had a chance to save her.

"Enough witty repartee. Walk into the den. Slowly." Intruder waved the gun toward the front hallway and the den beyond.

Brent stood still for a moment, trying to devise a plan. He considered running headlong at Intruder and trying to take him down with a football tackle, but the wariness with which his captor was watching him, and the gun, made Brent realize that such an

255

ill-planned, impulsive maneuver would never work. Forced for the moment to bide his time, he walked into the den.

"We need to compose your suicide note. It has to have just the right tone. Desperate, but not maudlin."

Brent sat down in the desk chair and crossed his arms over his chest. "Write it yourself."

"Come now, Brent. That would never do. It might tip off the police that the note was a forgery. My vocabulary is far superior to yours, and they would pick that up instantly. I don't make mistakes. Don't you know that by now?"

Brent uncrossed his arms, but he refused to put them on the keyboard. Instead, he let them fall into his lap. "And if I refuse to help you?"

"Let's just say I prepared a little motivational device in the event that you were feeling uncooperative."

"And what would that be?" He couldn't imagine anything that would make him help this bastard.

Joe tapped the muzzle of the gun at the bottom of the computer screen. "Do you see that minimized item there? Click on it."

Apprehensive, Brent reached out with his right hand for the mouse and clicked. A small box popped open on the left-hand side of the screen. He stared at it, unable to make sense out of what he was seeing. The green image was obviously infrared, but it was hard to tell exactly what he was looking at. A pair of eyes came into focus, and he watched them blink.

His heart leapt into his throat when he realized the image on the screen was Amanda. *She was alive!* Then elation quickly turned to fear when he saw she was visibly shaking, gagged, and bound to a chair. The camera captured the terror in her dilated pupils.

Enraged, Brent jumped up and grabbed Intruder by the throat with both hands. "Where is she?" Something struck him on the side of the head, and Brent was sent sprawling back onto the chair. A warm trickle ran down the side of his face, and he instinctively brought a hand up to his temple. His fingers came away red with blood.

Intruder leaned menacingly over him. "Start typing."

"You'll never get away with this."

Intruder let out a short bark of laughter. "Don't flatter yourself. You are hardly my first victim."

"But why?" Brent pleaded. "Why do you do this? And why me?"

"Why?" Intruder tapped a finger against his chin and seemed to consider the question for a moment. Then he turned and looked down at Brent. "People always ask that question. You were chosen at random, of course."

"At random?" Brent couldn't believe his ears.

"I only have two criteria for my nominees. The first, of course, is age. The younger the nominee, the more points I garner. Second, I prefer my victims to live in the Boston area."

"That's it?"

"Other than that, I tend to think of it as providence."

Brent gagged. "You're telling me this is fate?" It was completely incomprehensible. The fact that he had been chosen at random made this unending nightmare even worse.

"I suppose that's as good a word as any, if you believe in that sort of thing. Our game got off to a rather slow start, but it did get a bit better once Todd joined in the fun. And it was entertaining to see you in the flesh at the bar. I don't often get to shake hands with my nominees until D-day, or death day as I call it."

"I'll do anything," Brent said, hearing the raw desperation in his voice. "Please. Do you want money? Do you want—"

Intruder scoffed. "Don't insult me. If you had been a better player, you would be calling the shots now. Which is why I was so disappointed in your game-playing abilities. You're a very good RISK player, so I had hoped for more of a challenge. A better match, so to speak."

Chills came over Brent as he watched a slow smile creep over Intruder's face. He looked back at the computer image, the greenish glow of Amanda's terrified eyes. He couldn't live with himself if another person, let alone his wife, should die as a result of his decision to play this game. Todd was innocent. Amanda was innocent. Their baby was innocent. This nightmare was his fault and his fault alone. Brent dropped to his knees beside the chair. "Kill me. I beg you." His voice cracked. Unable to stop the tremors that shook his body as he pleaded with his captor. "If you kill me, you'll still win the game."

Intruder shook his head. "No. You still don't understand."

"Understand what?" Brent cringed at the madness he saw in Intruder's eyes.

"The reason Amanda must be killed today."

Brent shook his head as he continued to plead for his wife's life. "Make me your victim. You don't need her. Spare her life and I'll help you cover up my murder from the police. Please..." he broke off, still on his knees, his hands clasped in front of him.

"You see? That's why you'll never be the consummate game player. You overlook the obvious. She's more valuable than you."

"But—"

"Tomorrow is Amanda's birthday, right?"

"Yes, but why does that matter?"

"If I kill her tonight, before midnight, I get one additional point," Intruder said.

"One point?" Brent repeated, baffled. "But one point doesn't matter—"

"But it does," Intruder said. "I went to great lengths to take advantage of that fact. I pay attention to details."

"But you've figured out how to hack the list. The points don't matter." Brent's voice went up an octave. "Why not just wait for someone to die and then insert their name on the list?"

Intruder's expression turned serious. "You mean like with Randy? That was all Clive. I find no sport in such a game."

"This is not a sport, you psychopath," Brent said through clenched teeth. "It's murder."

"I prefer to call it my own little twist on the game. It's exhilarating."

"You are despicable."

"You simply have no appreciation for my skills. My plan to kill Amanda before midnight was my *piece de résistance*. But now, I'm afraid even that has become a moot point."

Brent felt the tiniest sliver of hope. "What do you mean?"

"Just days ago, I came up with a scheme so brilliant, I amazed even myself. An idea of pure genius. Look!"

Instead of replying, Intruder reached down and grabbed Brent by the back of the neck in a vice-like grip, lifting him up off the floor and onto his feet. The pain was excruciating, and it shot straight through Brent's temples. The edges of his vision began to darken, but he fought through the pain. He had to stay conscious. He had to get to Amanda.

"Your game-playing skills were pathetic. The game, for you and your family, is about to come to an end."

It took every ounce of Brent's willpower to pull back from the darkness. "I...won't let...you..."

"It's too late. It's over," Intruder said. "Watch."

Intruder shoved him back down onto the straight-back chair and then viciously slammed his head down onto the oak desktop.

"Look. Do you see that?"

Brent tried to lift his head, but Intruder's grip on his neck was unrelenting.

Intruder tapped the corner of the display with the barrel of his gun. "You see that?"

"No." The computer screen was so close to Brent's eyes that everything on the screen was a mass of meaningless dots.

"Come on." Intruder grabbed a fistful of hair and yanked his head back. "Take a guess. It's there. It's right there."

Brent blinked and forced his eyes to focus until he was able to once again distinguish the ghostly infrared image of Amanda on the screen. He held his breath, looking for signs that she was still alive.

"Come on, college boy, figure it out," his captor said.

A thin line snaked from out of the camera range down toward Amanda's hand. The first time Intruder had forced him to watch the video feed, he hadn't even noticed it. "What is it?" he asked, his voice hoarse with dread.

"It's an IV."

Intruder let go of Brent's hair. He cautiously straightened, still unable to make sense of what he was seeing on the screen. He turned and looked over his shoulder at his captor. The man's cold blue eyes were fixated on the screen. Brent was filled with dread, waiting for Intruder to tell him Amanda's death sentence.

"The IV bag is filled with Cytotec."

Brent's gut twisted as he watched the hint of a smile cross Intruder's face. "What is that?"

"You've no doubt heard of Pitocin?"

"It's a drug used to induce labor," Brent said.

"Right. I bet you learned that in childbirth class, college boy." Intruder sniffed in distain. "Cytotec is used to induce labor as well. It just happens to be cheaper and easier to obtain over the Internet. That's where I got it. That's the final irony of the whole thing."

"What irony?" Brent was having trouble following Intruder's logic. He spoke sheer madness.

"It's a brilliant idea, and how fitting to end the game with such an ironic twist."

"What do you mean?"

"I've figured out how to win the game without you or your wife." Intruder let out a burst of maniacal laughter.

Comprehension suddenly dawned within Brent. He retched, as hot bile rose, burning the back of his throat.

"No! You can't mean…" He knew now that he was in the presence of pure unadulterated evil.

"The baby added a whole new twist. No one has ever gotten ninety-nine points for a nominee before."

Brent felt dizzy. "But this plan…your plan…it makes no sense. You'll never be able to collect the points!"

Intruder didn't seem to hear him. "I must take advantage of every situation. That's what game playing is all about."

"Our baby! You can't take our baby. My God!" This couldn't be happening.

"There is a code of honor among the very best game players. You must know this adage, Brent, although you clearly don't seem to subscribe to it. Every advantage must be taken."

"What does that mean?"

"Your baby is worth more points than either you or your wife. I would be remiss if I won the game but failed to garner every possible point."

"Listen to me. There will be no record of the baby's birth." Brent tried to reason with Intruder. "You won't gain any points by murdering our child."

"I know you find it unpleasant, Brent, but surely you understand my position. I have no other choice."

"You're insane!" I won't let you do this!" Brent screamed.

Intruder struck him across the jaw with the butt of the gun. Blood filled his mouth, and his tongue found a loose tooth.

"Finish the suicide note."

Brent spat bloody sputum onto the carpet and laid his fingers on the keyboard.

"Start typing."

"No." Brent drew back his hands, leaving a bloody smear. "Not until I speak with her." He crossed his arms over his chest.

"You are in no position to ask for favors," Intruder replied.

"I want to tell her I love her one last time."

"Given your seemingly limited ability to understand where

things stand, I'll try to simplify it for you. The harder you make this on me, the longer your wife will suffer at my hands when it is her time to die."

Brent let out a moan. "You bastard." The eerie green eyes on the screen seemed to blink in agreement with him. Amanda was still alive.

"Your wife was much more cooperative. In fact, she started the suicide note for you." Intruder clicked on a document at the bottom of the screen.

"Read it aloud," Intruder commanded.

Brent took a shaky breath. "Dear loved ones, please forgive me for these acts which I am about to commit. I love my wife and unborn child with all of my heart…" He broke down, unable to continue.

"Not bad, huh?" Intruder said. "Short and sweet is best, I think. Now finish it. We need to move on to the main event."

• • •

Amanda woke up feeling disoriented. Her head felt heavy. She blinked several times, but whether her eyes were open or closed, the room she was in was pitch black and cold. Then she remembered Intruder and the gift box filled with the gun and medical supplies.

Her first instinct was to scream, but her lips felt glued shut. The thought that she was about to suffocate terrified her. She breathed deeply, and the pungent scent of adhesive filled her nostrils. Her mouth must be covered with tape.

Desperate to get free, Amanda struggled, tugging at the unseen restrains on both her hands and feet. Her wrists burned from her violent efforts. At one point the chair almost toppled over, and only fear of injuring her unborn child made Amanda stop struggling. But sitting still led to even more terrifying thoughts. Terror filled her mind as she tried to remember when she'd last felt her baby move. Unable to place her hands on her stomach, cut off from physically cradling her baby, caused profound pain.

Overwhelmed, Amanda gave in to tears once again. She let her head fall forward onto her chest as hopelessness settled over her. She was going to die here, in the cold, in the dark, without ever having seen her baby's precious face.

• • •

Under Intruder's watchful eye, Brent folded the note and put it in the envelope. Intruder made him lick the flap to seal it.

"Just in case they check for DNA."

Intruder then plucked the envelope from Brent's fingers and forced him upright, prodding him into walking back to the family room.

"Place it on the mantle" Intruder said.

Brent walked toward the fireplace. "I want to see Amanda," Brent said.

"I'm growing weary of your demands. Perhaps this will convince you of my consternation."

Before Brent could react, Intruder secured him in a headlock. Even as Brent struggled, he felt Intruder roll a finger under the bone behind his right ear. Pain exploded through Brent's skull, and a burst of white light flashed in front of his eyes. Pain rolled in waves from side to side in his skull. His captor's voice faded in and out, but he gradually beat back the blackness using sheer willpower.

In that moment, he realized he was not powerless. Each second he delayed Intruder from returning to Amanda was a personal victory. He would fight to the death. "Never. I'll never give up."

"Give in to your fate. Wasn't that what you called it before?"

"Then kill me. Get it over with," Brent taunted.

"It's not time. I must wait for the drug to do its job."

Intruder picked a piece of lint carefully off his dark jeans. "I've learned to be a patient man. A live birth must precede the next step."

"Tell me where she is," Brent pressed. "What does it matter if I know? You're going to kill me anyway." He hadn't been able to figure out where Amanda was being held from the infrared image. *A closet? The basement? Was she even in the house?* The only certainty was that she was in the dark and shivering, certainly from fear, but perhaps also from cold.

"I'm not that stupid, Brent. Still, I admire your—"

The doorbell rang.

Startled, Brent turned toward the hallway and took several steps in that direction before he heard the unmistakable sound of a gun being cocked behind him.

"Freeze. If you take one more step, Amanda will suffer beyond your worst nightmare."

Brent froze. He could see the porch light was on, due to an automatic timer he'd programmed to go on just before dusk. A delivery man in a chocolate brown jacket jogged away from the front door. A package lay propped up against the side of the house.

"Don't move. Don't even exhale. They'll leave," Intruder said.

Brent noticed Intruder had drawn all the house blinds. He also knew that Intruder, several steps behind him, was unable to see down the hallway from his position inside the family room. Brent watched the delivery man hop back into his truck, which he'd left idling at the curb. "Actually, she won't leave." Brent looked back at Intruder over his right shoulder.

"What do you mean?" Intruder stared at Brent with narrowed eyes.

"It's Amanda's mom." He smiled and waved. "What do you want me to do? She has her own key to the house. If I don't answer the door, she'll just come in anyway. She does it all the time."

"Let me check." Intruder took several steps toward him.

"She's reaching into her purse."

Intruder motioned with the gun toward the front door. "Open the door and get rid of her. Tell her Amanda's asleep. Convince her, or else." Intruder stopped at the wall that separated the family room from the hall. He spread his feet wide apart, taking a shooter's stance. "Don't try anything, I'm an excellent shot."

The gun was pointed dead center at Brent's back.

"Do it now."

Brent stepped onto the first marble tile of the entryway. Then without turning his head, he dropped to a crouch and grabbed the handle of the basement door, yanking it open. A bullet whizzed over his head and smashed through the hollow basement door, leaving a hole the size of his fist. *Oh my God!* Brent slipped through, grabbed the handle, and slammed the door shut behind him.

In the dark, he jumped the first half of the stairs in a single bound. As soon as he hit the landing, he turned and jumped the second, longer flight. Pain shot through his ankle when he landed off balance on the cement floor. He gingerly rotated his right ankle before testing his weight on it and ducking around the side of the stairway. A crash sounded from above as the door was flung open, and footsteps pounded down the raw pine boards, directly over his head.

Brent scrambled to his feet, ready to make a run for it when the footsteps overhead stopped on the landing. He froze, crouched under the stairs, unsure what to do. *Should he hide or run?* He was three steps into a mad sprint to the door when he slammed full force into a solid object and found himself almost toppling over a wobbly stack of moving boxes. He grabbed onto the top box for balance, and something inside made a loud clank.

"Running wasn't a wise thing to do, Brent," Intruder called out. "I have half a mind to go blow your wife's brains out for pulling that stunt."

Brent's heart leapt into his throat. He pressed a hand to his lips and remained silent. This was a game of cat and mouse, and he wasn't stupid enough to give away his position. What he needed more than anything was a weapon.

With the lightest possible touch, Brent lifted the cardboard flaps and felt around inside with both hands. His fingers closed around a strange rubbery object, and it took him a moment to identify the unfamiliar thing; it was a Gumby toy. He'd tripped over the box of Todd's office toys from Revolution.

One by one, Brent felt through various items in the box, identifying them if he could and then pushing them aside. The ridged edge of the two knobs on Todd's Etch A Sketch, plush toys, and then finally, his hand closed around the cold, slender, metal rod of the Emei piercer. It felt lighter and thinner than he remembered, but at least it was something.

"I'll go and tell Amanda you've made your decision," Joe taunted from above.

Brent heard a board creak. *Intruder must be headed back up the stairs. He had to do something!* Feeling exposed, Brent took several steps backwards, moving slowly and silently, until he reached the staircase. He slipped between two studs and then crouched down until he was directly underneath the staircase landing.

He peered cautiously up through the slats in front of him, remaining utterly still, barely breathing. He hefted the Emei piercer in his hand, realizing it was no match for Intruder's gun.

"Brent? Can you hear me? I've got a better idea. I'm going to increase the flow of Cytotec until it runs wide open. Either Amanda will give birth or be dead in twenty minutes."

It took every ounce of willpower not to respond to Intruder's threat, not to plead for mercy. The time for negotiation had passed, and speaking would only give away his position. The twilight that had softly illuminated the far corner of the basement had almost disappeared. Soon he would be in complete darkness. With only seconds to prevent Intruder from leaving the basement, Brent knew he had to act. *But how?*

"If you don't give yourself up, your wife will suffer an excruciating death," Intruder called out. "You have ten seconds to make your final decision. Todd died trying to be a hero. Now it's your chance to prove yourself his equal. Will one of your last acts be of a hero or a coward?"

The words slammed into Brent, along with overwhelming shame and guilt. As he stared between the slats of the stairs, horrific images of Todd's death pinwheeled through his mind. Then a miniscule movement on the steps banished all other thoughts. Intruder took a single step down the stairs, followed by a second, then he paused. *Intruder was headed down, not up, the stairs.* Intruder's legs produced two slim shadows, precisely at Brent's eye level.

Brent drew the tip of the metal shaft against his thumb, testing the sharpness. When he brought his thumb to his mouth, he tasted blood. Straining to see the two shadowy images in the near blackness, Brent brought the Emei piercer across his chest. He aimed for Intruder's Achilles tendons and slashed with all his might.

An agonizing scream filled the basement and something bounced from one pine board to the next. *The gun?* Brent's head swam as the smell of blood penetrated his nostrils. A heavy thump followed, and Intruder fell down the few remaining stairs. Still gripping the Emei piercer, Brent turned to make his escape through the exterior glass door.

The basement was now completely dark, and Brent dropped to his hands and knees to navigate back through the moving boxes to get out of the basement. From the opposite side of the staircase he heard a soft moan, followed by an indiscriminate shuffling sound. He waited a few seconds, listening, but all was quiet.

Was Intruder dead? He didn't care. He had to get to Amanda. Once again he scrambled on all fours toward the glass door, before realizing his mistake; he still had no idea where to start looking for his wife.

With a boom, the furnace kicked on, and Brent let out a startled gasp. A bullet whizzed over his head, and the glass door just feet in front of him shattered. Brent threw himself spread-eagle on the ground then rolled left to get out of the line of fire. A second bullet pinged off a steel header beam. Wood shavings fluttering down on top of him as the bullet buried itself in a wooden crossbeam somewhere above Brent's head. The heavy breathing resumed, and it sounded like Intruder was dragging himself across the floor.

"It's too late," Intruder called out, strain obvious in his voice. "I lied."

Brent refused to move. He listened to Intruder's labored breathing. In and out. In and out.

"You wife is already dead. It was just a recording."

Sudden laughter rang out. Rage surged inside of Brent, and he rolled to his feet. Heedless of the danger, he strode directly toward the staircase and the sound of Intruder's crazed laughter. He swung the Emei piercer out in front of him, like a ballplayer about to enter the batting box. "You lying son of a bitch. I know she's alive. Where is she?"

A gunshot exploded, and Brent felt searing pain in his shoulder. He was knocked back by the force of the bullet, but he managed to stay on his feet and maintain possession of the Emei piercer. "Where is she?" he demanded.

"You'll never win," Intruder said. He took a ragged breath. "You don't deserve to win."

The wound burned, but it only fed Brent's fury. The fingers of his right hand began to go numb, and he switched the Emei piercer to his left hand and continued to swing the metal shaft ferociously, blindly, in front of him. On his fourth swing he struck something solid, and he heard Intruder suck in a lungful of air.

Unleashing a flurry of blows, Brent heard Intruder gasp each time he made contact. "Tell me!" Brent screamed. Unable to stop himself, he continued to beat the mass on the floor. "Where. Is. She?" Brent issued a horrendous blow after each word. The last time he struck Intruder, he heard the gun skitter across the cement floor. Intruder had stopped moaning. Brent felt around on the floor until he retrieved the gun. Then he stood in the darkness, a weapon in each hand, and wondered for a second time today if he had committed murder.

Back upstairs, Brent walked into the den, eyes riveted on the eerie green image on the computer across the room. Heart in his throat, he was aware of each second that ticked by. At last the image shifted, and Brent was almost overcome with relief. Amanda was still alive.

The throbbing in his shoulder had increased, and Brent guessed the wound was more serious than he'd first thought. "Amanda! Amanda!" Brent yelled at the top of his lungs. He laid the weapons on the desk and examined his right shoulder. The sleeve of his shirt was soaked with blood. Not wanting to pass out from blood loss, he headed for the kitchen, turning on every light he passed. Grabbing a dishtowel from under the sink and using his left hand and his teeth, tied a makeshift tourniquet around his upper arm.

"Amanda, can you hear me?" Standing stock-still, he listened a minute for a response before heading for the family room. French doors led to the screened-in porch. At the same time, he opened the door and flipped on both the porch light and the floodlight. "Amanda?" he yelled. The floodlight illuminated the deck and the edge of the backyard, but he heard nothing, saw nothing.

He had to find another clue to her location. Back in the den, Brent clicked through all the recently viewed documents, leaving the mouse and the keyboard smeared red with blood. No new clues came to light and his heart sunk.

"Help me," Brent begged Amanda, gazing at her image on the screen. She blinked, and he ran his finger over her eyes on the screen for strength. *The answer had to be right in front of him.* Almost as if Amanda had answered his question, he realized in order to see the live image of Amanda, that a video camera had to be linked up to the den computer.

Brent dropped to his knees on the carpet and looked at the back of the computer under the desk. There were a myriad of cables snaking out both right and left, with the exception of one cable that disappeared through the wall. Intruder had drilled a hole and fed the cable through to the outside of the house. His adrenalin surged. *The attic!*

• • •

A hinge squeaked, and Amanda's head snapped up. Fear shot through her to the very core. Intruder was coming back! Was it her time to die?

"Amanda?"

Brent! A roar sounded in Amanda's ears, and she tried to call out, forgetting the duct tape across her mouth. She grunted, making unintelligible sounds, watching a tiny shaft of light cut through the darkness. She was in a cavernous room, the peak of the ceiling rose high above her. Then she spotted the artificial Christmas tree, and she knew she was in the attic.

The triangle of light near her feet widened as the pull-down staircase was lowered. White light flooded the room, and Amanda was blinded in the sudden brightness. Blue lights danced in front of her eyes until she became accustomed to the light after being in the pitch black for so long. She looked down at the rope which her captor had used to bind her. Then her gaze was drawn to a needle that was inserted into a vein in the back of her hand. Almost hypnotically, her eyes followed the plastic tube above her head to an almost empty bag of fluid. She began struggling harder than ever, trying to break free, knowing whatever was in the IV bag was making its way to her baby.

Brent's head appeared at the top of the stairs, and a sob escaped her throat.

He ran to her side. "Thank God!" He knelt down next to her. "You're alive. I know, baby, I know. Let me get this tape off." He pulled the tape off her mouth in one swift motion.

Her lips tingled, and she licked them, tasting the chemical adhesive while struggling to speak. "Get it out." Her lips felt thick and rubbery. Amanda jerked her head up, indicating the bag of fluid hanging over her shoulder. "Hurry." The drops fell in rapid succession. "Hurry." Amanda could feel the fear coming off Brent in waves.

Brent yanked the needle from the back of her hand and held his thumb over the puncture. With his teeth, he tore off a piece of duct tape and then stuck it over the puncture mark on the back of her hand, continuing to apply pressure with his thumb.

"What is it? What's in there?" Amanda's heart constricted with fear. "Will it hurt our baby?" Her voice was high and shrill.

"Let's get you to a hospital." Brent kissed her cheek and then began to tear at the knots in the nylon ropes that held her wrists.

It was only then that Amanda noticed his blood-stained shirt. "Brent, you're bleeding!"

"I'm fine." He bent down, using his teeth to help free the knot.

"But you're bleeding badly…"

"I'm okay. We need to go. Right now!"

Amanda shrank back against the chair. "You me…mean he's st…still here?"

"He's in the basement. I think he's dead."

"But the police? Aren't the police on their way?"

Brent had a piece of rope in his mouth, and he mumbled something she couldn't understand.

"We're on our own?"

Brent nodded.

Amanda's terror returned full force. Her teeth began to chatter as Brent freed the second rope. It fell away, and Amanda rubbed at the red rings encircling each wrist.

Brent tossed the ropes aside. "Can you stand?"

Amanda's head swam. She honestly didn't know if she had the strength or not. Then, placing her hands on her stomach, she knew she would somehow find the strength, if not for herself, for the baby. "Yes." Amanda pushed herself to her feet, leaning on Brent's good arm.

"That's right, lean on me. Are you okay?"

She nodded, wondering how long had she been locked in the attic. *Had it been minutes? Hours?* She no longer had any sense of the time that had passed. All she could do was follow Brent. He had come to her rescue. He was going to save their baby.

"I'll go first." Brent went several steps down the ladder, then held his hand out to her and motioned her to follow him.

Amanda backed down the wobbly ladder, holding tight to the railing. When at last she reached the carpet, she stood holding onto the second floor banister, still feeling woozy.

"Have you had any contractions?" Brent whispered.

Amanda shook her head, feeling dread rise within her at the thought of having contractions at twenty-six weeks.

Brent pointed over the banister and down to the front door. "Just a few steps. You can do it. Down the stairs and out the front door."

Brent wrapped his left arm around her waist, and they started down the stairs. On the third step, a gunshot exploded, and Amanda screamed.

Chapter 11

The bullet splintered the staircase spindle beside Amanda, and Brent yanked her body back to the top of the landing. He dove for the floor, pulling her down on top of him, cushioning her fall. They landed with their combined weight on his right shoulder, and pain ricocheted through him all the way up to his teeth. He bit back a cry of anguish.

"Amanda?" he whispered. No answer. Brent rolled her gently off of him and looked into her eyes. Her face had gone white with fear, and her eyes had a vacant look.

"Put your arm around me," he whispered, but her arms remained limp at her sides, as if she wasn't able to comprehend his words. "Help me, baby," he begged to no avail.

With one arm, Brent managed to pull and tug Amanda through the open doorway of the nursery at the top of the stairs, listening intently for the sound of Intruder's footsteps on the stairs.

Breathing heavily, Brent managed to get Amanda sitting down in the wooden rocking chair in the corner of the room before he ran back and closed the nursery door, pushing in the flimsy button lock on the doorknob. After a moment's hesitation, Brent pushed the wooden changing table across the room until it blocked the door. It wasn't much of a deterrent, but at least it was something.

Brent cursed himself for not taking all the weapons with him. *How could he have been so stupid to have left the gun on the desk in the den?* He'd been so focused on finding Amanda that he'd made yet another mistake. With the gun back in Intruder's possession, and once again without a weapon, Brent wondered if he'd just signed both their death warrants. A meager push button and a piece of furniture weren't going to save his wife's life. He had to do something. He would not simply hide out up here in their nursery, waiting to be killed.

Returning to Amanda's side, he knelt next to the rocking chair. Her head wobbled as if she might faint. "Stay with me, Amanda." Brent tapped two fingers against her cheek, relieved when her eyes met his. "I've got a plan. I'll be right back."

"No. Don't—"

Brent kissed her on the lips to silence her. He had no choice. "It's our only chance." He ran to the window and, with a last desperate look back at Amanda, threw it open and put one foot over the sill. The cool night air hit his blood-and-sweat-drenched shirt, and he shivered.

Standing on the roof, gripping the windowsill, Brent realized the slope of the roof was steeper than he had anticipated. Beyond the edge of the roof, the back porch light illuminated the deck far beneath him. Aware that every second counted, Brent forced himself to keep moving. His right arm pressed to his chest, he took one tentative step and then a second, inching down toward the edge of the roof, still clinging to the sill with his left hand.

Past the security of the window, Brent had only the edge of the thin cedar shakes to hold onto. It was a tenuous hold at best, and he held his breath and took another tiny step with his right foot.

A tiny avalanche began under the smooth sole of his dress shoe. Brent's foot shot out from under him, and he landed flat on his back and began to slide. Heart in his throat, he threw out both arms. His shoe caught on the gutter, and it creaked under his weight.

Cautiously, Brent peered below him, praying the gutter would hold his weight. All he had to do was drop down to the deck below. The height couldn't be more than ten feet, perhaps eight, but from this vantage point, it looked like a long way down.

Bracing his good arm against the roof, Brent said a quick prayer and leaped off. He hit the deck with a hard jolt and rolled the way he'd seen stuntmen do on TV. Burning pain seared his shoulder when he rolled over the bullet wound. Wasting no time, gritting his teeth through the pain, Brent ran down the flight of wooden stairs which led to the backyard. Dead grass crunched beneath his feet as he slipped underneath the deck to the basement door. Shattered glass glittered all around his feet in the dim light that filtered down through the cracks above him.

Brent pushed open the door and stepped inside, picking a path through the jagged pieces of glass and scattered moving boxes to the center of the basement. Hand over hand, Brent followed the rough wood of the two-by-fours and knelt down next to the box of Todd's office possessions.

The second Emei piercer took only a moment to find. Brent slipped the ring around the middle finger of his left hand, feeling the chill of the blade as it slid against his skin, hidden behind his forearm.

Brent eased noiselessly up the first four treads of the basement stairs heading toward the first floor. Heart pounding, he poked his head around the corner for a quick look up at the top of the stairs. The door to the basement was open. The light was on in the entryway. With nowhere to hide once he rounded the corner, Brent knew, if he wanted to save Amanda, he had to move now.

He walked gingerly up the remaining stairs, wincing each time a board creaked, until he was crouched on the top step. *Where was Intruder?* He had fired the gun from the entryway, and Brent guessed that Intruder had been unable to climb the stairs due to his injuries. He hoped Intruder was still holding his position at the bottom of the stairs.

He took a deep breath for courage and stepped onto the tile entryway. Instantly he felt the barrel of the gun rest against his left temple. He closed his eyes in utter despair.

"Well, isn't this a pleasant surprise," Intruder said.

Brent remained silent. At least Intruder was here, which meant Amanda was safe. Brent knew he only had one move left: give up his life in exchange for Amanda and their child.

"You have redeemed yourself somewhat in my eyes," Intruder continued. "Anyone except a true gamer would have given up in the face of such insurmountable odds. Sadly, however, I believe we've come to the final crossroad. How shall we end the game?"

Brent turned his head to look at Intruder, forcing him to draw the gun back, if only a few inches. "I'm sure you have a plan." Brent studied Intruder. The sparkle in his eyes was a telltale sign that he was certain of victory. Slight tremors also told him that Intruder was masking significant pain behind his outward smile. Only the slightest nuance, a grimace, the rigid set of his jaw, gave Intruder away.

"Yes. That's what makes this game so much fun. It's ever-changing," Intruder said

"Without a weapon, I'm afraid I'm at your mercy," Brent said, keeping his face a mask of defeat.

"The game was rather above your level of expertise from the very beginning," Intruder said.

Brent dropped his eyes and let his shoulder slump, beaten.

"No comment? A humble man, even when vanquished. Then let us proceed as planned. A birth, followed by a murder-suicide. How intoxicating."

Brent brought his hands to his face, covered his eyes in anguish, allowing a heartfelt sob to escape his lips.

"It will be over soon," Intruder said.

Brent steadied the movement of the concealed Emei piercer under his left thumb and interlaced his other fingers for strength. He knew he'd have only one chance. The timing had to be perfect.

"Now, I want you to—"

Brent sensed Intruder begin to lower the weapon, and he brought his arms crashing down onto Intruder's wrist. He felt the impact as the steel bar struck bone, and the gun was knocked to the floor, clattering across the tile entryway.

With a howl of pain, Intruder dropped to all fours, scrambling after the weapon. Without hesitation, Brent gripped the rod like a spear and jammed the point of the steel rod into the side of Intruder's neck.

Intruder gasped and stared up at him, a shocked expression on his face. A trickle of bright red blood began to seep from the wound as Brent slipped his finger from the center ring of the Emei piercer and picked up the handgun from the floor.

Brent stepped well out of his captor's reach, watching with horrid fascination as Intruder attempted to pull out the rod impaled in his neck. He held the gun on him even as Intruder fell backwards, screaming and writhing on the floor.

This time Brent would not underestimate his opponent. Breathing hard, he ran, gun still in hand, into the den. Unwilling to put down the gun, Brent reached behind the computer monitor and jerked the tangle of cables that snaked to the various pieces of computer equipment on the desk. Time was of the essence. He pivoted and started back to the entryway.

Feeling sudden resistance, Brent looked behind him. One of the cords was taunt, still connected to the monitor. He gave it another jerk, and the monitor toppled off the desk and powered down with an electronic moan.

Hearing sounds from the entryway, Brent knew Intruder was still alive. He raced to Intruder, who was thrashing around in pain on the ground, and pocketed the gun in his suitcoat pocket. Using his good arm and his teeth, he pulled both of Intruder's hands together and bound his wrists again and again with the computer cables. After doing the same with his ankles, pulling as tight as he could, and heedless of Intruder's outcries, he used a third cable to hog tie him.

A noise to his right startled him, and Brent whipped his head around.

"Amanda!" Brent jumped to his feet and ran toward her.

She leaned one hand against the wall for support and cupped the other underneath her belly. "My…my wa…water broke."

Fear constricted his throat. His gaze dropped down to the dark stain on the lower half of her maternity jumper. Her eyes drifted shut, and she slumped against him.

Brent caught her awkwardly in his arms and gently lowered her to the braided entryway rug. Heart racing, he put a finger on her carotid artery, relieved to find a steady pulse. "Amanda, stay with me. Please, baby!" He scooped her up in his arms and raced through the kitchen and into the garage. He peered through the driver's side window, thankful to see the keys dangling from the ignition, before he sat her gently in the backseat, leaning over to click the shoulder belt around her. Panting from exertion, Brent slid into the driver's seat. Her eyes met his in the rearview mirror.

"Hurry," she said.

At the emergency entrance, Brent laid on the horn. He careened into a spot marked "Ambulance Only" and jumped out of the car.

A big man dressed in scrubs came through the glass doors.

"My wife is having a baby. She needs help," Brent yelled over the top of the car.

Still walking toward the car, the man gave Brent a level stare. "You need to move your vehicle. See the sign? Ambulance only."

Brent ignored him and yanked open the passenger door. "Please help her!"

The man stopped. "Don't make me call security."

"Listen to me!" Brent shouted. "She's been poisoned!"

The man let go of the gurney and ran around the back of the vehicle. He shouldered Brent out of the way and leaned inside the car. In one motion, he had her draped across his massive arms. "What did she ingest?" he asked running through the automatic doors.

"Something similar to Pitocin," Brent said, running alongside him. "It starts with a 'C.'"

"How long ago did she take it?"

"I don't know," Brent replied. A woman came around from behind what looked like the admitting desk and took his arm.

"Sir, I need you to wait here."

"But—"

"She's in good hands, and you need that arm taken care of."

Brent watched helplessly as Amanda disappeared behind another pair of doors.

• • •

The bullet had been removed, and Brent's shoulder had been stitched up by a resident. It had seemed liked hours ago. Maybe it had been. Brent wasn't sure of anything anymore. The ER doc had immobilized his right arm in a blue sling, but Brent had refused all offers of pain medication.

As long as he felt the constant pain, he'd convinced himself that Amanda and the baby would be okay. She'd been whisked away into surgery so fast he hadn't even had a chance to tell her he loved her.

Now Brent paced in front of the wall of windows overlooking the mostly deserted parking lot and watched the clock as he held a cold cup of coffee in his hands from which he had yet to take a sip. He had given up badgering the nurses at their station about her condition. They claimed someone would come and talk to him as soon as they were able.

Brent had made yet another complete pass in front of the windows, fourteen steps across, fourteen steps back, when the double doors opened with a whoosh. A diminutive man dressed in green scrubs scanned the empty waiting room and then headed straight for Brent.

Liquid sloshed over the rim of the Styrofoam cup as Brent's

hand began to shake. Not taking his eyes off the doctor, he set the cup down on the metal ledge of the windowsill.

"Mr. Darby?" the doctor asked, pulling down his mask and revealing a closely cropped mustache and a narrow goatee. "I'm Dr. Uday."

"Is she…" The rest of the sentence refused to move past his terrified lips.

"Your wife did very well. The operation is over. My team is closing now."

"Thank you. Thank you for saving her life."

"Both your wife and the baby were in severe distress when they were brought in." He pulled off his surgical cap and mopped his brow. "The toxicology test confirmed extremely high levels of Cytotec in your wife's system. She's been moved to the intensive care unit, but I expect her to make a full recovery."

Brent exhaled and gave a silent prayer of thanks. "And the baby?"

"Your son was born weighing two pounds, four ounces. His lungs need further time to develop, so he has been taken to the neonatal intensive care unit."

"Two pounds? Will he survive?" Brent asked, blinking back tears. He focused on the surgical cap the doctor was rotating idly in his hands; it was imprinted with tiny pink and blue elephants.

"The survival rate for a twenty-six week old preterm infant is between fifty and eighty percent. Chances are, your son will remain in the neonatal unit for some time, but I've seen much smaller babies survive. Take hope in that."

Brent reached for the doctor's hand. "Thank you, Dr. Uday. Thank you for saving my family."

The doctor rose to his feet. "Getting your wife here when you did may have saved her life. You have much to be grateful for. I probably don't need to tell you your wife and your son are lucky to be alive."

Brent nodded. The doctor had no idea just how lucky.

Epilogue

September 16 – Wednesday

The front door of the rental apartment closed with a bang. *Amanda was home.* The wooden spoon jumped in Brent's hand, and his heart rate increased when she walked into the kitchen, unbuttoning her coat.

"How was your session?" he asked, concentrating on the marinara sauce.

"Good," Amanda replied. "Fall is in the air. Some of the leaves are starting to turn."

"Really? I hadn't noticed. I guess it is September." Brent was glad to see a bit of color in Amanda's cheeks, even if it was only from the brisk fall day. She shrugged off her coat, and he noted that she was still much too thin. "Are you hungry? We could have an early dinner."

She shook her head.

"Just a little something? The marinara sauce is nearly ready. All I have to do is heat up the pasta."

She shook her head again. "Is the baby still asleep?"

Brent nodded.

"I'll just go check on him."

Brent rinsed off the cutting board and dried his hands. He followed Amanda into the nursery, and they stood silently, watching their sleeping son. Brent so wanted to wrap his wife in his arms, but he knew better. Instead he bent his head and whispered into her ear. "I love you, Amanda."

"I know you do," she replied softly.

A familiar ache filled him when she didn't respond in kind. Walter began to stir, kicking his tiny legs in the air, and opening his gray-green eyes.

"Hey, peanut," Amanda said. She reached down and picked up the baby. "Are you hungry, little guy?" She kissed the top of Walter's head. He responded by sticking a finger in his mouth and sucking furiously.

Brent watched love shimmer between Amanda and her son. *Patience*, he reminded himself. Still it hurt.

"If you'll take him, I'll go heat up his bottle," Amanda said, turning and handing Walter to Brent.

"I'll make sure Walter Todd works up an appetite." After pausing to breathe in the warm, sweet scent of his son, Brent lifted Walter high up over his head, holding him securely with both hands. "Want an airplane ride?" Walter sucked on a finger, staring down at him. He spun Walter around in lazy circles as they made their way back down the hall. Walter pulled his finger out of his mouth, drooled on his shoulder, and gave Brent a toothless grin.

After strapping Walter into his bouncy seat which was sitting on the kitchen table, Brent popped an elastic bib over his son's head. "We have about ten seconds before he starts to scream like a banshee." Brent looked over his shoulder at Amanda, who stood at the counter pouring warm milk into a baby bottle. He looked back at Walter. "He's scrunching up his face..."

"I need just a few more seconds."

"Do you suppose all babies scream like this when they're hungry, or is it just our little peanut?" Brent asked.

"Oh, I forgot to tell you about Walter's checkup yesterday. The doctor said he gained two ounces," Amanda said. "The pediatrician showed me that Walter may even make it onto the growth chart someday. That's progress."

"Atta boy," Brent reached over and wiped a bit of drool off Walter's chin with the corner of the bib.

"He's bounced back faster than the medical team expected," Amanda replied, picking up Walter and inserting the nipple into his mouth. "They called our boy a born fighter."

"Uh-oh. Maybe it's the red hair," Brent replied. "Do you suppose he'll wind up a constant visitor to the principal's office?"

Amanda turned and gave Brent a shocked look. "My darling boy? Never."

Brent grinned, delighted at Amanda's teasing tone. "Mark my words…"

"Let's hope Walter has my temperament and your cooking skills. Your sauce smells delicious."

"Thanks. How about when Walter goes down for his nap we have a nice dinner together? You know, sort of like a date."

Amanda gave a soft laugh.

The sound gave him hope. "It's good to hear you laugh. I've missed your laughter."

Amanda wiped off a dribble of milk on the baby's chin with the bib. "I had a really good session today with my psychiatrist. I'm beginning to feel a bit like myself again."

A stillness settled over Brent, and he waited, heart pounding, hardly daring to breathe.

"I can't stop reliving what happened that night. My therapist said it will always be a part of me. But the harder part of putting this behind me has been trying to understand why you hid everything from me. Why you weren't honest."

Brent's heart sank. *She was going to ask him for a divorce.*

Amanda held the bottle up and looked to see how many ounces Walter had finished. "I'll never be able to make sense of what Intruder did to me. But my therapist says I've made progress. It's time for me to move on."

Without me. She's taking the baby and leaving.

Amanda turned her head, and her green eyes met his. The bottle trembled slightly in her hand. "I no longer blame you for what happened."

Relief coursed through him, and tears filled Brent's eyes. He struggled to speak over the lump in his throat. "I'm so sorry, Amanda. Words can't express…" His throat seemed to close up on him, overcome with guilt and shame. "I…I…"

Walter started to grunt, opening and closing his mouth, his eyes fixated on the bottle.

Amanda popped the nipple back in his mouth. "I'll always be sad that I won't be able to have more children." She bit her lip. "Intruder took away so much from me. From us. But what he did wasn't your fault. In therapy, I've discovered that what truly matters is that the three of us survived that night. We are together as a family, and that's all I ever wanted." She turned and looked up at him, her eyes shining with unshed tears.

Brent bent over and kissed Amanda gently on the lips. His heart was pounding as hard as it had during their first kiss. She was giving him a second chance, and he felt like the luckiest man in the world.

The baby began to fuss and wiggle in his chair, and they broke apart, laughing. "Life with baby," Brent said. He reached over and pulled the bib over Walter's head.

Amanda ran a wet washcloth around the baby's face while Brent unbuckled the safety strap and picked Walter up, settling him against his hip before he pulled Amanda into the embrace too. "I love my family," he said, almost unable to contain the joy in his heart.

Amanda nodded. "But there's one more thing."

Brent raised his eyebrows.

"You can stop walking around on eggshells. It's time things got back to normal. I want to start fighting again."

Brent gave her a look of disbelief.

Amanda shrugged. "I miss our makeup sex."

Brent grinned from ear to ear and did a little dance around the kitchen. "Done. Anything else?"

"As a matter of fact, yes."

284

"Anything," Brent said, becoming serious once again. "I mean that."

"You need to find a job so we can get out of this crummy apartment. Otherwise, I'm going to ask my mother if we can move in with her."

Brent shot her a horrified expression. "Then we'll never have sex!"

"Right, so go find a job."

"Talk about motivation," Brent replied, handing over Walter. "I'm on it."

Amanda wrinkled her nose. "Whew! Peanut needs a diaper change." She started down the hall. "In the meantime," she called out, "I'm going to set up my easel. I have a book to finish illustrating. Somebody has to start making money around here." She disappeared down the hall.

Alone in the kitchen, Brent couldn't help doing another celebratory jig around the kitchen, and then he grabbed the top advertising journal off the counter and strode into the family room. He sat down in the folding chair behind his old college desk and opened the back of the magazine to the listing for sales positions.

Nothing interesting. The usual collection of scams and too-good-to-be-true positions. He'd been looking everywhere, mostly online, but the job market was tight. Tighter, no doubt for him, since he'd been terminated from Revolution. He knew getting any job at all was going to be tough. *What was he going to do?* Still, he had new motivation, besides the fact that Amanda probably wasn't kidding about moving in with her mom.

Sometimes Brent thought the last five months had been even worse than what they had suffered at the hands of Intruder. Complications had arisen after Amanda's surgery, and she had been moved to the ICU. At the same time, Walter had fought his own battle in the neonatal unit. For a week, Brent ran back and forth between floors, feeling helpless.

Another week had gone by, and just when Brent thought

that his wife and son were finally through the worst of it, on the very day Amanda was to be released from the hospital, Walter took a turn for the worse.

Days turned into weeks while Walter struggled for survival in the neonatal unit. Filling out COBRA paperwork had been the furthest thing from Brent's mind. Months later, when he finally opened the stacks of untouched mail, he discovered his option to buy into the supplementary insurance had passed. Soon after that, came the staggering medical bills from the hospital.

He sold his new BMW directly from the parking lot of the dealership without ever having driven it. The house and every bit of furniture inside went as a package deal to a couple from New Jersey. Amanda refused to set foot inside the house ever again, and he couldn't blame her.

Walter remained in the hospital, and the bills kept coming. Brent started looking for a job, but with no business references and having been fired from the only job he'd held since college, he wasn't surprised that he didn't get a single call back, much less an invitation to come for an interview.

With nowhere else to live, Brent rented this crappy apartment. Amanda had barely spoken to him for the first three months. An apartment close enough to walk to and from the hospital had been her one request. She barely left Walter's side except to sleep. Neither of them had.

Now Walter was almost five months old, and Brent could see that Amanda had made tremendous progress. He marveled at her strength. Every now and then he could see bits of the old Amanda. A smile. Hearing her hum in the morning as she made coffee. She didn't jump at every sound like she used to.

But somehow he had to find a way to support them. Dejected, Brent set aside the trade journal when suddenly the answer came to him in a rush of adrenalin. He could start his own business. His corporation would be small and personal, yet edgy and filled with up-and-coming young talent.

Overwhelmed with a desire to get started, Brent decided the first thing he needed to do was to clear away all traces of the trauma that had filled his life for the past year. The right side of his desk was taken up with a huge stack of documents all pertaining to the Joe Kalaris case, otherwise known as Intruder.

Apparently, according to the police files and newspaper accounts, Kalaris had escaped from his house before the police arrived. They had tracked him to an old logging road a half mile behind their house in Garnet, but after few leads, the trail had gone cold.

Clive had been charged as an accomplice. He had allegedly provided information to Intruder in exchange for an assurance that his deadpool, Clive's Crypt, would end up in the money. It had come to light that Clive was awash in gambling debts; however, Clive's lawyer was spouting about his innocence to any media reporter who would listen, claiming he had no knowledge that Intruder's game involved murder.

Brent rocked back up on the two rear legs of his chair, contemplating all that had happened since January. Intruder, Joe Kalaris, was never far from the edge of his thoughts. The loss of Todd still physically hurt at times, and he had nightmares of Clive somehow beating the system.

He had to move on; it was time. Brent picked up a pile of paper relating to the Kalaris case and shoved it into the trash can next to his desk, piling up the overflow in a tall stack. He would personally take everything out to the dumpster later that night. Intruder had stolen enough from his life. As of this minute, Brent would never allow anyone or anything to control even a minute of his existence.

Control. That was his goal. Control would become the new cornerstone of Brent's life. Being in control. Having control. Maintaining control. Owning his own agency would fit right into this new mantra. Brent would be solely responsible for his success or failure. He alone would be in charge of his destiny. And that was of paramount importance.

"Okay, hotshot," Brent said out loud. "If you're going to do this, you better be prepared to work your ass off, beg for money to fund this venture, and hope to hell you haven't alienated every person in the ad industry on the East Coast. Oh, and you need to tell Amanda everything, every step of the way." That was another one of his new rules.

Brent rubbed his hands together and allowed himself to dream for a moment about starting his own agency. As he booted up his ancient computer and turned on the even older monitor he'd picked up free on the side of the road, ideas began to cascade into his head. He wanted to get to work on a business plan and couldn't wait to bounce his thoughts off Amanda.

He was about to get up and go talk to her when the perfect name for his company popped into his head: On The Rise. The name was ideal in so many ways. A tribute to Todd. A vision for his new company. And most of all, a talisman for his future with Amanda.

Energized, he decided to send emails to a few guys at Revolution who might be willing to jump ship. A few good men to start and he'd be golden. Brent opened his email program, something he hadn't done in weeks.

Halfway down was an email with no header information. Shock waves jolted through Brent's body. No sender. No date. No subject. He stood up, knocking his chair to the ground.

Unable to believe what he was seeing on the screen, he reached for the mouse. "It can't be..." Brent whispered aloud. "It can't be," he repeated. Brent moved the cursor on top of the envelope and clicked. The message was one long sentence, typed in all capital letters.

SHALL WE PLAY AGAIN?

About the Author

Anne Kelsey is the founder of *Dare to Write,* teaching creative writing throughout northern New England with her unique series of workshops that incorporate fun and laughter into each session. Anne's work has been recognized by numerous publications, including New Hampshire Writers' Project, *Writer's Digest,* and Amazon's Breakthrough Novel Contest. She lives in New Hampshire with her husband and her English cream golden retriever, Kaiah. Anne loves to hear from readers and writers. She can be reached at:

Website: AnneKelsey@DaretoWrite.com

Follow Anne on Twitter @daretowrite

Go to DeadlyIntruder.com for more information about upcoming books in the *Deadly Intruder* series.

www.ingramcontent.com/pod-product-compliance
Lightning Source LLC
Chambersburg PA
CBHW020346180626
46812CB00001B/362